PRINCESS OF STONE

FRACTURED QUEENDOM
BOOK ONE

Victoria Larque

I was never meant to rule
I was never meant to live in public eye
I was never meant to be important

Living my unconventional life
In secret
Doing as I pleased

But destiny is a fickle being
Forcing me to change my ways
Forcing me out of the shadows

Time is of the essence
Love the farthest thing from my mind
My family legacy is all that matters

For my people I will stand proud
For my people I will sacrifice
For my people I will do whatever it takes

by Helle Gade

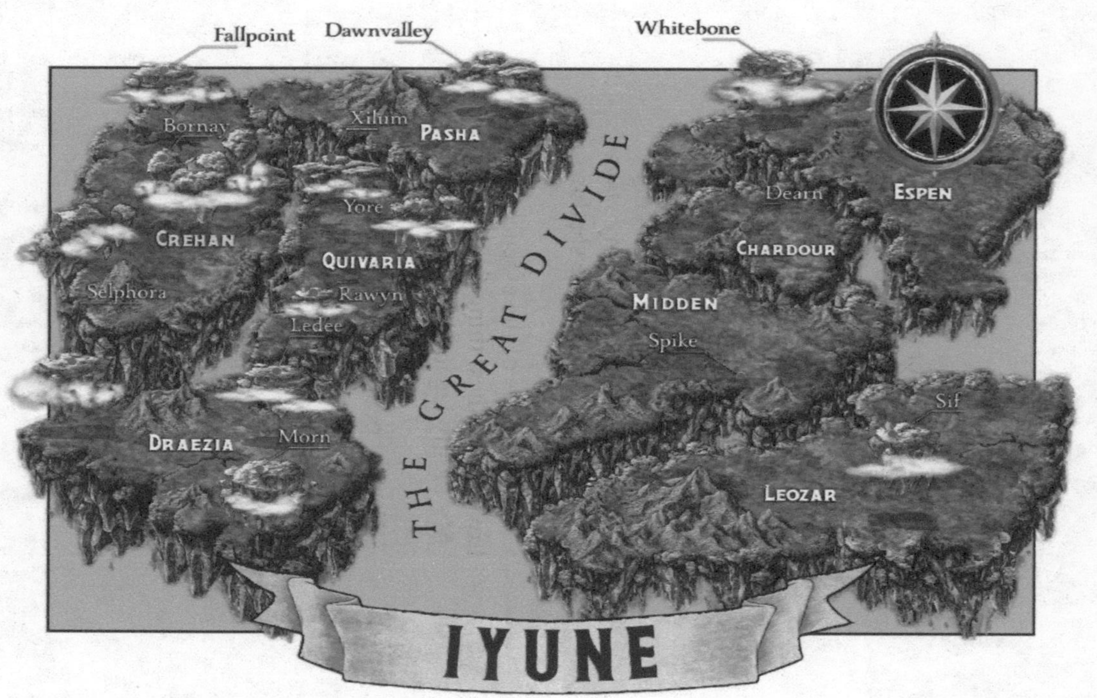

Fallpoint
Dawnvalley
Whitebone
Bornay
Xihim
PASHA
ESPEN
Dearn
CREHAN
Yore
QUIVARIA
Rawyn
Ledee
CHARDOUR
MIDDEN
Spike
Sif
Selphora
DRAEZIA
Morn
THE GREAT DIVIDE
LEOZAR
IYUNE

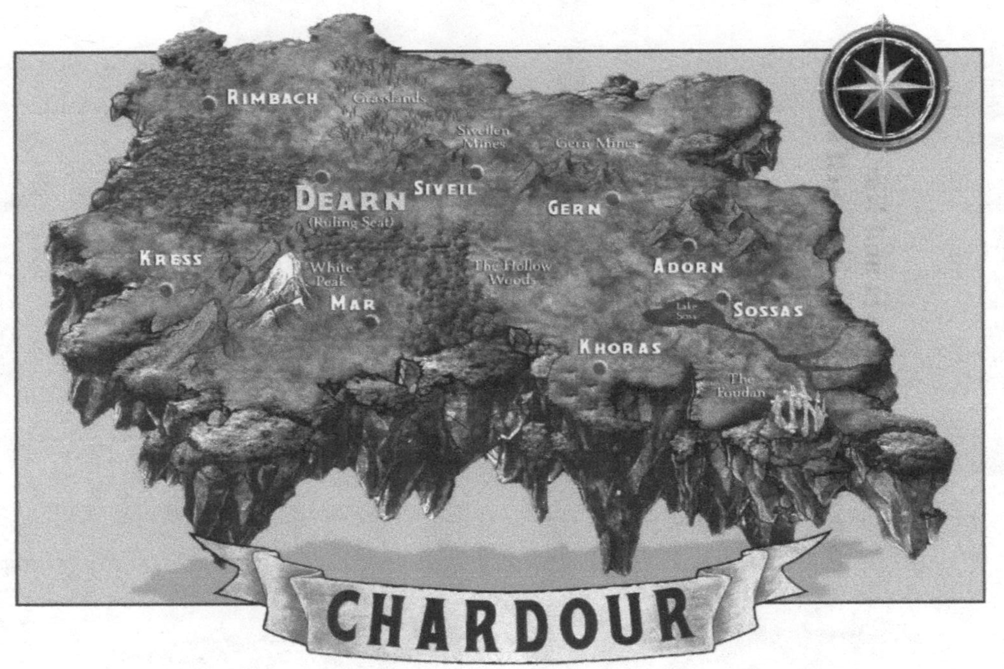

RIMBACH
Grasslands
Sivellen Mines
Gern Mines
DEARN
(Ruling Seat)
SIVEIL
GERN
KRESS
White Peak
MAR
The Hollow Woods
ADORN
Lake Sona
SOSSAS
KHORAS
The Foudan
CHARDOUR

For Liz, Rayla and Kay.
You made me believe in myself again.

Prologue

I have long since forgotten their names, their faces, even the sounds of their voices and the smell of their hugs. But every night, I practice what they have breathed. Standing on the edge of my spell-woven world, I speak to create a new piece. My breath befriends my body until every part of me moves in unison and toward the common goal. Voice grand, body dancing, I draw upon the ancient magic which makes my bones sing, and I call forth a piece, a thread, a slice, of materia, and add it to my island. This island that is threaded and stitched together by the magic of my foremothers and my own, stretching on for miles in every direction. Yet, it does not reach, it does not connect to anything, but that is why I do it.

Lonely as I am, I walk the length of floating magic to add and add anew, until the night is over and my power splinters away. I do as they all have done. Yearning. Searching. Waiting for the night I might set my bare feet on bare, unwoven ground. I know I am close now. I hear voices on the winds, smell alien scents through the mist, and my heart pounds faster with each glowing shroud I add to my home.

Once I am done, I will never return, but suck in the island, so many before me have built, and my power will grow beyond the dawn and into the sun. I will be bursting with strength. I will be goddess-like. And with the first step off, I will change the world I arrive in forever.

Fifty years ago, a Witch crossed the acidic ocean of Leigh and brought magic, death, and destruction to Iyune in a phenomenon known as the Breaking. Her arrival rearranged the very fabric of Iyune. Deep chasms mark the borders these days, and some kingdoms and cities float, while others cower in the shadows of those who do. Traveling is regulated for each kingdom and can only be achieved by magical crystals reacting with a portal. Every kingdom has one, called Foudan. As the lower kingdoms are forced to provide the floating cities with labor, resources, and even slaves, unrest rises. Some of the kingdoms have banded together and are opposing the rule of the Witchgoddess. War is imminent and suffering will follow.

The small kingdom of Chardour is one of the few neutral ones, but as its mines are rich with the coveted crystals, the neighboring countries are close to invading.

This is where our story begins, in Chadour and its capital, the city of Dearn…

Chapter One
Eliza
Dearn

Glowing crystals encased in grimy glass chased away the oncoming darkness of the early night and lit my way. My pulse fluttered in sync with my steps and I forced myself to slow down. It wouldn't do to be stopped and questioned by the patrolling marshals because I was dashing through the streets of Dearn like a madman. The thrill of sneaking away from my sentinels had my blood racing. Even if this wasn't new to me, this seedy part of town was, and I did my best to act casually.

For what felt like the hundredth time, I patted my left side, making sure my playing pieces were still in the leather pouch on my belt. An unnecessary move, as I heard them clinking softly with each hasty step. Again, I slowed down. My fingers fiddled with the fake mustache on my upper lip, then slid down under my cloak, to where I had bound my chest. There was hardly anything to bind, and what was there would surely be hidden by my cloak, but as nervous excitement ate at me, I fidgeted.

Men and women crossed my way, most of them laughing loudly and having a good time. The scent of smoke and alcohol was heavy in the air and I breathed it in as though it was perfume. Different. Intoxicating. Exciting. I loved Dearn at night, when all manner of people came out to escape the day. Just like me in a way. The baker, lounging on a chair next to one of the houses, still in his work-attire, playing cards with a few others, their conversation light and filled with humor. Two women walked past them, arm in arm, prettied up and giggling, throwing the baker and his friends a few choice words after one of them said something very inappropriate. The women scuttled on, giggling even louder as they went.

A smirk pulled at my lips when the sign I had been searching for came into view. The Tankard. One of the many drinking establishments in this part of town. This one differed from the rest in that women were expressly forbidden, and it hosted game-nights. More specifically, Trice nights. A game of calculating strategy, one I prided myself with being quite good at. But there was no way of truly knowing, as no one I played with dared to let me lose. And my siblings – the two people in the whole of Iyune who wouldn't mind insulting me – had stopped playing long ago.

After I dodged a few drunk men, singing and laughing while trampling along arm in arm, I turned and climbed the two steps leading to a heavy wooden door. Taking a bracing breath, I pushed the handle and swung it open.

Used to having eyes on me when entering a room, I was pleasantly ignored. Safe for a burly man, glaring at me from under bushy brows. He leaned against a barrel opposite the door, his muscly arms crossed.

"You here for the game, or to drink?" he asked, his impressive glare not getting friendlier as he spoke.

I cleared my throat. "The game." Seconds went by and I hoped that my voice had been sufficiently deep. For emphasis, I drew back my coat and jiggled the leather bag to make my playing pieces click.

The burly man raised a brow, eyed me up and down, then huffed. "They will eat you alive, boy. But as long as you have money, they will gladly take it from you."

"That's why I'm here," I said pleasantly.

This time he chuckled. "Well, go through then."

Happy with getting away with my costume, I strutted past him and looked around the room with wide eyes. A few lamps hung from the ceiling of the large room. The wax of the candles pearled from the holders, adding drops to the mottled wooden floor. I had no idea what made up half the stains on it, but I was fascinated by how dirty it was.

Most of the round tables were occupied by drinking men. The atmosphere light and loud. A flustered and strained looking servant had trouble keeping up as the orders for more drinks were shouted at him. In here, the scent of smoke and alcohol was even thicker, but coupled with sweat and the smell of food. It made for a truly unique odor.

Grinning like an idiot, I beheld smaller tables in the back, past a long bar, where two people sat opposite one another, boards and pieces out.

With excitement, I made my way through the throngs of people. Very quickly, I started dodging the mingling men, since no one seemed to care whether they bumped into me or not. It was a welcome change from the norm. No one knew who I was, and no one cared. It was elating.

When one of the men slammed his fist on a table, gathered his pieces from the board, grunted a few curses and stood, I slunk toward the vacated chair.

"Next?" the winner, asked. He had a toothpick between his meaty lips and was busy collecting the coins at the side of the table, sliding them over with unwashed fingers.

"Me. I-I'll go next." I cursed myself for the stutter, but my nerves ran rampant. What would happen if I was discovered in this part of Dearn? In this establishment? The thought was as exciting as it was daunting.

The man looked up and let the toothpick wander from one corner of his lips to the other. His small eyes were quick and calculating as he regarded me. He waved one of his unwashed hands at the empty chair. "If you want to lose, sit. Boy."

I plopped down, careful to not let my coat touch the floor. "Ale please," I addressed the passing, profusely sweating servant I had seen before. He took one tankard from the plate he was carrying and placed it in front of me. My brows rose when the liquid inside spilled over from his careless handling, and I swiped the puddle from the table with a hand before taking a careful sip. It was delightfully strong.

The man in front of me smiled, but it wasn't friendly and didn't reach his eyes. "Do you have pieces, or do you want to borrow some? I have an extra set, for a price, of course."

"No need." I unhooked the leather pouch from my belt and opened it, dropping my pieces onto the board.

"Those are…nice," my opponent said, ogling my seven-piece set carved from quartz.

When I noticed that everyone else seemed to play with wooden pieces, I could have kicked myself. Wow, I was off to a good start being inconspicuous.

"My father willed them to me," I said. "He was a grand player." I sent him one of my most charming smiles, but it seemed to unnerve him further.

"Stop grinning at me like that, let's play."

My smile fell and I focused. Setting up my part of the board lightning quick. Many people underestimated this step, but I knew it was an integral part of the game.

Placing my pieces with care, I took in the pieces of my opponent. Four would do for now. He played with heavy pieces, which dealt much damage, but had little reach. My pieces were a mixed bag of power, reach, and support.

Once done, I leaned back and crossed my arms. "Winner of the former round starts," I said.

My opponent rolled the toothpick from one side of his mouth to the other again, this time a small smirk appeared while he did so. "Four? Are you sure?"

I nodded, staring him down. He shrugged and began the game.

He was skilled, ruthless, and apparently used to winning. The game went from him attacking and me dodging, taking in his playstyle, to a hard and short fight during which we both lost most of our pieces.

He had two left, I one. Now the toothpick rolled from side to side every two seconds and he couldn't hide a smirk now and then, a sure way of telling that he thought victory was within reach.

I pulled my piece back and waited for his action. As I had planned, he went for his stronger piece to chase mine, leaving the other one to sit neatly, and defenseless.

In one move, I took out his forgotten piece, too many spaces away for his remaining piece to reach mine. Then I finished him. The toothpick cracked and broke as he bit down, his meaty lips snarling at me.

"I won," I said.

"Seems like you did." He spat out the remainder of his toothpick and glared. "Rematch!"

"If you want. Two out of three?"

He huffed and set up his board, but nodded once.

I didn't need three, as I beat him again. Joy and pride flooded through me, leaving me with a rush and that was when I made a fateful mistake. A victorious whoop left me – too girly to pass for a man and he scrutinized me. I grabbed my mug of ale and gulped it down, to gloss over my misstep. Swiping at my lips I felt the mustache loosen and cursed when his eyes widened.

"Your facial hair seems to be giving you the slip," my opponent said and leaned back, with a grin. "Barkeep, please get a marshal in here, it looks like we have been duped."

"What?" a large man shot from behind the bar and appeared at the side of our table. "Is there a problem?"

"Absolutely not!" I said.

"Yes," my opponent said at the same moment. "Your doorman has let in a woman."

His voice rose as he said it and the chatter around us died. Chairs scraped the dirty floor as men turned to look at us. At me. The barkeep gasped and sped off.

I felt like sinking into the ground, but straightened instead. "What exactly are you accusing me of?" I demanded. "I might be young, but I am definitely a man."

My opponent got another toothpick from his jacket pocket and stuffed it between his lips. Did he have more where they came from, and if so, why? He didn't look like the kind of person who took pride in his hygiene.

Stop it, Eliza, I told myself. This was not the time for wondering about these kinds of things.

"I don't think so," the man opposite of me said. "But it looks like you can take that discussion up with the marshals." He jerked his chin to a commotion behind me and a second later I felt a heavy hand land on my shoulder.

"Shit in a chasm," I breathed when I looked up into the stern face of a marshal. My night out was officially over.

****

"Really?" Brown eyes met mine as I was helped into a chair at the marshal's station. "Again?"

"Marshal Jentz," I said, beaming at the man.

Jentz waved at the two marshals, who had taken me across town and to the station, and they left the stuffy little room Marshal Jentz called his office. Papers and books covered every open surface and he even had a second table-plate set up, with four bricks on the corners of the first. A crystal lamp shone light onto his chaos, glinting in the square glass-ashtray set atop a pile of more papers.

I waved at the two men who had brought me in, with a wide grin. It was not reciprocated.

I shrugged and turned to look at my favorite marshal. Now he had an impressive full beard, making me a little envious as my silly little mustache tickled the side of my mouth, hanging on for dear life as it teetered off the corner of my lip.

Marshal Jentz sighed, plucked the fake thing from my face and shook his head. "How many times do I have to tell you? Sneaking off is dangerous for Your Highness. What if the people found out who you are?"

"That should not pose a problem, right? I hear the people love the royal family." I batted my lashes. "Or was that a lie?"

Jentz wrung his huge, calloused hands on the table between us and didn't meet my gaze.

The truth was – as I had discovered on my many grand escapes – that while our kingdom was rich, the revolt from surrounding countries against the Witchgoddes Ivey, had led to serious problems of our exports. Which meant less money, less work, and more

15

hunger, desperation, and violence. And as long as my father, the king, didn't magically make all of it go away, discontent steadily rose.

Jentz and I both knew this, even though I shouldn't. I let him off the hook by leaning back and changing the subject. "Besides, no one would expect the lame, third-born to troll the streets of our glorious capital." I wiggled my brows. "Especially not in these times. Much too dangerous."

"Please, Your Highness, I fear I will find you dead in a ditch if you continue this madness."

"Why? Other people live and thrive." I bent forward over his desk and winked at him. "Even the women," I whispered, then looked shocked. "Scandalous, isn't it?"

"Those are not the kind of women you want to be associated with, your Highness."

"What? Ladies of the night? From what I have seen so far, they make a good living and always laugh last. Which is kind of admirable if you ask me."

Jentz groaned and pinched the bridge of his nose. "Please, Your Highness. You will be cause for my early grave. Gregor!"

A young marshal stuck his head through the door. "Yes?"

"Go to the palace and get a message to Prince Reagan. Tell him that the mouse is caught."

Gregor's shoulders fell. "Again? What does that even mean?"

"Just do as you are told. Now!" Jentz roared, making Gregor's face whiten, before it vanished from sight quickly.

"My brother? Really?" I whined. "He will never let me hear the end of this."

"Better him than your father," Jentz said. "And maybe that is exactly why I call on him. One of these days he will get through to you."

I snorted, happy with the fact that all I got in response was a raised gray brow from the marshal, and not an endless litany on how a princess should conduct herself at all times. "I doubt that. Reagan is a stick in the mud, one I will happily ignore."

"You really shouldn't, Princess Fabienne. Times are getting increasingly dangerous."

"How many times have I told you to call me Eliza?"

"Countless, Your Highness." He smiled at me and shook his head. "A game house, really? Why?"

I pulled up one shoulder. "It is forbidden, which makes it fun."

"Did you win?" he asked.

I laughed. "Did I win? Marshal Jentz, how long have we known each other?"

"Four years, Your Highness." He swiped over his graying beard. "I allot every single gray hair to you, by the way. Now tell me. What happened?"

I proceeded to tell him about this newest adventure and while he tried very hard to look stern, Jentz couldn't help but smirk from time to time at my story.

"I will never understand Your Highness."

"Oh, Jentz, I enjoy our encounters, too."

The door flew open and a woman entered, followed closely by a gasping and wheezing Gregor. "My apologies, senior marshal," Gregor said. "But sh-she headed me off at the castle gates and…demanded to come straight here."

Marshal Jentz's answer drifted into background noise when I met the gaze of the woman. Her eyes were gray as steel, her armor-clad frame tall and toned. Braids of deepest black pulled the hair from her stunning face, revealing sharp cheekbones and contrastingly curved lips. But nothing about her hit me as much as her stare. It was intense. Like being too close to an open fire. She felt like that. Bright and burning.

It might have been the fact that she wore the armor of a Dovani, matt black steel with gray edges, but I doubted it. No. Her presence was electrifying and for the first time in my life I was shocked into silence.

Chapter Two
Rayla

With one hand, I closed the door on the still profusely apologizing marshal, not taking my eyes off her. She could have passed for a man on a quick glance, but I knew exactly who she really was. Once we and the senior marshal were alone, I nodded at her. "Princess Fabienne Eliza Vaster?"

Stark, forest-green eyes blinked at me. "If you say so," she said.

"Come. I am taking you home."

"Excuse me," the senior marshal said, getting up from his seat. "Who are you and how do you know the princess?"

It took me a second to unglue my gaze from hers as there was something in the depth of those green eyes that seemed to spellbind me, but I did and regarded the marshal. "I am Rayla, a Dovani from the twin cities. And I have been called by the royal family to be the personal guard of Princess Fabienne. I heard she was missing, so I waited and kept an eye out."

"Personal guard?" The princess grimaced

"A Dovani?" the marshal asked. "But why?"

I raised a brow at the marshal. "We are in the marshal's station, are we not? In the middle of the night. With a princess who is clearly dressed as a man and not at all where she is supposed to be."

My gaze flew back to her and the adorable little scowl growing on her features. "It does look like she needs a personal guard. The king and queen were obviously not lying when they told me how their daughter gives her usual sentinels the slip all the time."

"Ugh. This has to be a mistake," Princess Vaster said and stood from her chair. "Fine. I will go with you to the castle so we can clear all of this up." She raised the hood of her cloak over her head and strutted through the room. "Till our next little chat, Jentz."

"Princess Fabienne, wait," the marshal followed her, giving me the hairy eyeball as he came closer. "I will come along and make sure she is who she says she is."

I looked from him to my newest and first charge, then I decided to let him come along. Neither of them knew me, and he was right to question my truthfulness, even if others of my order would have smitten him clean from his marshal boots for questioning their authenticity.

The marshal's station was close to the castle grounds and it took the three of us little time to get there. And while I hung back a little, making sure nothing and no one suspicious crept up from between the houses, the princess marched steadily, her shoulders bunched up in what looked like anger. The senior marshal threw me glances over his shoulder from time to time, his full beard bristling each time he did.

Even if the trip was on the short side, it gave me time to take in a bit more of the city. I had arrived in Dearn late in the evening, traveling from the Foudan of Chardour in the east. I had never been to one of the semi-floating kingdoms, as I had grown up and lived most of my life in the floating city of Xilum. The twin cities Xilum and Yore trained and harbored the greatest warriors in all of Iyune. And only a handful of us ever reached the state of Dovani. The fact that I had been called upon the royals of Chardour told me a couple of things.

They had to be desperate and very rich. My kind was not normally called upon as guards, and if we were, it was a costly affair. My captain had given me this assignment to 'broaden my horizon,' but I knew he'd been lying. Partly. Women rarely became Dovani, and many thought I didn't deserve my station. I had no qualms in showing them they were wrong, which meant I got into trouble with my captain regularly. He had to be ecstatic that I was gone. One less thing to worry about. I, for one, didn't want to be here and I would be gone soon. All I had to do was make it crystal clear to the king and queen of Chardour that they didn't really need me. What I should be doing was get ready for the looming threat of a rebel war. Until then, I would do my job as well as any of my guild.

Dearn was what would be called quaint from where I hailed. The houses were old, rickety, and made up a maze of cobble-stoned alleys and narrow streets. Simple folk lived here. Providers for the floating cities. The condition of the streetlamps and cobbled streets did tell of comfort and care. There was no trash, no gunk, and no drunkards around. This might have to do with the proximity to the castle and marshal's station, but from what I had seen so far, most of the city looked like this. Quaint.

High, white walls encased a large iron gate, opening to a sprawling park of meticulously kept gardens, through which a wide alley of trees wound, leading to the castle. The castle was huge, white and gray, with towers, glass-windows and smaller buildings on either side.

Once we reached the gate, the stationed guards bowed deeply for the princess and nodded at the marshal, before seeing me and bowing again. I didn't like the attention and reverence, feeling a blush creep up the back of my neck.

The marshal fixed a stern look on me. "Seems you are who you said. A word of advice; she will do what she sets out to do, you can either stay at her side and protect her, or be made a fool of."

A smile breached my lips as I watched the thin wisp of a princess storm off in the direction of her home. "A fool? I think not."

The marshal shrugged and turned toward the city. "Famous last words, Dovani." He strolled off into the night and I huffed out a laugh. Strange people. This kingdom seemed a lot less boring than I had originally thought.

I sped up my steps and caught up to the princess about halfway to the castle. Leaving the appropriate distance to her, I lagged behind, then stopped when she spun around after a few moments.

Her startlingly green eyes met mine. "However long you are here, I will not have you looming behind me like a guard-dog. You walk at my side, or you get lost. Choose." For someone so small, she had an impressive glare and I tilted my head to the side, suddenly feeling a lot shorter myself.

"Fine," I said and walked up to her, falling in step with her when we carried on.

"The absolute nerve," the princess said. "What were they thinking? A Dovani... As if anything would warrant such an expense."

Her words caught me by surprise, the royals I had gotten to meet in passing didn't care about things such as expenses. Least of all princesses. But then again, I had never seen a princess sneak out of a castle dressed as a man. For a moment I wanted to ask why she had done it, but refrained from doing so. It was none of my business.

From time to time, she glanced at me, only to keep on muttering and huffing as we went, clearly angry at me being there.

When we reached the castle entrance, the stationed guards bowed and opened the gigantic door. Marble floor greeted us and a large hall made our steps echo as we traversed through it. The white walls on either side of the hall were decorated with a myriad of crystals. They sparkled in the light provided by gemmed chandeliers hanging from the high ceiling. The crystals ran over the walls like a relief, depicting a scene that was sprawled across the entire entrance hall. It told the story of the Breaking fifty years ago, and how the House of Vaster had built up Chardour after realizing the Breaking had set free magical crystals. In a space between the crystals, five gold-framed pictures sat. Each one held a likeness of one of the royals residing here. King Edrick, Queen Mauve, Princess Pavette, Prince Reagan, and Princess Fabienne. When I had arrived earlier this evening, a manservant had shown me around the hall, explaining the paintings and rambling about the lineage of the House of Vaster. As it had done the first time, the sheer amount of crystals used across the walls left me breathless. The manservant had told me they were without magic, 'unfit to be of use and practically waste,' he'd called them. I had never seen the like and was astounded at how many of those 'unfit' stones made up the walls. How many would the mines have to extricate in order for these to be merely waste? It was unfathomable.

I tore my eyes away from the splendor and spotted that the bag I had brought with me was gone from where I had left it next to a set of plush futons surrounding a grand fireplace. Prince Reagan had met us, telling me his sister was missing, again. Seemed like someone had taken my bag to whatever lodgings the Vaster's deemed adequate for me. As I had left right away, I had no idea where that was.

Princess Fabienne led the way to curved stairs, leading from the hall and deeper into the castle. The hallways were white, and each one was sparkling with another scene of gems. They reflected the light, chasing all the colors imaginable across the floors and ceilings. It was as though one walked into a waking dream.

We passed many sparkling hallways that led into other wings, heading straight for the middle. The princess threw open a pair of double-doors and stormed through, into a set of resplendent chambers. My steps faltered when I realized this had to be the joined chambers of the king and queen.

"Keep up, Dovani, will you?" the princess snapped. She hurried on, bursting into what looked like a cozy, private library. Shelves upon shelves of books spanned the walls, a fireplace was lit next to a front of windows overlooking a beautiful part of the gardens. Armchairs and couches stood around the fireplace — filled with people. The same faces we had passed in the hall downstairs.

"Whose glorious and absolutely harebrained idea was it to sic a Dovani on me?" Princess Fabienne asked.

The whole royal family stood, the sister rushing over, taking Princess Fabienne's hands in hers. "You are back! Thank the Goddess."

"Fabienne," King Edrick said. "We will discuss this in private." His eyes met mine and he nodded curtly.

I was about to turn and leave the room when the princess wound one hand from the grip of her sister and snatched my arm. The pads of her fingers brushed past the hem of my sleeve and landed on skin. A prickling sensation wandered up my arm from where she touched me and quickly, the princess let go. Her eyes met mine and a strange expression flashed across her face. Had she felt the same thing? "Stay," she said to me, then turned her head toward her family. "Since you all thought to make a Dovani my personal guard, I intend to keep her personally close until she can leave." Her voice was even enough, so I banned what just happened from my thoughts.

"You left us no choice, sister," Prince Reagan said. "Mother and father have told you time and time again that your excursions are dangerous and that we are in a delicate political climate right now. What if enemies of the crown found you? You never think of anyone but your own pleasure and fun."

"Says the princeling who visits the Lotus at least once a week," Princess Fabienne said.

The prince glanced at his parents, blushed and scowled at his sisters. "I-I do not."

"Right. At least my visits of the city are educational."

"Fabienne!" Queen Mauve thundered. "Enough. We stayed up, sick with worry. Your brother is right, it is dangerous to leave the castle right now and you will–"

"But a Dovani, mother? It must have cost an arm and a leg."

"Do not interrupt me, child." Queen Mauve looked at her daughter, showing off the same impressive glare I had been introduced to earlier. For the first time, Princess Fabienne shrunk in on herself, guilt flashing across her features.

"I apologize, Mother."

Queen Mauve nodded, the shine of the fire glowing on her copper hair as she did. "Now. Never you mind the cost, you will stay inside these very walls, your new guard will see to it." She looked at me and it felt like a fist was grabbing hold of me. Pure authority. "You will not leave her side, Dovani. Wherever she goes, so do you. And you will make sure she does not leave again."

I bowed. "As you wish."

"Mother. Please…"

"Your mother is right," King Edrick said. "Enough is enough. Now go to bed. We can all use a good night's sleep after your shenanigans. We have set up the Dovani next to your bedchamber."

I was taken aback by that tidbit and had it been possible, I would have protested. It was not my station to have lodgings inside a royal palace. These people really were desperate to keep her out of the city.

Princess Fabienne turned her head and looked me up and down. "Fine, follow me then."

Her sister Pavette did not let go of her hand and they walked off together. I bowed to the royal family and followed my charge.

Princess Pavette had the same golden hair as her father and she was a bit taller than her sister, with a soft and wholesome face. Princess Fabienne whispered at her sister as they went but she shouldn't have bothered. I could easily hear what she was saying.

"Can you believe them? A Dovani? Why? And why now?" Princess Fabienne whispered.

"You know they mean well, Eliza. And right now, you will need all the protection you can get," Princess Pavette said in a perfectly normal tone of voice.

"Shhh." Fabienne threw me a glance over her shoulder.

Princess Pavette shook her head. "Really, sister, we have acquired a Dovani, which means she took an oath to serve and protect. And she has to honor the code of secrecy. Isn't that right?" The last question was aimed at me.

"It is, Princess. Whomever I serve, I do so fully. Your secrets are my secrets and your life is mine to protect."

"See?" Pavette said, patting her sister's hand gently.

Princess Fabienne did not seem convinced as she kept silent during the rest of the way. They did stay together, even when we entered Princess Fabienne's chambers. As the two princesses opened a door leading to a spacious bedroom, I lingered right outside.

Princess Fabienne glanced at me and sighed. "I am done for one night, honest. You can take the adjoined room." She pointed to a powder-blue door next to a white closet. I bowed curtly and crossed the room to get into my lodgings.

My bag sat in the middle of a much too large bed in a too big room. It was beautiful and so luxurious, it made me uncomfortable. Even this room was graced by a chandelier – gemmed, of course – which could be turned on by a latch next to the door. The latch had an almost clear crystal embedded, which reacted to the same crystals set in the chandelier. Sinusai, they called it. A gem to capture light. Here in Chardour, even the streetlamps had them. My eyes widened when I saw a tiny, yellow gem sown into the bedsheet. If I was not mistaken, it was called Micra, and would be able to heat the sheets if found the corresponding latch to activate it.

I closed the door but kept my focus on the conversation happening on the other side, pushing past all the strange and marvelous things in my room. It seemed I had been called not only because Princess Fabienne snuck out regularly, but there was something more going on. I needed to know what, in order to do my job right.

The more I listened, the better I understood that I

would not be gone from Chardour any time soon. And while I certainly expected to feel disappointment at that, the information coming from beyond the door was interesting, nearly as intriguing as Fabienne Eliza Vaster herself, striking-green stare and sizzling touch included.

Chapter Three
Eliza

"What is going on, Pavette?" I asked as soon as my newest sentinel had closed her door. I believed my sister that the Dovani was sworn to secrecy, but I didn't know her. And right now, I was not sure if her presence was so exciting because she was dangerous, or because I found her unbelievably attractive. Either way, I needed to know why my sister was being so cryptic.

Pavette plopped down on my bed and waved me over. "Let's get that out of your hair."

I grumbled something not very nice under my breath and sat down in front of her, giving her my back. Pavette gently went to work on my disguise.

"You know father can't stay neutral in this uprising much longer. Someone will make us choose, or take us over soon." She tugged off my short-haired wig and unpinned my hair from where I had fastened it.

"But we have riches, and an army to protect our Foudan or any part of the kingdom."

"Yes," Pavette grabbed the brush from my bedside table and began brushing my hair. "We do. But for how much longer? What do all the kingdoms opposing the Witchgoddes need? Our crystal. Not just so they can travel from kingdom to kingdom, but also for other magical purposes. They will force us to produce more for less, just as Selphora and those loyal to it will. If we don't, there are many kingdoms who would happily usurp Chardour and exploit our people and mines for the coming war. What we need are allies, and to pick a side."

"But there isn't even a war going on. I have heard that Selphora invited the revolting houses for peace talks." I had never been to the ruling city of the Witchgoddess, but had heard things about it. Grand and terrible.

"Since when has the Witchgoddes ever taken the road of peace?" Pavette continued brushing my hair softly. "No, dear sister, war is coming, one way or the other. Which is why you need protection."

"Me? Specifically?"

"Yes. Father has made arrangements for me to marry Prince Marcus of Leozar. Their country is large and strong."

I twisted my head to face her. "He did what? And you are fine with this?"

My sister smiled mildly. "I will do what is necessary. For my family and for Chardour." She stuck her fingers into my hair and turned my head back. "We will be leaving for Sif soon. But father has decided you will stay behind."

It felt like a block of ice slid into my stomach. "I-I have to stay here? While you go and get married off to some bored, spoiled princeling, like a fattened-up goose? No way! I have to see this guy first and then—"

"Sweet sister, you would ruin my marriage before I even had a chance to say my vows. We all know you aren't what one would call sociable."

I snorted and my sister tugged on a strand of my hair.

"Proving my point, Liz."

"I am plenty sociable." I crossed my arms.

Pavette laughed and leaned down to hug me. "You are my dearest and most favorite sister and friend, but are too sharp, and you let people know it. You have no impulse control and are way too curious about everything." She kissed me on the top of my head and straightened to continue working through my tousled hair. "Not to mention, you tend to let people know when they are wrong."

"People *should* know when they are wrong."

"Maybe. But they don't want to hear it from someone as young as you, never mind a woman."

I had no idea what to say to that. She was right, I was not built for the delicate dance of politics and nobility. Since I had been a girl, I had upset almost every member of aristocracy I'd met. Whether intentionally or not. Most of them I severely disliked.

As we sat in silence for a few moments, I mulled over everything Pavette had told me. The ice in my stomach turned to a sour sensation and climbed to my throat.

"You can't go. Who else will I talk to in this stuffy house? Reagan? He stopped really speaking with me the moment he decided he had become a man. Always with the scolding and the 'a princess doesn't do this or that, a princess behaves, a princess doesn't speak unless spoken to.' He is insufferable. And who will you confide in?" I turned to her and my dark-red tresses fell from her hands. "I should come with you. To keep you company and protect you from the vultures in Sif."

Pavette chuckled. "Vultures?"

"I'm sure there are many. Leozar is known for their ruthlessness in battle and for their conniving political ways." I took one of her hands in mine. "Besides, I'd love to see the capital city. Sif is floating, right?"

My sister nodded. "It is. And I wish you could come, I truly do. We would have fun and…" Her blue eyes misted up. "I will miss you. I'll miss this." She squeezed my hand. "But father has decided and there is nothing to be done."

"I won't even be there for your wedding, how… Why would he keep me here?" My throat closed up and I felt tears brim my eyes. "Aren't you scared?"

"A bit. But we always knew this was to be my fate. Reagan will rule one day, and I will always be Chardour's ally, even from far away." She swiped away a tear running down my cheek. "And you know the rules and yourself, sweet sister. The family can't leave the kingdom as one, if ever something should happen, we need at least one to carry on the legacy of the House of Vaster. And besides, you'd go exploring at the first opportunity."

"Rules shmules. If I have to uphold the name of our house and govern Chardour, we are all going to be in trouble."

Pavette laughed. "No, the world would be in trouble." We hugged each other for a long time after that, both crying a little. And once my sister had left me to my miserable thoughts, I lay awake for hours, hating that she was right. Rules were rules, and I had made my own bed by being the impulsive hot-head I was. A few times I debated whether I would be able to smuggle myself into their entourage, but that would only work until we reached the Foudan. Travelling was closely watched and documented. There was no way of hiding who I was at the portal.

Still, I was angry and of half a mind to wake my parents and tell them that they were making a mistake. I couldn't imagine this place without Pavette and her reasonable cool. She was the weight attaching me to my family, to my station. She was the only one who understood me, and yet followed protocol herself. I had always looked up to her, wishing I could be more like her, but there was no point to that. There was no other way for me to quench my thirst for knowledge and adventure other than going out and finding what I was looking for.

And now I had a Dovani to watch over me. While I understood the why of it – my family going off to Leozar and not willing to leave me behind unprotected – it still seemed redundant. Way too expensive.

I glanced at the door, a weird feeling building in the pit of my stomach. I hadn't seen many female warriors as of yet, and certainly none like her. While she was technically below my station – even if she was my guard – I felt small and insignificant next to her. When I had kept her from leaving my parents' study earlier, my fingers had brushed the skin of her arm. Remembering her surprised face and the tingle I'd felt at touching her was exciting. She was foreign, undoubtedly having seen things I couldn't even imagine, and she was forbidden in more ways than one. She would either become an obsession, or an annoyance very quickly. But as I lay in the dark, I was inclined to think it would be the former. And why not? I needed something or someone to obsess over, to help stem the sting of being left behind, left for good by my dear sister.

****

"Do you want me to plate your hair, Eliza?" Marie, my handmaid asked, brushing out my hair. "It is such a lovely color." Her round and kind face lit up when I smiled at her through the mirror I sat in front of.

"Do whatever you like, Marie. You have a much better eye for these things than me."

Now she beamed, sectioning off strands to begin her work. Behind her, I saw the door to the Dovani's room open and my guard emerged. Her steel-gray eyes met mine in the mirror as she walked across the room to take up position beside the entrance to my chamber.

"How did you sleep?" I asked her, receiving another glance from those hauntingly beautiful eyes. This time they widened slightly in surprise.

"Good, Your Highness."

Marie's fingers had stilled during our interaction and she tried really hard not to look at Rayla.

"Marie, this is Rayla, a Dovani from the twin cities. She is here to protect me. Rayla, Marie is my handmaid."

Marie shyly looked to her side and curtsied, while Rayla gave her a curt nod. A few seconds of awkward silence ticked by and I could tell from the slight shake in Marie's hands, that she was intimidated by my new sentinel. I immediately understood why. Rayla was tall and carried herself with the kind of lethal grace I had only ever witnessed predators in the wild display. She reminded me of a Sauvey, a kind of large cat, native to the grasslands in the north of Chardour. I had only ever seen one, during the time my father had taken me along with his hunting party. It had been swift, deadly, and graceful. Not caring about us, but solely focused on a group of deer she was stalking. Rayla had the same quiet intensity.

Also, guards normally weren't around in personal chambers, and we had none who were female.

And while I felt my pulse quicken at her presence in the room, I decided to try and ease the tension. "How long do you have to train to become a Dovani?" I asked, hoping that having Rayla talk would make her less daunting.

"It differs, Your Highness."

"Right. But there has to be a norm."

Rayla's lips tightened almost imperceptibly for a heartbeat. "The norm would equate to six years. After the three years of basic military training."

"That is a long time," Marie said, the shake gone as she curled the braids up and pinned them in place. "We only train for half a year to be able to work in the castle, unless you get to work as a direct servant to one of the royal family, like me. I had to take additional tutoring for a year." She shook her head. "I'm so glad that is over."

Rayla raised a brow.

"Miss Grant, the head of house, is unbelievably strict," Marie continued. "Learning from her was as educational as it was scary."

I snorted, thinking of the older woman who had been my mother's handmaid since she was young, until she turned head of house when mother became queen. "I'll say. I'm surprised she can't breathe fire."

Marie looked me dead in the eye. "I'm not so sure she can't."

We broke into laughter after a moment, while Rayla stood silent, her brow still raised.

"Word of advice, don't cross Miss Grant," Marie told Rayla, her nervousness forgotten.

"I will keep it in mind," Rayla said.

My handmaid sighed happily and wove the last plated strand onto my head and pinned it down. I turned my head from side to side, taking in her handiwork. Most of my dark-red hair was left long, falling past my shoulders, while Marie had woven the plated parts up and through each other, so it looked like I was wearing a delicate crown. "I love it, Marie. Thank you."

She fiddled here, plucked and smoothed there, then stepped back and grinned. "You look stunning, Eliza." Her brows shot up and she clasped her palm to her mouth, her gaze flicking to Rayla. The casual way she acted and felt around me when we were alone had gotten to her, and for most it would come off as disrespectful. Normally, Marie was very careful when it came to these things, as Miss Grant would figuratively have her head if she knew, but somehow, my cautious friend had slipped.

I spun around on my stool and reached out my hands. She slowly lowered hers from her face and placed them into mine.

"You did good, Marie. Don't worry about it."

My handmaid gave me a shaky smile, quickly eyeing Rayla, before excusing herself and exiting my chamber. She seemed very flustered when passing my new guard and my heart sank for a moment. It seemed my attempt to loosen the tension had worked too well.

"I would appreciate it if you didn't tell anyone how Marie acts around me," I said, standing up. "It took me quite some time to have her be comfortable enough around me to lose that stupid 'Your Highness' business. I'd hate for her to be scolded for it."

Rayla stood still as a statue, only her eyes following me as I sank down on my bed to slip on a pair of shoes. "Why would you care?" she asked.

I frowned. "Because she is my friend. One of the few people in this place who won't lie to me to keep in my good graces. She speaks her mind if I ask her about something, which I value highly. I'd detest seeing her change that."

"And you think me ratting her out to Miss Grant would do that?"

"Undoubtedly."

My guard tapped an index finger to one of the sliver scythes hooked to her belt. "As I said last night, your secrets are my secrets. I did not plan on talking to anyone."

"Good. And I would appreciate the same from you. If you could, please feel free to call me Eliza, I am not comfortable with the whole devoted servant thing. It gets tired rather quickly. And leads to all manner of lies and deceit."

Rayla met my stare and I felt heat wash over me at the intensity of it. "I am not your servant, so it won't be a problem. I am here to protect you from harm. That is all."

"Right." I let my gaze sink and walked up to her, in order to leave my chambers. Next to her, I halted. "How long did you train, to become a Dovani?"

Once again, her index finger tapped the top of her right scythe. "Eight years." Her voice betrayed her then, as she was unable to ban a certain amount of anger from it. I wanted to ask, but feared she would not answer. She didn't know me, so it wasn't surprising. As I opened the door and left with her in tow, I hoped that one day I'd find out why the length of her training angered her. There were many things I wanted to ask, so many things I wished to know, about the rest of the world, the twin cities, if she'd ever visited Selphora, the ruling city, or where she was from originally. Had she maybe even met the Witchgoddes? But more than that, she intrigued me. Who was she? Other than a Dovani, whose presence was like a live flame. Bright and hot.

Part of me knew I was trying to find ways to distract myself from what Pavette had told me the night before, focusing on the most intriguing person around me, but another part of me knew that I would have been curious regardless. And even other parts of me came up with forbidden questions. Would touching her again result in the same prickling sensation it had last night? Why did

I feel like turning around trying it right now? My breath grew short and my heartrate picked up. A blush crept up my cheeks. I felt giddy in a heavy way, which was an oxymoron, but didn't change facts. How did someone I knew so little about, who was so quiet and serious get to me like that?

Chapter Four
Rayla

Eliza's shoulders rose and sank with a deep breath as she led the way through the castle, down past the entrance hall through an arch beneath the stairs. Down here, the walls were free of any sparkling gems. Soon, sounds and smells of the kitchen reached us and she offered to let me leave through a door to the left for breakfast. It would come up to the servant's kitchen. I declined, following her into what looked like a smaller breakfast room. A big, dark-brown table was set up, with five chairs surrounding it.

This had to be the family dining area when they were not entertaining. The king and queen, along with Eliza's siblings were already seated, with no servants around. It was strange and I felt a little uneasy intruding on a family moment like this, but I took up vigil next to the door while my charge rounded the table and sat down, facing me.

Her family greeted her in various tones from chipper to loving, and sleepy.

"Your hair looks pretty," the queen said. "I wish you would let Marie do it up more often, she is good at that."

"Right?" Pavette grinned over a spoonful of egg. "I should snatch her away and take her with me. She could do my wedding hair."

Everyone stopped eating, staring at Eliza's sister instead. Pavette placed her now empty spoon down and looked from one to the next. "What? You all really thought I would keep Eliza in the dark about the decision? And then? We would have just packed up and left, or would any of you have talked to her at all?"

"Of course, we would have," the queen said. "But if you had let us handle it – as we agreed – we could have explained."

"Pavette explained, Mother," my charge said, cutting into a buttered toast. "And while I think it is a mistake to align with Selphora through an allegiance with Leozar, I also know that my vote does not count." She bit into the toast and closed her eyes at the taste, ignoring the stern look from her father.

"And what would you know of such things?" Reagan asked. "You have not been trained in the delicate dance of politics as I have. One day, you will also strengthen Chardour through a favorable marriage. It is your place in this family."

"Reagan," the queen said, glaring at him.

The prince shifted uneasily under her stare but scowled. "What? It is about time she comes to terms with who she is and what is expected from her. I'm not keeping her opinionated self around when I am king."

"Reagan Vaster!" the king thundered. "You will not speak about your sister with such disrespect. She is a member of this family, just like you and Pavette."

Prince Reagan was not dissuaded by his father's tone of voice, however. "You have been spoiling Eliza since birth, furthering her ridiculous need for exploration and adventure. Now you sit with the problems, we had to pay a horrendous amount of money – money we could have spent on more important things – to keep her safe and in this palace while we are gone." His green eyes – so much like Eliza's – found his sister and glibness shone on his features. "And while I also question the wisdom of aligning with Selphora, you are absolutely right in saying that your vote simply doesn't count."

The king inhaled to start shouting at him, but Eliza shot him a gentling smile, cut off more from her toast and addressed her brother. "Reagan, you might have been tutored to rule since shitting your pants, but you let people influence you way too much. Why are you against aligning with Selphora?"

He looked taken aback but quickly caught himself. "Because more kingdoms oppose the Witchgoddes than take her side."

Eliza stuck the toast into her mouth. "And who told you that?"

He frowned. "Senator Gilles."

"Aha. Senator Gilles. The one you have been seen with in the Lotus, if I am not mistaken."

Reagan spluttered something while the queen tried to keep a straight face and the king looked angrier by the second. "You see, brother, many kingdoms may oppose the Witchgoddes, but she and her allies control the floating cities. Cities she can move at will. If Selphora and the twin cities attack from above, it won't matter how many kingdoms oppose them, because every single one of them will fall. I'd stay neutral, align with a neutral kingdom and profit off both sides. The rebel kingdoms will need our crystal to move their armies and Selphora needs to stock their weapons with Doran. Not to mention all the other crystals we export, for various magical uses, whose demand will only increase if a war breaks out. We are too small to not break under the coming pressure, but if we aligned with Espen instead of Leozar, we could bolster our forces and stay out of the war."

The silence that followed was only interrupted by Eliza continuing to eat as if she had spoken about the weather.

"Preposterous," Reagan said. "We won't be able to stay out of the war."

"Just because you want to prove yourself doesn't mean the people want to fight."

"The people?" The prince chuckled. "The people do what we tell them to do."

"It is funny to me how you have been 'tutored to lead' while understanding nothing about how kingdoms work. We rule, because we look after our people, our kingdom used to thrive because Father kept them safe, fed, and bettered the working circumstances in the mines. Chardour was insignificant before the great divide and Mother and Father built it up with foresight and equality in mind, making it one of the richest in all Iyune. Choosing a side now will alleviate the strain on our citizens, but when the war breaks out, it will cripple us. That is why I think it is a mistake." She casually finished her toast.

Reagan snorted. "As if you have any idea what you're talking about."

"Enough!" the king said. "Reagan, you should listen to your sister more often than to dubious Senators and Eliza, while I appreciate your input, the choice has been made. This is our way forward, come what may. Besides, Espen is joining in talks with the rebels as we speak, they will surely not stay neutral for much longer, which makes your point moot." He smiled at his daughter with obvious pride. "But your reasoning is solid and I commend you for it."

Prince Reagan looked like he wanted to say something, but his mother shot him one of those impressive glares and he clapped his mouth shut, then continued to sulk into his breakfast.

As for me, I stood surprised. Eliza's wit was sharp, while her knowledge of her kingdom and people surpassed that of many royals I had met. Coupled with how she was around her handmaid, her personality started to impress me. It was a far cry from what Prince Reagan had told me about her last evening.

How she was young – barely twenty-two – childish, selfish, and reckless. I could see recklessness in her behavior and even a hint of childishness, but that all seemed to stem from curiosity and interest. She'd asked me about my training after all, not many people did.

And there was the fact that I had held my breath seeing her this morning when entering her chamber. Her dark-red hair complimented her forest green eyes in such a stunning way, I'd had trouble not staring at her. Even now, my eyes were glued to her. Her porcelain skin was covered in freckles and shone in a sliver of sun, peeking through the windows behind her. Her eyebrows were darker than her hair and moved with each expression, telling anyone who looked how she felt. It wasn't a good trait to have when in my business, but on her, it was fascinating to watch. She glanced at me and my thoughts froze, but before I knew it, she averted her eyes and I fought to let my gaze wander.

The room itself was cozy, missing the splendor of a typical royal dining room. The floors consisted of sandstone blocks, the furniture looked old and well used, and the two dressers standing on either side of me and the door, were laden with all manner of things. From vases with meadow flowers, to a clock inside a dome of glass, to piles of books. The windows behind the table overlooked a part of the gardens I hadn't seen yet, revealing a square building further away. It looked like a garrison and I wondered about it. Did it have military stationed there? Where there training grounds? Maybe I could ask Eliza about it later. She didn't seem to mind talking to a guard, or a maid, or marshals.

I felt her look at me and a startling feeling bubbled through my stomach. Something close to nervousness, but warmer and more exciting. I inwardly shook myself to get rid of the feeling and luckily, it passed as quickly as it had arisen.

The topic of discussion changed to Pavette's future marriage and the travelling details and Eliza soon only poked at her food, quietly distancing herself from the conversation. It did seem unfair to leave her behind when she cared so much about her sister and surely wanted to be with her during such an important time as beginning a new life, far away. But the rules – similar in this regard in every kingdom – made sense, but it seemed more like a punishment than a precaution. They could have left the prince in charge, if he was to lead the kingdom one day, it would have been a good practice for him.

King Edrick rose from his chair and rang a bell next to his plate, upon which the door opened and servants arrived to clean up. "I will head for the throne room to go through a few details with the senate. Join me?" he asked his wife.

Queen Mauve nodded and the two left together, followed closely by a still sulking Prince Reagan. Left alone, the princesses chatted a bit, before deciding to head to the gardens together. As I turned to follow them, a maid came up to me. She was older than most of the others, thin and with a stern face. "I am Miss Grant," she introduced herself. "Have you eaten yet?" Her voice was as clipped and short as her demeanor suggested.

"No, Miss Grant."

She handed me a bundle of cloth. "You can do so while watching over her, the Goddess knows she needs someone to." With that, she turned on her heel and strode away to scold a young maid who had spilled a bit of milk on the table.

I weighed the cloth in my hand and left the room, knowing exactly what Marie had spoken about when talking about Miss Grant. Still, she had been thoughtful enough to leave me with something to eat.

****

The day was warm and other than trailing the sisters through the garden while eating what Miss Grant had offered me, I had nothing to do. When we passed the back of the castle, with the square building sitting in the distance, I wondered yet again whether it was being used as a garrison, but I didn't want to disturb the sisters and what little time they had left together. Although I itched for some training, trying out the effect the altitude change would have on my body and my fighting. Not that I overly worried about it, but it was good being prepared.

During the time we wandered over paths leading through meticulously kept greens, flowers, and fountains, Eliza threw me looks over her shoulder from time to time. And while her face was very expressive, I was unable to tell whether she was angry at me being there and watching over her – intruding – or if there was another reason for her glances. I ignored it as best I could and took in my surroundings instead.

The sheer tranquility of the gardens was foreign to me. In Xilum we lived under a tight regiment, following a strictly planned day of training, sparring, and tactical lessons. Even after becoming a Dovani, most of us stayed, training and learning until we were needed somewhere. Xilum was a city of brick and mortar, gray and dark in almost every corner, this amount of green and warmth was nearly overwhelming. But I felt myself warm to it. I didn't miss my comrades, yet there had been comfort in knowing exactly what the day would bring. The routine had done wonders for the anxiety I had felt in the beginning and it had kept the dreams at bay.

I clenched my fists, pushing the thoughts about them deep and out of sight. But I couldn't stem them completely. They had come again last night, probably because of the change in scenery. And I had awoken panting and sweating.

It was always the same dream, filling me with dread and letting the feeling cling to me after I woke up. But I hadn't had one in a while. All I could hope for was that it would lessen and pass, so I could focus on my charge and do my job.

The sisters approached a large tree and sat down beneath it, using its trunk as a backrest. The trunk was enormous, looking like it would take at least three grown people to join hands around it.

If I was not mistaken, it was one of the rare elder trees, many of which had been destroyed during the Breaking fifty years ago. They were sacred to many cultures, said to keep evil at bay. I didn't believe in such stories, or the old Gods. Even if they did exists, we had a living Goddess among us, ruling us. It was stupid to think this rebellion would result in anything other than a massacre. Eliza had been right, the Witchgoddes had flying cities – two of which were Xilum and Yore – and she would attack from above. The rebels didn't stand a chance. I thought it was wise to align with Selphora on this, because it would be the winning side.

I took up vigil not far away, a bit higher up, to keep everything within my view. And while I got out my whetstone and sharpened one of my scythes, I opened up my senses to ascertain that no one else was around. This was a trait I had discovered long ago, as a child. It had been purely by accident and I had honed and used it ever since. I slowed my heartbeat and let my pulse radiate through me, feeling it in every part of my body. Pushing the feeling out in what felt like waves, the sounds grew louder and clearer. At first, the noise was incredible. Birds chirping, wind whistling, and the voices of the gardeners from closer to the castle drowned me, but I soon sifted through them, getting them in order. I wasn't trying to listen to the princesses, muting their conversation to focus on the bigger picture, when I heard my name. Helpless to my curiosity, I tentatively listened.

"Eliza, you have to stop staring at your Dovani," Pavette said. "It is only a matter of time before someone else notices, and that will not end well for you or for her."

"I am not staring. I look at her because she is interesting, and I want to ask her a million questions, but it's not like I know her well enough to just ask."

Pavette giggled. "Please, sister. I know you. And while you may have convinced yourself of the afore mentioned reason, I see you blush every time you look at her. I understand, she is beautiful and exotic, but be careful, if anyone finds out… Well, you know what happened to Princess Sayn of Midden."

An exasperated sigh floated across the distance. "Princess Sayn was knocked up by her coachman, and decided to be an idiot about it. She could have easily married some prince and pretended the child was his. Instead, she professed her love for a commoner and was exiled for it. Even if I become…infatuated, what would be the worst that could happen?"

"Her kind is dangerous, sister," Pavette said. "And I don't think she would reciprocate."

Eliza laughed. "Whatever, it's beside the point, because I have no interest in Rayla other than what I told you before. She is a Dovani, she might as well have come from the stars. Doesn't that excite you?"

"No, Eliza, it scares me. I'm scared that we live in times where people like her are necessary. It scares me that we have to have her here for you. Promise me to keep your distance and not get too friendly. It will only lead to problems and possible heartache."

I had stopped sharpening my scythe, my hands stilling in my lap. The feeling from before was back, that warm nervousness. Taking a deep breath, I reeled in my senses and put away my weapon and whetstone. For some reason, I didn't want to hear Eliza promising her sister she'd keep her distance. Why, was beyond me, but I remembered how her intense gaze felt on me and how that one little touch had prickled on my skin. I snorted and shook my head. This meant nothing. My only reason for being here was to protect her. Nothing more, nothing less.

Shortly after, the sisters got up and went back to the castle. Pavette left to prepare for their journey tomorrow and Eliza waited, at the side entrance her sister had vanished in, for me.

"I have a lesson scheduled for this afternoon." She frowned. "Embroidering. I severely lack talent for it, but I doubt anyone will attack me inside the castle. If you want, you can do something else instead."

I scrutinized her with a raised brow. "You are trying to get rid of me, aren't you, Your Highness?"

The princess gave me a dazzling smile. "I wouldn't dream of it, but if you want, we can skip the lesson and take a closer look at that old garrison you seem to be interested in." She pointed at the building.

I was taken aback. "How did you–"

"I notice things." Eliza eyed me up and down, leaving me a bit short of breath. "You want to go check it out?"

"I don't think it's a good idea."

Before I could add anything, Eliza had snatched the hems of her dress and bounded off. I fell into a sprint to catch up with her. She was a lot shorter than me, so it didn't take long, but when I reached her, she dashed on, laughing loudly. Short of snatching her up and throwing her over my shoulder, I was out of options to stop her.

Chapter Five
Eliza

Sneaking out and running from marshals, dubious men, and my sentinels had left me with more stamina than I had thought. Soon, the walls of the old garrison at the edge of the gardens loomed over me and I gasped when speeding through the open iron gates.

Rayla was neither out of breath, nor did she have trouble keeping up, but her steel-gray eyes were dark when she looked at me. She was not happy.

I twirled and let my skirts fall down, reaching out my hands to either side. "Welcome in the abandoned garrison," I called out. "We used to train fighters here, but since the military has moved to Khoras, closer to the Foudan, this was left empty."

"Where do the watchmen and soldiers of Dearn sleep and train?" Rayla asked.

Swiping back tendrils of hair that had come loose during my run, I took a few deep breaths to calm my pulse and breathing. I walked through the inner courtyard and out the other side, to the training grounds. "They live in the city, with their families. And they have training facilities right outside Dearn's gates. Mother didn't like having them here, within the palace walls, and she insisted that those with families here, should be with them, rather than stationed somewhere else." I grinned at the Dovani. "The military loves my mother for that."

"I bet," Rayla said, her face as stony as ever.

"Impressed?" I asked, waving at the training grounds. I hopped onto one of the horizontal wooden poles encasing the sandy grounds and lifted my legs over it. Frowning at my shoes sinking into the soft sand, I crouched down and pulled them off my feet.

"Hardly. These are fairly adequate training facilities, if a bit worse for wear." Rayla slunk through the enclosure smoothly, reminding me of that Sauvey once again. She came to stand next to me and glowered at my naked feet. "How am I going to explain your state when we get back?"

I laughed, threw my shoes down next to the enclosure and raised my fists, then circled her. "Don't worry about that, Marie has me covered. Want to show me some of your moves?" There was no rhyme or reason to my actions, other than that I wanted to know more about her, thinking this would be the way, but I was a little disappointed at her calm.

"No."

"Come on, please?" I punched the air next to her shoulder.

Rayla, who had her arms crossed, stood still, only her dark eyes followed my movements. "Absolutely not."

I jabbed out, this time hitting her shoulder softly. "Just one move?"

"Stop it, your Highness."

"Come one, I told you to call me Eliza." My fist flew out again, and before I knew what was happening, she caught my arm, twisted me around and brought my hand up behind my lower back, her free arm circling around my chest. My back smoothed against her armored torso and her breath tickled my neck. What felt like sparks travelled up my neck and forked down my back.

"Satisfied?" she rumbled.

I turned my face to her, meeting those daunting gray eyes. "Not even close."

Rayla let go of me immediately and stepped back. "I apologize, Your Highness."

My breath heavy and my heart pounding, I grunted, disappointed in the absence of her body against mine. Maybe Pavette was right, and I was fooling no one but myself. I wanted Rayla close, this show I was putting on was laughable and stupid.

"No need, Rayla. I am the one who should be sorry. And I am. I goaded you into reacting." I huffed out an embarrassed laugh. "This isn't me, you know. I have no idea why I did that."

"I do," she said to my surprise. "You are curious, thinking you need to gain my trust or favor in order to ask me things."

I tilted my head, looking at her, taken aback by her perceptiveness. With a nod, I wanted to pass her, to retrieve my shoes, but she gently clasped my upper arm and when our eyes met, her gaze was like cold fire.

"You have need for neither," she said. "If you want to know something, just ask, and I will do my best to answer to your satisfaction."

I swallowed, the fact of our renewed proximity catching up with me and my body.

Rayla brought her lips close to my ears. "As for the other reason… You should stop your thoughts about that. I am not made for, nor fond of flings with royalty. Not even when they are as beautiful and intriguing as you." With that, she let go of me and walked away. She picked up my shoes and held them out to me. My heart hammered and a blush crept up my cheeks as I took them from her and we exited the enclosure. Feeling like an absolute idiot, I stayed at her side as we made our way back to the castle. It took me the entire way to shake off my embarrassment.

She knew. So what? She had also said to ask the questions I had, which was far more important than the pesky butterflies in my stomach that had fluttered like crazy when we touched.

****

The next morning was busy. Servants dashed through the castle, gathering and packing, while Pavette oversaw the emptying of her chambers herself. Miss Grant barked orders in her stern, dusty voice and I tried to keep out of the way but wanted to spend as much time as I could with Pavette.

So for the most part, I tried helping her with smaller stuff, or lounged in her chambers. Rayla was never far away and kept a close eye on me. It both unnerved me and led to slight blushes now and again as I replayed the scene in the garrison over and over in my head. Even though I tried not to let my embarrassment get to me, it often did and I avoided talking to her. Not that it was difficult with everything going on and I soon dragged my focus to Pavette and her nervousness. I tried to calm my sister, telling her how visiting Sif would be amazing. A real, floating city. One hovering above the land. I had heard they used a certain type of gem to float up and down. I could not imagine the view from a floating city, much less floating up to one.

"Just imagine, you'll be able to see Leozar from the air. The view has to be fantastic." I picked up some of her perfumes and creams, placing them carefully in an ornate box that could be closed and carried around.

Pavette sighed and pointed at a heap of dresses on her bed. "This one goes into the big trunk, this one in the smaller one. I need to have some adequate clothing for when we arrive." The maids buzzing around us followed her orders quickly. "It's not that I'm not excited to see Sif," she said to me. "But what if…what if the people there don't like me? What if I don't like them? And what of Prince Marcus?"

"Pavette." I closed the lid of the box, handing it to Marie, who smiled and carried it to one of the big trunks near the bed. "They will love you, everyone does. As for Marcus, he is lucky and blessed to be marrying you. And you like most people, I wouldn't worry about either." I walked up to my sister and drew an arm around her shoulder. "Besides, if you hate it, write to me and I'll come over."

Pavette leaned her head on my shoulder, making her adorable dimples appear as she smirked. "Not that you visiting would better my circumstances, should they be bad. But I would always welcome you." We hugged and I kissed her temple, wishing I could go with her. The notion of just doing it and hiding in the entourage woke once more, as did the reasonable side of me, telling me I couldn't

"Princess Fabienne," Miss Grant's dusty voice snared behind us. "The king wants to see you in the master study."

"I'll be there shortly, thank you, Miss Grant."

The older maid nodded, looked around and homed in on a poor young thing who was busy folding underdresses – in a way that would apparently rumple them, as we all found out from the resulting tirade.

I still heard Miss Grant's squawking all the way down the hall to my parents' chambers, acutely aware of Rayla following me. Silent as a shadow.

When I entered the study, my father stood in front of the tall windows, looking over the gardens as the sun steadily rose.

"Father? You asked for me," I said and walked closer.

He turned, his brown eyes finding me, then my guard. "Dovani, will you be so kind as to wait outside? I have a private matter to discuss with my child."

Rayla bowed and closed the door behind her.

I frowned. "What is this about?"

My father reached out a palm, capturing my hand in his, then walked me over to one of the couches. We sat down and he stared into the empty fireplace for a while. He was a handsome man, my father. With kind brown eyes, dark-blond hair and an even darker beard. Both were streaked with gray and the lines around his eyes grew deeper when he smiled. I knew those eyes could look dangerous, as I had cowered beneath his stare often being the child I had been. And I had seen the authority he radiated when speaking publicly. Right now he looked kind, and tired.

"Eliza, I hate leaving you here, but our rules have a reason." He squeezed my hand gently and pointed to a sealed scroll on the table in front of us. "I have left you instructions to follow during our absence. Please read them and do the tasks I have set for you. Other than that, our good steward Stefan will see to everything."

"Of course." I was astounded and blinked at the scroll, not expecting my father to entrust me with anything.

"You are my joy, daughter. Your sister is my pride, your brother my legacy, your mother my heart, but you are my joy. I know what drives you, as I have been the same in my youth, where that you had been born a son, I would have named *you* my heir."

I didn't know what to say to that, not sure if I even could speak as tears clogged up my throat. His smile was warm and he squeezed my hand again. "Be good while we're away."

He pulled in a deep breath and stood from the couch.

"Father?"

"Yes?"

"If Pavette doesn't like it there… I mean, if she and Marcus don't get along, or if he doesn't treat her right–"

"Then we'll take her right back home."

I nodded. "Promise?"

"I promise. We might be in dangerous waters, but I'll make sure Pavette is happy, as much as she lets me."

"Good."

My father walked back to the window and gave me his back. "Now go, be with your sister for as long as you can."

I stood, picked up the scroll, went over to hug my father and then left him to what looked like deep thoughts as he stared out into the new day.

****

Too soon, midday came and with it the carriages were loaded up. Then everything went very quick. I hugged Pavette for a long time, whispering to her how Father would not force her to marry if she did not want to. She pulled back and smiled at me with tears in her eyes.

"I will be fine, sweet sister. You be good." She squeezed my palms then turned and entered the royal carriage. My mother and father hugged me as well, telling me they loved me and to be on my best behavior.

I would have rolled my eyes at them, but I knew I'd miss them, no matter how soon they'd be back.

Even Reagan gave me hug and tousled my hair. "Stay away from the city, sister," he said with a smirk. "If you can."

"If you stay away from Sif's brothels," I said and winked at him. My brother bristled and quickly followed our family into the carriage.

The four horses in front of the carriage fell into step and pulled, their hooves echoing off the wall of the palace. I waved at my family as I watched the carriages drive down the alley. For a long time, I stood and stared after them, missing my sister already.

I threw Rayla a glance, getting something back that was almost close to an encouraging smile. The expression floored me and I thought that a real smile would weaken my knees for sure.

As we headed back into the castle, I went to my study to read the scroll my father had left for me, just to know what he expected of me in the coming days. My study was small, but I loved it dearly. Other than rest of the rooms in my chambers, it had Sinusai crystals embedded into the walls all around the room and I could flick them on with a latch next to my favorite armchair. What was so special about this was how I was able to dim the light by turning the latch. Something very new my father had ordered to be installed here for testing. The palace cutters and inventers had worked on it for months, finishing it only a few weeks ago. I loved how it had turned out.

Rayla stood watch next to the door, her quiet presence calming my nervousness and exciting me at the same time. I had never been without my family before and the castle seemed all the quieter in their absence. It wasn't true, of course, but somehow felt like it.

Something akin to fear rumbled through my gut as I broke the seal of the scroll and rolled it out.

Sitting in my favorite armchair, I read the scroll, nodding through all the points my father had written up. With his elegant handwriting, he had jotted down a few decrees I would have to make, some things to go over with our steward Stefan, and… My eyes widened. I would have to sit passing judgement. In three days. Bringing the scroll closer, my hands shaking, I read that part again. It couldn't be.

"Shit in a chasm," I whispered when the words stayed the same. Sitting judgement. It meant receiving the public, passing judgement on disputes. While I had watched my father and mother do it countless times, and generally thought it an acceptable way to connect with our people – even if it could get difficult – I had always hoped never to be in their place. Nausea swirled through my body and I eyed the door, debating whether I would make it to my privy, or spill my guts right over the woven carpet in front of me.

"Your Highness?" The voice came from far away, then a hand landed on my shoulder, shaking me softly. "Eliza?"

I looked up into steel-gray eyes, as Rayla bent over me with a concerned look on her face.

"What is it?" she asked.

Too nervous to speak, I handed her the scroll and tapped the last entry of my father.

Rayla squinted and read his wishes. "Sit judgement at new moon."

"Hmhm," I made.

"What does it mean?"

I grunted. "It means I have to pass judgement on the public for a day. But I can't, that is too much responsibility. I have no idea how my parents do it."

"You'll settle disputes?"

"Yup."

"And you are afraid of it?"

I glanced at her, seeing that raised brow. "You wouldn't be?"

"No. While there are always two sides to every story and blame can be shared, so can punishment, if it gets too hard to decide."

"Right."

"I am confident you will do well."

I chuckled. "That makes one of us. I have seen lives destroyed by judgements."

"You just need a bit of time to wrap your head around it." Rayla pursed her lips, seeing I was still having a hard time calming down. "Do you play?" She waved at the Trice board on the table to our right.

"I do."

"Let's have a round, to get your mind off this. Once you get used to the thought, you'll feel better."

"Promise?" I asked, hating the weakness in my voice.

This time she actually smiled at me and I had been right, it was radiant and took my breath away. For a moment, I wanted to suggest she just keep on smiling like that, in order to make everything else disappear.

"I promise."

She had no trouble winning against me, which was refreshing. Still, I couldn't help feeling a little embarrassed as time passed and I calmed down. She'd been right, I only needed to get used to the thought. I had seen my parents do it every month for as long as I could remember, it would be fine. But my breakdown in front of Rayla ate at me and I was not able to really talk to her as we played. Besides, being this close to her was awfully distracting. I kept watching her long-fingered hands move about her pieces, wondering how they would feel on my skin.

It was truly pathetic and I kicked myself inwardly. It wasn't like she'd go away any time soon.

"Why did it take you eight years to become a Dovani?" I asked, mainly to distract myself, but also because it had been one of the questions I wanted to ask her since the beginning.

Rayla threw me a quick glance, then swiped a few of her braids back behind her shoulder. "I am a woman."

"That is your answer?" I gaped at her. "Really?"

She sighed. "There aren't many women in Xilum and Yore, not those that train in fighting at least. And even the few that are soldiers, rarely become Dovani. We have to prove ourselves more, train harder, and fight the stigma of still not belonging or being enough."

"That is awful." I slid one piece closer, setting a trap for Rayla. "I bet it leads to an awesome sisterhood though."

Her lips thinned and she moved away from my trap. "Not really."

I moved another piece next to my first, fattening my trap. "How so?"

"I am an outsider, even among my warrior sisters." She took the bait and kicked my two pieces off the board.

I grinned and moved in with another, swiping her strongest piece.

"Hey!"

I couldn't stop the giggle rising from my chest at her surprised face. "You fell for it."

My guard smirked, making my breath shorten again. If she kept this up, I would have a hard time remembering her words in the garrison.

"Rematch?" I asked.

"Rematch."

We set up the board again." Why are you an outsider? And please tell me if my questions are invading or overstepping a line."

Rayla only shrugged. "It's not a secret, so I see no problem in telling you." She started the next round. "I was found by a group of soldiers as a child. They had been patrolling the outskirts of Leede and there I was. I grew up in Xilum and while that would suggest me belonging, my fellow trainees always thought the captains were treating me differently. They did. I was treated harsher and had to train harder. But they also saw me as kind of a little sister, or at least some of them did. Which meant while they constantly pushed me, they also joked and laughed with me. My fellow trainees grew envious and I distanced myself. It resulted in me being a loner. But I don't mind it."

It was the longest she had ever spoken in one go and I hung on every word. "You grew up in the training facilities of Xilum? Wow. What a place to raise a child."

She raised one brow and slid a piece closer to one of mine. "It isn't a good place to grow up, cold and colorless. But I was lucky to have a home and someone who cared about my upbringing. Even if that upbringing consisted of fighting."

I couldn't imagine Rayla as a child, growing up around hardened warriors, although it did explain her detached calm. I wondered what she thought of me, probably that I was spoiled and reckless. Growing up in a pretty palace with servants to wait on me. No wonder she wasn't interested in me the way I was in her.

My eyes met hers and I quickly looked down, feeling my cheeks heating. She did say I was beautiful, though. I'd take that.

Chapter Six
Rayla

The next two days went by fast. Eliza and I got into a certain routine. Or rather, she got into a routine and I was always by her side. I'd wait for her to get up, dressed and ready, before we headed down to the dining area. Eliza asked me to sit with her on the second day and I wanted to decline, but she looked so lonely sitting at that huge table, so I gave in and sat with her. None of the servants said anything, but Miss Grant threw me peeved looks whenever we crossed her way. I did not react to it, but the animosity was a familiar feeling.

After breakfast, Eliza took a walk around the gardens and then met up with the steward Stefan in the throne room to discuss the tasks of the coming day. Planning and carrying out her tasks usually took up some time and, in the afternoon, we settled in her study playing Trice, or she would read. I was fascinated by the sheer amount of books she called her own, and stared at the rows, wishing I could get lost in them. There was so much knowledge, so many stories, to get to know… It was something I'd never had growing up. To my dismay, my charge noticed me staring and said I was welcome to sit with her and read.

For a moment, happiness flooded me, but I quickly clamped down on it. "No, Your Highness, thank you. Reading would distract me from being vigilant."

Eliza looked saddened by my answer and I was surprised by how much it bothered me. Why did she care? She shouldn't care.

That night, she took along a few books – probably for nightly reading – and we went to her chamber. Eliza passed her bed and opened the powder-blue door adjoining our rooms with an elbow. She walked to my bed and set the books down on my bedside table. With an enchanting grin, she turned to me. "Maybe you can read before going to bed," she offered. "Or when you wait for me to wake up."

I had no idea what to say. Gratitude swallowed me, but the sight of her sheepish and nervous grin made me want to hug her. I shook myself inwardly. This trail of thought had to stop immediately. She was likable and beyond beautiful, but her actions made me feel more than a physical pull. It endeared her to me. And that was dangerous.

"Thank you, Your Highness," I said, sure that my face had betrayed nothing of my surprise or feelings, I saw her shoulders sink.

"Well, they're there if you want them," she said in a small voice.

I bowed curtly and she passed me on the way to her room without looking at me.

"Sleep well, Your Highness, and thank you. Again."

Eliza halted, but then slunk through the door and closed it softly. A sigh escaped me and I had to control myself to not go after her. What I wanted was to assure her that I was ecstatic about her thoughtfulness, but I couldn't. As that heavy nervousness swirled in my stomach, I wasn't sure whether I would be able to put into words what I felt, without reaching for her. Which was something I constantly wanted to do, after feeling her in my arms at the garrison, when she had goaded me into reacting to her. If I did, I knew she would let me, and that, right there, was the problem.

Blowing out a frustrated breath, I unhooked my scythes and placed them under my pillow, then I undressed and washed up in the bowl of clean water, sitting on a small table opposite the blue door. I smirked unwittingly when I felt how cold the water was in comparison to the days before. I bet Miss Grant had something to do with it, as the servants normally warmed the water in the evening. Sitting with Eliza at the breakfast table was not my place, and the older woman let me know it this way. I lay awake for hours, flicking through the books on my bedside table, until my lids grew heavy and I fell asleep.

****

I floated. Drifting through misty clouds, through swaths of cold moisture. Underneath me, far away, an unknown country woke to a new sunrise. The golden light of the morning blanketed hills of green and a peak of white, standing out against its surroundings like the tooth of a Sauvey. Small towns littered the valleys and a big lake, fed by a river sat to the left. Directly beneath me was the biggest town, more like a city, and the walls and dark roofs, greeted me with a feeling of welcome. Tranquility. Peace.

A sound shook the earth and my head snapped up. The white peak seemed to vibrate, tips of snow falling down. I was pulled toward it, unable to fight back. Pulled, faster and faster, until I shot through the sky like lightning. Ridges and slopes soon became visible. Sharp edges under a blanket of white. Deadly and hard.

My face stung from the cold air, and my breath was heavy with fear. Still accelerating, the peak got closer. I tried to close my eyes, knowing I would smash into the mountain any second now, but my lids didn't listen to me. Dread wove through me like tendrils of smoke, lashing, clinging, and binding. A fear I had never felt before ate away at my very soul, devouring who I was.

Spikes of stone greeted me on impact, skewering and breaking my body. Shattering me. I screamed.

****

"Rayla. Rayla! Wake up."

My eyes opened and I sat up, scythe in hand, pouncing on a figure looming over me. We crashed to the floor, me on top of the figure.

Eliza's pretty face froze when my blade settled on her neck. For a second, I could not make sense of anything, then I realized I was grabbing the throat of my charge, holding a weapon to her. I crawled back, my head hitting the wooden frame of my bed with an audible thud. I didn't even register the pain, as I tried to get off her as fast as I could.

Sweat clung to every part of my skin and my heart hammered like mad. I had nearly hurt her.

"Goddess, I am so sorry, Eliza," I rasped. "I never meant to… did I hurt you?" Shaking with the dread, lingering from my dream and with what I had done, I clasped my knees to my chest, unable to reach for Eliza.

The princess sat up, fingers running over her throat. "What happened, Rayla? Are you – you're shaking." She very slowly moved closer, laying a palm on my naked shoulder. "I heard you scream and came running. You jerked around in your bed, so I tried waking you."

"Did I hurt you?" I asked again.

"No. You just surprised me, that is all."

"I almost sliced your throat. I am so sorry."

Eliza grabbed my shaking hand and pried the scythe from my fist. She got up to her knees and placed the

66

blade on my bedside table, then sat down next to me so our sides touched. I realized she still had my hand in hers, squeezing it softly, then she rubbed her thumb over my knuckles.

"You're fine. You're safe now." Her words loosened something within me and I was powerless not to let my head sink to her shoulder. A voice in my head said to keep my distance, to send her to her room, to tell her everything was fine. But nothing was fine. The fear from the dream had followed me, icing through my veins. I shook with it, not able to resist.

Eliza wound her arms around me and pulled me close. She stroked through my hair and hummed, while rocking from side to side.

"I've got you. It was just a dream."

It wasn't and I knew it. I've had the same dream all my life. Racing toward that mountain, barreling into it, fearing it. I did not fear dying, and it wasn't the impact that made my skin crawl. It was the mountain itself. A peak of evil so gruesome and dangerous, it was able to end the world.

This time was different, I had never been comforted before and it calmed me, while making tears gather in my eyes.

The princess still hummed and rocked us, cradling my head and shoulders in her arms. My breath returned to normal slowly and my heartrate steadied, now I fought tears from spilling. One shaky breath after another, I concentrated on her. She smelled like a field of flowers in the sun, her skin was soft and warm, her palms stroking me gently. I knew harshness, and I knew lust, both combined well. But what I felt in Eliza's arms was comfort, safety, and protection. Things sorely lacking from my world. It lit me up with a warmth I had not experienced before. And yes, there was lust as well.

But it was more like an undeniable pull, something I had to react to. Like gravity.

The fear faded, as did my shaking, making way for that heavy nervousness I had come to associate with Eliza. She was too close, and not close enough.

I lifted my head from her shoulder, coming up to her face.

Worried green eyes searched me. "Better?" Her palms now slid to both sides of my face and her thumb wiped at a single tear running down my left cheek. I was hopelessly caught in her gaze, sinking ever deeper into those pools of green.

My skin beneath her hands started to prickle and come to life, thrumming with a sudden need and want that took my breath away. I needed to touch her alabaster skin, count every freckle on her entire body and taste her lips. But I shouldn't. I warred with myself for a while, when her gaze dipped to my lips, only to flick back to my eyes and heat up.

I was nearly lost to her then. All I wanted was to surge forward and kiss her, as the tension between us grew to an unbearable degree. I forced myself to lean back so her hands dropped from my face. Our eye contact broke, as did the moment.

"Y-you need to sleep, your Highness. Tomorrow is a big day for you. You will have to sit judgement in a few hours."

Eliza folded her hands in her lap. "Right. Will you be fine?" her tone was soft, but shaky.

I didn't have the heart or self-control to look at her, so I just nodded, staring at the clawed feet of the dresser sitting against the wall. "Thank you, yes."

She got up and walked to the powder-blue door. "There is no shame in wanting what's forbidden," she whispered and my eyes rose to her face. "And there is no shame in bad dreams, or the fear and desolation they can bring. Know that."

Before I could answer, she was gone, leaving me feeling more alone than I had in all those years in Xilum.

I pulled myself to my feet and sat down on my too soft bed, my gaze fixed on the door. Everything inside of me wanted to open it. To go to her. But I stayed where I was, fisting the sheets on both sides of my legs. Eliza was right, there was no shame in wanting the forbidden, but it was something entirely different to act on that want. I could not. She was a princess, I was her guard.

"Shit," I breathed out. A guard who she had to comfort like a child after I had attacked her. Wow. Some guard I was. How pathetic.

I sprang to my feet and dressed in my soft, black training gear, then I took the training sticks from my bag and tip-toed to the second door, leading me directly into the hallway, connecting all the rooms of Eliza's chambers.

The castle was mostly empty, and the few guards I found on their posts bowed when they recognized me. Leaving through one of the many side entrances, I jogged through the garden and toward the abandoned garrison. The grass and flowers around smelled lovely. Crickets chirped in the bushes and even an owl hooted from one of the trees further away. They were soft and gentle sounds, comfortingly normal, yet amplified in the darkness.

Once I reached the training grounds, I began to practice on the damaged dummies made of straw. It took me longer to go out of breath and work up a sweat than usual, but it was what I needed right now. I didn't stop when my breath eventually grew ragged or sweat ran down my face and back. Only once the birds started singing and the horizon grew pale, did I let my arms sink. Feeling my body burn and hum with exhaustion, I left the enclosure and jogged back, planning on being ready when Eliza woke up.

When I got to her chambers, I quietly opened her door a fraction to peer inside. She was still asleep. Like the idiot I was, I snuck into her room and toward her bed. Why, I couldn't say, but the closer I got, the more dread stole itself into my chest. Where was her dark-red hair? It was so long, it had to peek out everywhere. With a shaking hand I pulled back her covers, to reveal a bunch of pillows, formed roughly into the shape of a body.

I let the blanket fall, gasping. She had snuck out, just like me. "Fuck," I grated out and glanced around for any clues. One of her closet doors was slightly ajar and I nearly ripped it from its hinges to look inside. What looked like hair peeked out from a drawer and I pulled it out. Wigs, facial hair, and long rolls of cloth. Eliza's drawer of costumes.

I cursed and stormed off. Still only clad in my training clothes, I sprinted out of the castle and searched the gardens. Nothing. I hadn't had much hope, knowing she was probably in the lower city, escaping.

As fast as I could, I ran to the marshal station, not knowing Dearn enough to simply look on my own without guidance.

The men stared at me as I mowed past them, barging into marshal Jentz's office. The older man looked up from the chaos of papers on his desk. He eyed me up and down, then folded his fingers over his belly and smirked. "Lost her, didn't you?"

"I have no time for your gloating. Where could she have gone?"

Marshal Jentz scratched his chin, the sound of his nails in the beard beyond unnerving. "Try the inner city, you'll know it when you hit it. There is one street that is broader than the rest, it has all sorts of pubs, gambling places, and brothels. She loves spending time there to do what she calls people-watching. I'd start there and work my way out."

"Thank you," I said and turned away.

"Dovani."

Biting my teeth together, I faced him once more. I had no time for lectures or whatever the hell else he wanted to impose on me.

"Find her. Follow the loudest crowd, and she'll surely not be far."

I nodded at him and left. It was already dawning and during my way into the city, I wondered what kind of establishments would be open this long.

I found the wide street easy enough, and while the atmosphere changed from quaint to seedy within one turn, I was astounded by the many people milling around.

Smoke and the scent of sweat and alcohol was thick, as was laughter and cackling. Of course, I was noticed right away. I wore tight black clothing, not something any respectable – or in this part of town – unrespectable woman would wear. When I was in my armor, people knew what it stood for and showed me respect. Right now, I was just running around a bad part of Dearn, wearing something skintight – not leaving much to the imagination.

Any crude words, or whistles, or groping hand was met with a warning glare, and for most, that was more than enough to keep them at bay. The others, I swatted to the side, continuing my search.

I ran up and down the street, growing frantic, when I remembered what marshal Jentz had said. I halted and listened for a few seconds, but a drunken man soon stumbled into me. Fleeing into a narrow side-alley, I calmed my breathing, steadied my heartbeat, and listened. The cacophony was overwhelming. Music, slurred voices, laughter, and groaning. Filtering the sounds and voices I focused on them, one by one, to push them to the side.

Then I heard loud laughter, and a question. A voice answered, deepened, but unmistakable.

"Eliza," I said, sprinting from the alley and back into the crowd, following her voice like a hound would a blood trail.

A nervous laugh led me through another alley where a group of men had surrounded a smaller one, the princess. She was backed into a corner, talking fast, but the men closed in.

"I have no idea what you're talking about," I heard her say.

"You know. You cheated. Now hand over the money, boy," one of the men sneered.

"I have not cheated. I won against you fair and square."

A knife blinked in the hand of the man and I lunged at him. Twisting his arm so hard he yelled, I snatched the knife from him and elbowed him in the face. I pushed him away and he collided with one of his peers. Quickly, I put myself between the men and Eliza.

"Rayla?"

"What in the ever-loving – who the fuck are you supposed to be?" another man asked. He was tall and burly, his nose crooked from one too many punches. His friend still held his wrist, cursing.

"The lot of you will leave now," I said. "Or face the consequences."

Three stares met me, before the large man chuckled. "You may have caught Jimmy by surprise, but not rest of us. Step aside, make your little friend give us what is ours, and we will go." He held up his hands. "No harm done. But stay in our way and we will hurt you, little miss."

A small hand wound around my right upper arm from behind. "Let's just do as they say," Eliza whispered.

"Did you win the money, as you said, fair and square?" I asked over my shoulder.

"I did."

"Then we will give them nothing." I raised my fists and took a stance.

Again, I was met with chuckles. This time, I smiled. Being underestimated always gave me additional drive, and the upper hand.

The large man with the mashed-up nose came at me. I ducked beneath his grabbing paws, letting my fist fly up, soundly connecting with his jaw. His head flew up and I socked him in the stomach with my other fist. The air left him with a huffing sound as he snapped forward. Stepping back a bit, I raised my knee, letting his nose bounce on it. He grunted and teetered to the side, meeting the cobblestones like a felled tree.

"Leave now. And take your buddy with you," I told the two remaining men. They gaped at me for a few seconds, then at their fallen and groaning comrade, who wheezed and rolled across the ground.

Quickly, the two scooped their buddy up and dragged him from the alley.

I turned to face my charge, feeling like an absolute failure.

Just as I opened my mouth to apologize, Eliza blinked at me, her green eyes as round as saucers. "That was incredible. You just felled that overgrown man like a tree. Within a second."

The urge to grin at the comparison snuck up on me but I denied it. "You can't leave like that, Eliza."

"Oh, stop it. I was perfectly safe." She waved me off.

I stepped toward her, bringing our faces so close that she hit the wall behind her with her back. "You. Can't. Leave. Without telling me. How am I supposed to protect you?"

Eliza gasped, her lips below that ridiculous mustache opening slightly. "Y-you left first."

"To train. In the middle of the night. When you should be sound asleep."

"I wasn't though, was I?" That glare I had come to know scalded me. "I held you in my arms, feeling something happen between us, and you sent me away."

The panic I had felt while searching for her ebbed away, leaving room for need. I swallowed as the feeling rose. With another step, I wedged her between the wall and myself, powerless to stop myself. When our bodies touched, my skin tingled.

Eliza rose onto her toes and kissed me. I was too surprised to react and she sank down looking mortified. "I-I apologize," she stammered. "I know this isn't what you want."

My lips burned from her kiss and I pressed against her harder, cupping her face as I brought my face down to hers. Our lips met again, soft, searching, then hard and filled with abandon. I pulled back, only to tug the scratchy mustache from her face. Then I dove right back in. Our kisses grew heated and her hands met my back, pulling me closer. As her nails dug into my muscles, I groaned and nipped at her fuller lower lip. She tasted like heaven. Igniting a spark within me, fanning it into flickering flames that singed me from the inside out. Her mouth opened and our tongues met. I sucked her lower lip into my mouth and ran my tongue over it, making her whimper. My hands clung to both sides of her face as our kiss grew deep and frantic, mirroring the desperate need I felt for her.

One of her legs sank between mine and she undulated against me, making me tremor with lust. This was insane. But I didn't care. I kissed her as if my life depended on it.

"Not what I want?" I whispered against her lips, then kissed a path down the side of her neck, relishing the goosebumps I created. "I wanted you since the moment you first touched me."

"Oh, Goddess," Eliza murmured, skimming her hands down to cup my butt. "This is madness."

Her skin smelled like a sea of flowers and tasted divine. I would have happily spent the rest of the dawning day exploring her, but I forced myself to back up. "We should go," I said, my breath heavy.

Eliza looked delicious, panting with reddened cheeks. "Yes. You are right." She reached out and took my hand, entwining our fingers. When I looked at her questioningly, she shrugged and pulled me with her and out of the alley. "Might as well enjoy touching you while I can."

I had nothing to add as I never wanted to let go of her. We hurried through the busy street and into a still sleepy city, up to the castle. Shortly before reaching a piece of wall that was overgrown with vines, Eliza haltingly let go of my hand. She climbed over and jumped into the gardens. I followed quickly and as soon as I landed on the other side of the wall, Eliza grabbed my hand once more, as though she also couldn't stand not touching me.

We dashed, ducked, and snuck our way through the gardens, hands always touching. Hiding behind a bush of roses from a pair of guards on rotation, Eliza palmed my face and kissed me again. Our breath was ragged and I almost moaned when the kiss deepened. The excitement of getting caught fanned the flames of passion I felt for her. It was nearly impossible to push her back, but I did. We grinned at each other then went on.

To our great pleasure, many guards walked the grounds and we had to find hidden spots throughout and wait for them to pass. These little moments resulted in more kisses, wandering hands and muffled gasps. It was dangerous and stupid, but we were unable to stop ourselves. Finally, we found a free side entrance and snuck inside.

Eliza seemed to know exactly how the servants came and went at this hour, and she led me through the waking palace undetected.

"You do this a lot, don't you?" I whispered when we turned a corner and headed toward her wing.

She smirked over her shoulder. "Whatever do you mean? Sneaking around kissing beautiful women? Not that much."

We both chuckled and entered her room. The second the door closed behind us she pinned me against it, using her entire body to corner me. I sank my lips down on hers, threading my fingers through her short-haired wig.

Her hands slid underneath my shirt and traveled up my back. I gasped with the sensation of having her skin on mine, while her body was flush against me. My heart felt like it was going to jump from my rib cage when she pulled back a little, looking at me while she slid her other hand over my belly and up.

"You are so gorgeous," she whispered, giving me a slow kiss while softly cupping my left breast. "I want to see and feel all of you."

I barely stifled a moan in answer, fisting the linen shirt she was wearing, ready to rip it in half.

A knock on the door behind me made me jump.

"Eliza? It's me, Marie. Are you awake?"

Eliza's eyes widened with shock and we scrambled away from each other as fast as we could. "I'm awake, just a moment, Marie," Eliza called out, pointing at the powder-blue door.

I walked past her, stealing one last kiss before entering my own room.

"Come in," Eliza said.

The door to her room opened audibly. "Oh no! Eliza!" Marie said in a chiding voice. "You snuck out? What will your Dovani say when she finds out?"

I had to hold a palm to my face to keep from laughing.

"We'll just make sure she won't," Eliza said, her voice strained. Probably from trying not to laugh. "Help me out of this, will you?"

Chapter Seven
Eliza

"This can't be right," Senator Gilles said, watching me sit down on Father's throne. I had hardly slept, but the night itself left me feeling energized and wide awake. I tilted my head questioningly, grabbing hold of the armrests to my side. They were as black as the rest of the throne, intricately carved with decorations. Darkroot, my father had told me. The two thrones – his and Mother's – were made from one single, mighty tree.

"Excuse me, Senator Gilles, but what can't be right?" I asked, smiling at him with a confidence I didn't feel.

"You can't sit judgement, Your Highness. In the king and queen's absence, that duty falls to the steward. Stefan? Why is Princess Fabienne sitting on the throne?"

While his question was harmless enough, the tone was almost venomous, and I felt even more intimidated than I already was.

Behind me, to my right, I heard a footstep. It was Rayla, making herself known to me. I glanced back and she gave me a near-invisible nod, her gray eyes firm and believing.

I faced forward and breathed in deep. If she thought I could do this, I could. Still, my knuckles turned white from how I was grabbing the armrests. As nervous as I was, my mind circled the early morning…the alley, the garden, my room…and Rayla's lips on mine. I had never felt such maddening lust before. She was like a magnet. She was a flame and I the moth. In her arms I had come alive, her body so foreign, yet so similar to mine.

"King Edrick has decreed that Princess Fabienne sit judgement in his stead this month," Stefan said, ripping me from my unchaste thoughts. He sat on the steward's seat, to the right of the two steps upon which the thrones stood. The steward was a man of great calm and I had known him all my life. He was about the age of my parents and had shoulder-long, silver hair, a sharp-angled face, and a straight, long nose. While he wasn't overly kind, or mean, he always exhibited a certain dryness, coupled with a sharp wit and no sense of humor at all.

"The king decreed?" Senator Gilles asked. "Without consulting the senate?"

The five senators all sat in their allotted seats, on the left side of the thrones, opposite of the steward. Two of them nodded along to Gilles' words, throwing me disdainful looks.

"She is too young and inexperienced," Senator Margaret said. "What if her judgement leads to an uproar, or a civil dispute?"

"It is the king's wish," Stefan said, his face showing nothing.

"I, for one, would like to put it to a vote," Gilles said, looking at his fellow senators.

I knew little about court, and even less about the senate and how it operated, I did know however, that a vote against the direct decree of my father was a bad thing. It could lead to more down the line. He wouldn't have stood for it, so I couldn't either.

Gathering all my courage, I cleared my throat until all eyes were on me. "No one was more surprised than me, by the king's wish," I said, smiling at Gilles sweetly. "But I have had three days to think on it and prepare. If I – at any time – am unsure about what to do, I will confab with Stefan and he will surely be able to help. Other than that, I am positive I will rise to the occasion."

Gilles glared at me, the corners of his mouth dropping, so he looked like a fish. "But the vote–"

"We have no time for a vote, Senator Gilles," I said, putting as much firmness into my voice as possible. "The people are waiting. They have come from far away. Do you really intend for them to stand around longer, because you have concerns regarding my aptitude?"

Senator Gilles swallowed, but sat down. "No, Your Highness. But take note that I have warned you. Sitting judgement is no easy feat."

Again, I felt my Dovani move behind me, reminding me of the fact she was there, literally having my back.

"Noted," I said, unclasping one hand from the armrest and waving at the guards at the end of the hall. "Open the doors."

Swiftly, they swung open the two doors, revealing countless people gathering before it. They filed inside of the throne room in throngs, unnerving me. Their feet shuffled across the marble floor, many glancing around open-mouthed at the splendor of it. No doubt none of them had ever seen the inside of the castle the way they ogled the reliefs of non-magical crystals lining the walls, telling the story of the founding of our mines in Gern and Siveil. There were so many people.

I saw Gilles smirk gleefully and tamped down on my nervousness. I would do this. It was time to follow through on my brave words from before.

Steward Stefan rose, unrolling a scroll as he did. He looked to me and at my nod he read the first names on the list. "Renata Mate, owner of a cutting house in Dearn and Mireille Dobe, owner of a bakery in the same street."

Two women came forward, their animosity to each other clear as day as they scowled at one another. They both bowed to me and Stefan focused on his scroll.

"Renata accuses Mireille of trying to sell her special cutting technique to an exporting firm close to the mines in," he squinted at the scroll, "Siveil."

I shifted in my seat. "What kind of cutting technique are we talking about?" I asked. Stefan looked at a loss for words, so I nodded at Renata.

The woman curtsied again and spoke. "I use a method of cutting that allows Rigna – the brown crystal – one additional travel, Your Grace. I sell my crystals only to local people, no exports. And since most of my customers are only allowed to use Rigna, they have to buy another crystal in the country they travelled to from here. Buying crystals as a foreigner is costly, as you surely know, Your Grace, and I ease that cost by a lot."

Many senators had leaned forward in their seats, their eyes glued to Renata.

"How does this way of cutting work?" Senator Margaret asked.

Renata glanced at the senator, then looked back at me. "It is a secret, Senator."

"I demand an answer, now," Senator Margaret snapped.

I swallowed but straightened in father's throne. "As far as I know, cutting houses are allowed to cut their product in any way they see fit, provided the crystals work as advertised. Renata does not owe you an answer, Senator Margaret."

Margaret glared at me, a stern crease appearing between her brows. The lines around her mouth deepened as she pursed her lips in disdain.

"Besides, your work is not at discussion here, your accusation is. How did Mireille come by your secret in the first place?"

Renata wrung her hands. "Mireille is my sister in-law, Your Grace, and we used to be friends. I taught her all I know about cutting, and once she learned how to cut, she wrote up instructions and sent them to Siveil, to one of the export firms who will exploit that knowledge for profit."

"First of all, I did no such thing," Mireille said. "Secondly, you are making a fine profit yourself, selling the Rigna at a much higher price."

"Of course, I sell it at a higher price, you stupid cow, they have double the travel amount. The difference is, *I* invented it. The firm you tried to sell it to, didn't."

"There is all this talk about tried," I said. "Did the instructions she allegedly sent to the firm not work?"

"No, your Grace," Renata said. "I found her drawings and instructions and changed them. I wanted to know if she would truly go through with it, which she has. Now she owes the firm a large amount of money, because she signed a contract she can't uphold."

"You did what?" Mireille screamed. "I'm in this position because of you? Not only did you throw me out of the house you and my husband owned, you betray me and–" She looked at me, shocked about her outburst. "I-I mean, I didn't… I…"

"Finally, you admit it!" Renata yelled.

"You did sell your sister in-law's secret, Mireille. Why?" I asked.

"My husband died in a mining accident a few years back, Your Grace, and Renata blames me for it. It became unbearable to live with her."

"My brother went to the mines because he couldn't stomach living with you, you drove him to his death," Renata hissed.

"Berto loved me. How dare you say such a thing? You couldn't stand that he wasn't around as much to cater to your every whim." Mireille gasped and wiped at her eyes.

I sighed deeply. "While I begin to understand this is about more than cutting crystals and selling secrets, Mireille, you did what Renata accuses you of. But on the other hand, the secret stays with you, Renata. There was no harm done, but ill will. Mireille, you are in debt because of what you did, I find it an adequate punishment."

"But Your Grace—" Renata began and I lifted my hand.

"You lost someone you both loved. Someone who surely wouldn't want you at each other's throats. Do you really want to continue this fight? You are staining his memory by bickering and blaming, instead of finding comfort in each other."

Both women looked sheepish, as they curtsied and stepped back, vanishing in the crowd. I received a lot of raised brows from the senate, but nodded at Stefan to carry on. He called forth the next pair, and the next pair after that. Some cases took time, others were fairly straight forward and while Gilles huffed and puffed at my mild judgement, I felt set in my decrees. After a while, my nerves had calmed somewhat, even if all eyes were on me.

"Felicity, Fabian, and Chris," Stefan read from his scroll. "They stand accused by neighbors of influencing the children and surrounding community with their way of life." The steward cleared his throat, glanced at me uneasily, and looked back at his scroll. "The three live together."

"I do not see how that would cause an accusation?" I asked, confused.

"Your Grace," Felicity said. "We live together as a family. We love each other."

"Ah. That explains it. Well, the laws of Chardour are clear on this, any form of relationship is valid, as long as the people involved are of age, and no one is forced into a union. Does this apply to you?"

"Yes, your Grace," Fabian said. "We are all willing and loving members in this relationship."

My heart fell when I saw the three people standing in front of me, holding hands, while many of the others behind them glared and scowled at them. Half the senate looked appalled, the others didn't seem to have any opinion on it.

Gilles rose from his seat. "The law your father laid down is meant for same gender marriages, your Highness, not for polyamorous… relationships."

"And if it was a man with two wives?" I asked. "Those are widely spread and tolerated in many cities. Khoras, for example. Are you saying they are all invalid, Senator?"

Gilles spluttered. "I-I don't think you can–" He stopped himself from saying whatever was on his mind, luckily for him, because I had the distinct impression it was something along the line of 'you can't compare the two' which would have made me blow up in his face. Instead, he thought hard, then grinned and said, "We are not in Khoras, are we? Dearn is a beacon of hope, comfort, and normality. We are a city that sets example. We cannot allow depravity such as this–"

"Depravity? You, Senator Gilles, want to speak to me of depravity?" My voice shook with anger as I regarded the man, watery-blue eyes and laughably thin mustache included. I knew better. I shouldn't let myself get as riled up, but I'd had enough. I opened my mouth to verbally behead him, when Rayla stepped up to my side.

"He isn't worth it, Eliza," she murmured, quietly enough so only I could hear it.

My nostrils flared as I breathed out, yet she was right. Attacking Senator Gilles would not only make me look bad, it wouldn't help the people in front of me. Refocusing on the three, I said, "The laws of this country are clear in this matter. You have done no wrong. Go home and be happy."

They smiled at me, then each other and bowed before walking back into the crowd.

"For the rest of you," I focused on the intimidating sea of people watching my every move. "I will not tolerate slander of innocent people. Next time, I'll want the names of those who accuse falsely in such matters."

Several faces paled, some looked grateful, and very few seemed angered. Before I could think too much on what I had just said, the doors burst open and a man – an envoy, judging from his brow-blue uniform – barged inside, waving a scroll.

"Make way! Make way!" he shouted as he forced himself through the crowd. Soon, his shoving and yelling had the people stepping to the side so he could jog through.

"Your Majesty," he gasped when reaching the stairs to my throne. He collapsed to his knees and thrust out his hand, offering the scroll he was carrying. His face was a mix of horror and panic, unsettling me.

Stefan hurried over, snatched the scroll from his hand and upon my nod, broke the wax seal and unrolled it. The scroll shook in his hand and his face mirrored that of the envoy within seconds.

He looked up. "Out. Everyone. Sitting judgement is over."

Voices of protest grew loud throughout the hall.

"Out!" Stefan yelled. "Right now!"

Slowly, with many glances at me, Stefan and the scroll, the people shuffled out of the hall.

Our steward climbed up the steps to my throne and leaned down. "You Highness, I pray that we take our leave. To a more private place."

I swallowed at the shaky sound of his voice. "What is it, Stefan?"

"Not here, Princess. We cannot let them see your reaction." He jerked his chin in the direction of the senate.

"What is going on, steward?" Senator Margaret asked.

"This is a message for the princess, first and foremost. You will be informed." Stefan turned on his heel and I followed on unsure legs. A feeling of dread stole itself into my chest. Heavy and sharp as broken crystal.

****

"Tea, princess?" Stefan asked when he, Rayla, and I sat in my parents' study. Well, I sat, Rayla stood behind me, and Stefan paced in front of the fireplace, the scroll still in his hand. By now, the parchment was crumpled where he fisted it, softly crinkling when he moved.

"Stefan," I said, but he seemed not to hear me. "Stefan!"

He stopped and blinked at me.

87

"What is it?" I asked, pointing at the scroll.

The steward swallowed, the professional composure he always wore like a second shirt had dropped, leaving him with nothing. "I… My Princess…" He sighed and came over, holding out the crumbled scroll on his palm. "It is better if you read it for yourself."

Hesitantly, I reached out a hand to take the scroll. It took a second until Stefan let go and I could tug it from his grasp.

With apprehension, I unrolled it on my lap, smoothing over the crumbled-up parts with my fingers.

The words I read made no sense. I read them again. And a third time. They didn't register in my brain. "This can't be right," I said. "This… this is…"

…with a heavy heart we inform the kingdom of Chardour that the royal convoy of the House of Vaster was found destroyed, half a day from Sif, all members of the family slain by unknown hands…

I looked at Stefan. "It has to be false. A jest. Or some kind of mistake."

The steward pointed to the signature on the bottom of the scroll. "King Onis himself signed and wrote this message, princess. I am so very sorry."

"No. Stefan. No. I refuse to…"

He knelt before me, this dry and unmovable man taking my hands in his. "I fear it is true, my Princess. My deepest and most earnest condolences." He cleared his throat as I stared at him, not seeing him.

"I-I will leave you to… The senate has to be informed. As do the people. Excuse me, Your Highness."

Stefan rose, letting my hands fall onto the scroll in my lap. Then he left. I didn't register either as the terrible truth sank into me with the weight of utter desolation. Pain bloomed in my chest, radiating from it, overtaking everything. My vision blurred when tears gathered in my eyes.

Father, Mother, Reagen, Pavette. My family. Gone.

Arms came around me as a figure sat down at my side, pulling me into an embrace. I smelled Rayla's unforgettable scent of lilies and metal, feeling her warmth and hearing her lovely voice. I had no idea what she was saying as she rocked me gently. The pain grew, searing through me with a raw heaviness. Pulling at me from between my heart and shoulders, ripping me into myself until I had the feeling I broke from the pressure.

Hot tears streamed down my face and I screamed. I screamed until my voice broke and vanished. Like they had.

Chapter Eight
Rayla

The minute the steward read the words on the scroll, I suspected, and when Eliza read the lines, unbelieving, I knew. Still, sitting next to her, her nails digging into my skin with a vengeance as she held onto me for dear life, I read the words on the crumpled-up scroll myself.

I hadn't known the Vaster family that well, but I had witnessed love amongst them. And while I felt this undeniable pull toward Eliza, I also didn't really know her yet. Still, my heart broke for her.

The pain she felt was palpable, and nothing I could say or do would make any of it better. It made me feel an impotent hopelessness, the likes of which I had never experienced before. Her entire family.

I read and reread the letter from King Onis, trying to find more information, snippets of knowledge. I came up with nothing. Anger grew inside of me, cold and brittle. The sudden need for vengeance consumed my thoughts, even if this wasn't my family. But as I held Eliza while she screamed until her voice was raw, then further until it was gone, leaving her to whimper and sob, I would have set the world on fire to make her feel better. To help.

Finally, after what seemed like hours, Eliza's death-grip on my arms loosened, her sobs quieted, and she fell into some kind of shock-trance. Not seeing or hearing me.

I gathered her up in my arms and carried her from the study to her chambers. The servants I met on the way seemed to have been informed, because their eyes told of sadness and no one judged or said anything.

Marie was inside of Eliza's bedroom, she cried silently when she saw me carrying her mistress and quickly pulled back the blanket so I could lay my charge down. Eliza didn't move and I tucked her in, my heart breaking all over when I saw her empty eyes staring at the ceiling, while tears ran down the sides of her face.

"It is true?" Marie whispered, sniveling into a handkerchief. "The entire family…"

I nodded, but placed my index finger to my lips to keep her from speaking any further.

Marie nodded, her kind face a mask of sorrow. She sniffed and went back to work. Dusting here and there, then flicking a latch next to the fireplace. Yellow crystals, the size of my forearms, ignited and let a gentle warmth seep into the room.

I felt unable to leave Eliza, so I took to standing next to her door, while Marie dusted some more and then sat at Eliza's side. She took her hand and stroked it, squeezing it gently, before getting up with a stricken sigh.

"Look after her, yes?" she asked me as she walked past me. "I still have chores in-in the k-kitchen."

"I will," I said.

Marie smiled with teary eyes, raising a palm as if to touch me, then let her hand sink again. "I am glad you are here, Dovani." With that, she slipped through the door and left.

Alone in the room with Eliza, I managed to stand at my post for about half a minute, before I went over to her bed and sat down, taking her hand. I stroked some of the deep-red strands from her face. I sat with her until night came, until her eyes closed and she drifted away into an uneasy sleep. Still, I didn't leave.

She woke several times, crying and wailing. Each time, I would be there, hug her and assure her I was there. The words coming over my lips made no sense to me, but hearing my voice and feeling me close seemed to help. Eventually, I sat on her bed, my back resting against the headboard, while she was cradled in my lap, her arms wound around me. I had no experience with consoling anyone, but I did my best. As close as she could get, she snuggled up to me and eventually fell into a fitful sleep. I guessed her body had to be exhausted, blessing her with a bit of rest.

I sat in the darkness, my thoughts dark as well. Again, the need to alleviate her pain soared through me. But was there anything I could really do? Besides leaving her and hunting the people responsible for her suffering?

The thought was unbearable, and yet it kept me awake through the night.

****

Morning came and we were in the same position. When the sun peaked through the windows and crept up the bed with golden light, waking the birds outside, Eliza stirred. She breathed in deeply, hugging me. Reddened eyes wandered up to meet mine.

"You stayed," she rasped, her voice broken.

"I stayed."

Groaning, she sat up, resting her back next to mine. Eliza took my hand, entwining our fingers. "I hoped I had dreamed it. But you being here means it was all true. Th-they are g-gone, aren't they?"

"I fear so. I can't tell you how sorry I am. I—"

She squeezed my hand. "I just c-can't believe it. Why? Who would… I don't understand."

"Me neither, they should have been safe in Leozar."
The anger from before iced up my veins once more. "If
you wish it, I will go to Leozar and find whoever did it."
I left out that I would take them apart piece by piece, it
didn't seem like a good idea to let her know just how
enraged I was on her behalf.

"No. I fear if you leave, I will completely fall
apart." She nibbled on her lower lip, then tears ran down
her face again. "N-not that I have been a bastion of self-
control. I am s—"

I leaned over, cupping her face and turning it to me.
"Eliza. You do not apologize to me for that. Ever. I am
here, and I am not leaving unless you send me away.
Understood?"

She nodded. "I can't believe I never get to…see
them…again."

I opened my arms and she sank into my chest.
Tremors of sobs raked her, quieter than yesterday, but
they felt even more hopeless, tearing at me like claws.

"You need to eat," I told her.

"I don't feel like it."

"Doesn't matter. I can go and get something for you
if you want to stay here, but you have to eat."

"I don't feel like doing anything, Rayla."

"I know. I'll get you something and then you can do
nothing all you want, deal?"

She sniffed but nodded against my chest. "Deal."

I unwound myself from her and quickly headed to
the kitchen. To my surprise, Marie stood behind a
trolley, packed with food and drink. She looked
devastated, but tried to smile when she saw me. "Is the
princess awake?" she asked, making all heads in the
kitchen turn to us.

"Yes. I told her she needs to eat."

"Thank you," Marie said. "I prepared something, I'll come with you."

Together, the maid and I went back to Eliza's chambers. We found her rolled up in her blankets, her head nowhere to be seen. For a second, a feeling of déjà vu slammed into me and I thought she might have run off again, but when Marie rolled the trolley up next to the bed, the blanket moved, revealing red hair and red eyes.

"Eliza," Marie said. "I can't tell you how sorry I am. I-I mourn with you."

"Thank you, Marie." Eliza sat up and let her handmaid set up breakfast on a tray that had feet. She placed the tray in front of Eliza, making it into a small table. The princess forced herself to eat something, drink some tea and assure Marie that it was great.

The handmaid seemed happy to have helped in some small way as she reloaded her trolley after Eliza said she was done.

"Leave the bread, and some apples," I said.

Marie placed some food on a plate and set it down on the small table in front of the fireplace. Then she rolled the trolley out of the room.

"You need more, Eliza," I said when Marie was gone.

"I am done, Rayla."

"You barely touched anything." I took the plate and sat down next to her. "One apple. Then I'll leave you be."

Her look turned to a scowl, but she took the apple form the plate and bit into it. "You are insufferable," she said.

"True. Eat up."

It took forever, but Eliza ate the whole thing, then she rolled into herself and closed her eyes. Her hand reached for mine and I took it, stroking her hair with the other. "Rest, Liz," I whispered.

My charge clasped my hand with both of hers and soon drifted off to sleep. I took a deep breath and even though it was hard, I slipped my hand from her fingers and got up. It was time to find Stefan and find out if he knew anything more.

****

The steward was in the throne room. A table had been set up in front of his seat, it was overladen with pages and scrolls. He poured over them, writing down something on a blank page. The senate was thankfully absent, I didn't care much for half of them and wouldn't have had the stomach to listen to what Gilles or Margaret had to say.

Only some guards were stationed at the doors and a servant was busy polishing the claw-footed candleholders around the room that stood as tall as me.

The steward looked up when he heard me approach. He looked beyond tired. "How is she?" he asked.

"As well as one would expect after such news."

His lips thinned and he nodded. "It is a tragedy. But we will have to act soon. Princess Fabienne will have to act soon."

"What do you mean?"

"Chardour is without a king and queen. I can stall and lead in their stead for a while, but we need the princess. I have the distinct feeling that someone will make a grab for power soon."

I frowned. "Why? The princess will ascend to the throne and that will be that."

Stefan gave me a listless smile. "No offense, but you have no idea of royal workings." He leaned back in

96

his chair. "Princess Fabienne was never meant to rule, so she hasn't received the proper training and knows little of politics. Not to mention, she has a reputation of being too straight-forward when it comes to dealing with aristocracy. Some will see that as a weakness and will make their claims known. She is young, unprepared, and inexperienced. And she is unmarried. She cannot take the throne unmarried."

His words sliced into me like a blade. The thought of Eliza marrying, somehow, made the anger still simmering within me blaze to life.

"She has to marry to become queen? What kind of a rule is that? Aren't there many unmarried kings throughout Iyune?"

"Kings, yes, queens, no. The only instances of a lone queen ruling – apart from the Witchgoddes herself – are widowed queens who have lost their kings."

"That is bullshit."

The steward raised a brow at my words. "I agree. But the law is the law. We have to be vigilant. The coming days will be very important. If the senate calls a meeting, I have no doubt that they – or some of them – will try to enforce the law of overtaking. It is a law meant to protect the kingdom if a ruler is unfit to rule. The senate will take over, anointing another aristocrat, or one of their own," he added when I looked confused. "If Princess Fabienne hasn't made an absolute claim, with the intention of marriage, she will lose Chardour. We can't let that happen. The Vaster line has ruled these lands for hundreds of years and under their rule, our kingdom has prospered. But I fear it will be a battle." He shrugged. "As I said, the princess is inexperienced and young."

"The way she sat judgement should have shown everyone how capable she truly is." I thought back on yesterday, before that envoy and his terrible news had entered the palace. A feeling of pride and affection had stolen itself inside my heart as I had watched her. I had known she was nervous, seeing her knuckles whitening with how she had grabbed the armrests, but she had shone like a beacon, speaking sound judgements.

"I agree, Dovani. And I believe she would be a formidable queen. But as this tragedy is so fresh… She needs to make a choice. And she needs to make it soon. We only have mere days to solidify her claim." Stefan folded up the paper he had written on and sealed it. "You seem to have an…unusual connection with her. Will you speak with her?"

I swallowed, the magnitude of the situation weighing on me. "I can try."

"Call for me when she is ready to speak, and I will help make things clear. Also, give this to her at an opportune moment." He pulled a letter from under the rest of the papers and scrolls on his table and handed it to me. It was thick, sealed and bound in string.

"It is from her parents. They always left letters for their children when travelling, in case anything happened to them." His lower lip trembled for a second.

I took the letter. "She will get it. And I will do my best to talk to her."

"Good."

I turned from him and strode away.

"Dovani?"

I pivoted to see him hunched over the table once more, but his eyes were set on me. "And be careful, she might be in danger, too. We have no idea who killed the royal family and why."

Unease froze my insides as I bowed curtly and headed back to Eliza. Whoever thought they could get close enough to my charge to harm her was in for a quick death.

Eliza was fast asleep when I got back and I placed the letter on her bedside table. Then I snuck through the castle. Listening to the chattering servants and guards, hidden away in dark corners and nooks as I did. Nothing much came off it, as all of them seemed genuinely saddened. None of them spoke much, to be exact. I nearly gave up on my spying endeavors, when I found two maids huddled together in what looked to be a supply closet, between the kitchen and the servant's quarters.

"You can't be here, Chrissy," one whispered. I quickly hid behind the next corner when Chrissy closed the door softly. Forcing my breathing to deepen, I opened up my senses, eavesdropping through the cracks in the wooden door.

"Shh. I know. But my master told me to come."

"Ugh, that vile man. I hate that you have to work for him, sister."

"He pays well and we both know we need the money right now," Chrissy said.

"I know…what does he want to know?"

"He asked about the princess. How she is and if anyone has seen her."

"Marie saw her, I could ask her how her Highness is feeling."

A moment of silence passed.

"Is there any way you could make up a reason to enter her chambers? I need first-hand information."

"Not while that scary Dovani is around. She never leaves Princess Fabienne's side."

"Right, I forgot about her."

"Oh, but I saw her not long ago, Chrissy, in the throne-room, talking to the steward. Maybe she is still gone?"

"I can't chance her seeing me or you, especially you. You must know something, though."

There was another small pause.

"What…what does he want to know, truly? I don't believe he cares for Her Highness."

"I can't say. He never tells me why he wants me to do certain things."

"Well, from what I have heard, the princess is in distress and she hasn't left her bed since this morning," the other maid said.

I was on the brink of storming into the closet, my hands grabbing hold of both my scythes to calm myself. The familiar feel of them helped in most situations. I bit my teeth together and stayed where I was.

"At least I can tell him that. Thank you."

"Chrissy, be careful not to let anyone see you when you leave."

The door opened and footsteps echoed off the corridor walls. "I am always careful, sister."

A cloaked figure passed me and I waited a few seconds before following her.

She was right in telling her sister how she was always careful, as she led me out of the castle, through the gardens and past a green maze. Ducking behind bushes and walls whenever someone was near.

Chrissy finally arrived at one of the outer walls, that was overgrown with ivy. She pulled at the leaves closest to the walls and revealed a hidden, old door through which she swiftly disappeared.

Chrissy was fast and I nearly lost her as she wove through Dearn, passing several parts of town until we entered a section with large houses. They looked like small castles and had to either house nobility, the senate, or both. The maid entered one of the houses – with peach-colored walls and ornately carved columns – and I snuck into the garden, glimpsing through windows.

I heard voices from the terrace and crept along the side of the house, halting behind a couple of rose-bushes.

"Thank you for meeting me here, and not at my own house. We have to be careful in these times. Now, what news, dove?" a man's voice asked. It was deep and agreeable, but I couldn't place it. I tried to get closer and sneak a peek, when a gardener appeared from the direction of the terrace, whistling and snipping at the rose-bushes. I ducked further down, hoping he would leave soon.

No such luck. The maid, Chrissy and her employer went inside and out of my earshot, as the gardener kept snipping and whistling with all the finesse of a teapot. There was no rhyme or melody to his musical musings and I was left aggravated and unable to concentrate long enough to truly listen.

By the time the gardener was done, I heard whinnying from the street, then the door of a carriage shut audibly and hooves stomped on the cobblestones, growing quieter by the second. The gardener slowly waddled off and I shot from my hiding place, ran through the garden and vaulted over the fence, but the carriage was already gone.

With a few choice curses and feeling like an absolute failure, I hurried back to the castle. It seemed as though no matter what I did, I failed my charge. I should have found out who was so keen on knowing how she was – to what end could only be guessed. The feeling that it wasn't good sat with me as the day grew darker and I arrived at the castle.

One thing became clear though, Stefan was right, we had to be vigilant. Things were afoot and we needed to counteract as soon as possible. My heart bled when I thought of Eliza. No matter how inconsolable she was, she would have to face much more in the coming days.

Chapter Nine
Eliza

Pain thrummed through every part of my being, leaving me unable to think clearly. I tortured myself by replaying memories. Trying – like a fool – to make myself believe they would come back to me. Trying to tell myself that all of it had been a mistake. Not true.

I sat in my bed, staring at the gauzy curtains billowing in the wind, next to the glass-door leading to my balcony. As if to mock me, the sunset was gorgeous, painting the atmosphere with breathtakingly beautiful golds and reds. All of it was lost to me. How could the sun set on a world where my family was gone? Surely, everything should have stopped. Halted. Dropped from existence. *I* wanted to drop from existence. I wanted to sink into my bed and fade into the mattress. Never to be seen again. Maybe then, the pain would cease.

I knew better. This pain would stay with me forever, and I couldn't bare knowing I would have to spend my life feeling it. A part of me – the best part – was gone. In the space of a few words on a scroll, I had lost my world.

"Eliza?" A voice found me, but I was busy trying to fade to nothing, so I ignored it.

"Liz." The voice was comfort, the only thing tethering me to reality.

I turned my head, seeing Rayla stand at the foot of my bed.

"You were gone," I said, hating how weak I sounded. Also, the accusatory tone wasn't lost to me.

My beautiful guard nodded, then came around the bed to sit at my side. "I know. And I am sorry I wasn't there when you woke. I wanted to be."

I believed her as Rayla had never said anything to me she didn't mean. She took my hand and squeezed it.

The usual effect of her touch was curiously muted. I wished back the spark it would have caused a day ago. When kissing her had been all I could think of, even with hundreds of eyes on me. Her. My solace. A nudge of fondness twirled inside of me, surprising, given that I thought all I could feel was thrumming agony.

"Come with me," she said and stood, then pulled on my hand.

"Where?"

"Please. Just…do?" Her gray eyes pleaded with me and I was helpless to deny her. She helped me heave myself off the bed. My legs felt shaky and unsure as my naked feet hit the tiled floor.

Rayla drew my right arm around her shoulder and walked with me through the room and toward the balcony.

Wind stroked my face, tangling my hair, and I looked down past the balustrade. From here I had a spectacular view of the gardens, the maze within, and Dearn. My beloved Dearn.

I tried hard to focus past my staring into space and the fresh air, coupled with Rayla's arm around my waist did help some. I leaned my head onto her shoulder, wanting to stay like this forever.

We didn't talk, just stood and watched as the sun sank below the horizon, as darkness prompted the streetlights to be lit, making Dearn twinkle and shine. After a while, a chill descended on us and Rayla pulled me into a full on hug. She held me silently, letting me breathe in her scent of comfort and lilies.

"No matter what happens, Liz, I am here," she whispered into my hair.

More than anything, her presence helped. "W-will you stay with me tonight?" I asked, feeling stupid and small, but I had to know. "Like you did last night?"

Rayla didn't answer right away and a sudden rush of anxiety made a shiver fork over my back.

"I will stay with you."

A held breath exited me and I pressed my lids shut. "Thank you." This strange need to have her close was embarrassing, and it wouldn't do, but right now, I allowed it to engulf me as it was the only thing keeping me marginally sane.

We went back inside and while I would have positively vibrated with excitement and lust by the prospect of sharing my bed with Rayla, I was barely able to keep my eyes open.

My guard tucked me in, then unclasped and unhooked her armor, before undressing to her undergarments. She slid into the bed at my side, the only light glimmering through my room coming from the Micra crystals in the fireplace. Marie seemed to have been here while we were on the balcony. For a heartbeat the thought of her seeing us embrace unsettled me, but Marie was my friend, she would never betray me by talking about it.

"Get over here," Rayla said.

I didn't have to be told twice. Sighing deeply when her arms came around me, my body curled into her as tightly and closely as possible, and I closed my eyes. And even as new tears flowed from me, I was grateful for my Dovani.

****

My rest was short and interwoven with nightmares of my family's demise. As bad as those were, the good dreams were worse. The dreams in which I laughed and lived with them, only to come to and feel the pain of losing them all over again.

I had no idea how Rayla stood being around me, cradling and holding me through all of it. It seemed to have taken its toll, as I felt her even breath at my back. She was sound asleep. Slowly, I turned and sat up. My Dovani frowned in her sleep, snuggling closer until her head came to rest in my lap.

The alien urge to smile tugged at my lips. It felt strange, almost painful. As if my face had turned into a mask of sorrow, hard to break. I tucked a strand of her black hair behind her ear and stroked over her hair and face. She had loosened her braids, and the sheer black sleekness felt unbelievable. And the scent rising from her was exquisite.

She looked less intimidating when she slept. Younger, too. The arch of her brows, her long, thick lashes, the curve of her upper lip… There was only one word for her. Perfection. Even the tiny scars running over her shoulder blade, vanishing in her chemise. I wondered if her body was littered with scars like these. They would have to be from her training and whatever assignments she had before me.

My fingers stroked over those small scars and I wished something else would have brought her to my bed. I wished for many things to be different. But they weren't.

I heaved out a shaky sigh and let my head roll to the side. I frowned. A thick letter lay on my bedside table. I hadn't noticed it when I got up yesterday.

I reached for it and let the string run through my fingers. A groan fought up my sore throat. 'Eliza.' The word, written in the unmistakable lines of my father's calligraphy hit me like a punch.

Rayla stirred and I gently caressed her shoulder. A small sound came from her, then she stilled again.

With shaking fingers and a pounding heart, I opened the string, broke the wax seal, and opened the letter.

There were two. One from my father and one from my mother.

I let them sink, unsure whether I would be able to read them at all. Taking a bracing breath, I started with the one from my mother. Very soon, tears ran down my face, falling onto the blanket. Hearing her voice, as I read her words, made agonizing warmth spread through me. I knew in that moment, I would hang onto this letter for as long as I lived. They were words of encouragement, telling me I was loved beyond measure, and how I was to stay the stubborn, curious woman I had grown into.

After I was done, I needed minutes to look at the letter from my father. My soft crying didn't cease and I had to wipe my eyes repeatedly to even see what he had written.

It was much of the same my mother had said, in his own words. When I came across him writing, *you are my joy*, I suppressed a whimper.

I know I have told you before, but you are my joy, daughter. Every day I had the privilege to know you, to live in your presence has lifted my heart. You are exceptional in every way. Clever, tenacious, always searching for answers and kind. Never lose any of it. Not even when faced with loss and grief. Promise me this.

I swallowed at the lump in my throat, wanting to fade from this world once more. They left me and now I had to face all the world without them. How could I possibly stay who I was? How could I possibly keep on living? Trying seemed futile.

Behind his letter was another. This one was rational and clear, telling me about things going on in our kingdom. About the senate and who I could trust, about who was important when it came to the nobility. He had listed a few names, dukes and barons who had claims to the throne in one way or another. Who of those were likely to try and realize these claims, and those who were not. He warned me of a law that could anoint a member of the senate as leader, as king. I was taken aback by reading about this, dread sneaking into my stomach. If this was true, I had no doubt Senator Gilles would try and rally the senate behind him to ascend and steal the throne.

At the very end of the letter my father got more cryptic.

Chardour is the biggest supplier of powered crystals in all of Iyune, you know this, which means you have to keep it safe. The mines of Siveil and Gern are to be prioritized in security and subsidizations. That being said, the one true secret our kingdom has, lies hidden. If ever Chardour is invaded, you must protect the White Peak and the fortress of Mar. If need be, station the entire army there. The Witchgoddes does not know what lies within the mountain, and she never may. If all is lost, the mountain will provide. Protect it with your life.

I let the letter sink, thoroughly confused. The White Peak? Mar? Both were tucked away at the very edge of Chardour, behind the Hollow Woods. I knew little of the people living in Mar, as they were said to be a secretive and strange bunch. But what could be more important than our people? Than the mines? Than my life?

Yet again, dread sliced through me, leaving me afraid of my father's words. What had he been hiding?

I folded up the letters and thought on where to hide them. Especially the last one had to be safe. Words of love from parents to their child posed no danger, but the vague warnings of my father were much too important to leave lying around.

"You found it," Rayla said, making me jump. She slowly sat up, looking from me to the letters in my hand.

"You put it there?"

Rayla nodded. "Stefan gave it to me yesterday and said to make sure you got it."

My guard rubbed her eyes and yawned, then pressed her shoulder to mine. "Are you well? Did you sleep?"

"I am...I *am*. That has to be enough for now. And yes, thanks to you, I did sleep."

She smiled at me warmly, making a dimple appear in her left cheek. It was utterly charming. Then she frowned and pointed at the letters. "I am sorry if the letters caused you grief, but I thought it was important for you to read them."

"They did, but that is none of your fault. Thank you, Rayla." I turned my head to face her. "I mean it. Without you..." I got lost in the deep gray of her eyes for a moment. "You tether me."

Rayla leaned her cheek against the headrest and looked at me. Her gaze was as intense as a touch, without being intimidating. "We have to talk about a few things, Liz."

"I like that nickname."

She placed her palm in mine and laced our fingers. Her thumb stroked across my knuckles, then she picked up our hands and kissed the back of mine softly. "I never had reason to use a nickname for another before. You are the first."

I swallowed, my skin heating a bit despite everything going on inside of me. "You wanted to talk about something?"

"Yes. And it is not pleasant. We should get up and dressed before we do." She sniffed at me and crinkled her nose. "And you need a bath."

The suddenness of that statement, coupled with her face, made me huff out a surprised laugh. Just like the smile she had almost coaxed from me, it felt misplaced but it eased some of the tension knotting my insides together.

Rayla grinned for the first time since I met her. She threw back the cover sand climbed from the bed. "I'm going to get Marie to run you a bath." She quickly dressed, then dashed by to kiss my forehead before she left.

I stared after her, grunted and rolled myself off the bed. Treading around my room, I looked for a good place to hide my father's words. My eyes stuck on the row of porcelain dolls on my lower dresser. Next to the mirror, they sat in a neat line. I remembered that one of them had unfortunately lost her head during a tea party with Pavette, which had evolved into a massacre. Miss Grant had scolded us and then tried to attach the head, but it has always been slightly askew since then.

Trying not to think of my sister, I plucked the doll from her place and took off her head. Rolling the last letter up firmly, I slid it into the doll's hollow body, then placed the head back on and sat her down again.

"Apologies, Tina," I said. "But I need a guardian for my secrets."

Footsteps outside announced Marie and Rayla shortly before the door opened. I turned from my dresser and poor Tina, to see them both enter, each carrying two steaming buckets of water.

"Good morning, Eliza," Marie said, a shy smile on her face. "Follow me, please."

I held out a hand to take one of the buckets from Marie, but she shook her head and walked from the room quickly. Without a choice, I was left to follow my handmaid and guard down the hall and into the bathing room. While Marie and Rayla poured the buckets into the large copper bathtub, I looked around.

Since I could think, I have loved this room. Ceramic tiles filled most of the walls, painted with delicate blue flowers, and the white crystals embedded into the wall behind my tub shimmered in the morning sun. These crystals held a certain sway over water.

Marie twisted a handle – also holding crystals – so it aligned with the stones on the wall. A hollow and echoy gurgle came from the pipe protruding from the wall and soon enough, clear, cool water joined its heated counterpart in the tub.

Rayla took the empty buckets and stacked them into each other, while Marie rounded me and unlaced the back of my chemise.

I stared into the distance, listening to the gargling water and felt an empty heaviness descend onto me. The feeling was foreign and I could not discern it. Tiredness? Numbness? No. The grief still thrummed through my body at every second, but this was added. A sort of hopelessness that seemed unending. How was I to carry on? To fulfill my father's wishes? The letters of my parents swirled through my mind, clamping down on my throat.

Marie patted my legs and I stepped from the chemise, then from the pants. She gave me another smile, silent, and opened some of the flasks standing close to the tub. Pouring some of this and some of that into the water, then running her hands through it, she made the room smell divine.

"Do you want me to wash you?" she asked, knowing I usually would have sent her on a break while I undressed myself, put in the oils and bathed. Doing it myself might have seemed strange to anyone else in the aristocracy, but I never minded it and Marie had a few minutes to herself.

"No, Marie. Thank you. You can go."

My handmaid curtsied and shuffled off. Rayla, who had her back to me started to leave as well.

"Stay?" I asked.

She went ramrod straight and froze. "If you wish." She did not turn to me, however, and when I looked down my naked body, I felt something chase away the empty heaviness. Self-conscious, I quickly lowered myself into the tub. My eyes focused on Rayla's reddening nape and ears.

"You can look now," I told her.

Her shoulders rose and fell. "I'd rather not, Liz."

Taken aback, I swallowed. In the grand scheme of happenings, the sinking sensation on behalf of her denying to look at me was stupid. But it further nudged and poked at the empty heaviness, which I was grateful for. Not that it was nice.

Rayla's hands closed into fists at her side, then she opened them again. Her shoulders rose and fell visibly. Was she...aroused at the thought of me naked? This time, the emptiness was blown away as if by a bracing breeze. My self-consciousness was back though, but this time it prickled with something close to excitement. Barely notable, but there.

I blew out a breath and grabbed the huge sponge from the table next to my tub. "You wanted to speak of something. You said it wasn't pleasant." I dipped the sponge into the water and began washing myself.

Slowly, Rayla turned toward me, her eyes set on the floor at her feet. She did look beautifully flustered and her cheeks had reddened, too. "I do. But it can wait until you… until I…"

"Rayla?"

My guard glanced up. Her steel-gray eyes darkened and a shaky breath left her open lips. "I will go now."

"Why?" It was a curious feeling to have my heartrate pick up, like a drum beating through hollow space. My breath quickened at the sight of her expression. Daunting. Dangerous. Unearthly beautiful.

"Because my thoughts are not where they are supposed to be right now." Rayla's lips thinned. "I should not see you like this, I should not be holding you while you sleep. And I should definitely not think of the kisses we shared. I understand you need comfort, but it feels selfish to indulge in your wish."

"Selfish? From me?"

She vigorously shook her head and took a few steps in my direction. "Absolutely not. I am the selfish one. Being close to you…it is as painful as it is soothing. Knowing exactly what our proximity means to you during this time. Yet it grows into something else for me. Every second it gets worse. I can't satisfy my selfish needs while you grieve. I will not use it as an excuse to be close to you. To see you like this… It has to stop." She knotted her fingers, bowed, and turned on her heel.

"Rayla."

She halted a foot away from the closed door.

"You are the only thing keeping me sane."

Rayla sighed.

I stood in my tub and watched her freeze up. Not caring about the drops of water I left on the floor, I walked up behind her. "Don't you think I feel the same way? Isn't it selfish of me to use your closeness as solace? You help keep my thoughts in this world." I raised my hand, seeing it was shaking. Placing it on her shoulder, I gently pulled her to face me.

"Please, Eliza. You have to let me go now," she breathed, her eyes palpable heat as our gazes met.

"Why not both be selfish?" I whispered. An echo of the lust I remembered feeling for her ignited in my bones. Small, fighting its way to the surface. It did nothing against the pain, but it was something else to focus on. Something alive and beating. Something I could sink my being into.

I cupped her face and rose a little, placing my lips on hers. She groaned but held perfectly still.

"Please let me forget for a while. Make me feel something other than this sorrow," I whispered against her lips.

Chapter Ten
Kay

The scene was loud and rowdy. Pulling my hood deeper into my face, I followed the patrons of the bar closely from my table in the corner. He was here, had to be. All my leads had pointed to this establishment, in a town by the name of Hem, in the middle of Midden.

A bar like any other in Iyune. Smallish, dirty, dimly lit and heavily laden with the scent of sweat, alcohol, and food. The tables and chairs didn't fit together, a raggle-taggle of different woods and styles. The floor was compressed dirt, soaking up the spilled drink and everything else that fell onto it.

All around me, men and women drank, laughed, danced, and played Trice. None of them knew who I was, or what I was doing here. Hopefully.

I took a sip from my ale and scrutinized each person separately, hoping for some kind of tell.

"Another, love?" a barmaid asked, pointing at my tankard.

I didn't look up, but shook my head. "I'll have something else, though." Fishing out a couple of coins from my pocket, I laid them on the rickety table in front of me. "Information."

The barmaid discretely swiped the coins off the surface and bent lower. "What do you want to know?" she asked.

"I'm looking for a man named Aaron. He is also known as the Mace. Do you know him?"

A small hiss reached my ear. "You should not be looking for him, love. He is trouble."

I couldn't help but smirk at that. "So, you know him?"

"Everyone knows him." She sighed. "See the round table in the back? The one with the five burly men? He is the one in the corner."

"The small one?" I asked, taken aback.

"He only looks small in comparison to his men. But make no mistake, he is vicious. You'd do well not to approach him, stranger."

"Thank you," I said.

She straightened and left, catering to the needs of a drunken fellow two tables over.

My gaze homed in on Aaron. So, this was him. I had expected more. As I regarded him, the bald head, the missing front tooth, and the scar leading from his jaw to his left ear – which was only partly there – he didn't seem like the type of person I was looking for. The one who had been in my waking and sleeping thoughts for over a year.

I emptied my tankard and stood, the chair scraping over the dirt. No time like the present. I twisted the crystal band on my wrist, rotating the crystals in a certain manner. The daggers in their sheaths on my belt vibrated in answer. Ready, like me.

I wove through the throngs of people, my eyes on Aaron. Eventually, I was at his table.

In the middle of a loud conversation, one of his men noticed me and nudged him with an elbow.

Aaron looked up at me from his seat, his holy grin fading slowly. "Looking for something?"

"Many things, actually. But I'll settle for your head on a spike." I smiled at him.

"What did you just say?" Aaron asked, springing to his feet. His men followed his example, their chairs toppling over. The entire bar quieted down, all eyes on us.

"You heard me, Baldy. Tell me, can you whistle through that missing tooth hole?"

He blinked, then all his men lunged at me at once. I let a few punches through, dodging others, as I was shoved, pulled, and manhandled through the bar and out the door.

My feet left the ground when one of the larger guys picked me up by my cloak and threw me. The impact was hard, but I rolled over and sprang to my feet. Spitting out a mouthful of blood from a jab to my cheek, I turned and wiped my face with the back of my hand. This was right where I wanted to be. Outside, where no innocents could get hurt. It was time to get to it.

Aaron and his men piled out of the bar, some of the other patrons, were glued to the windows, others followed us outside to witness the show.

"You are looking for a beating, pretty boy," Aaron roared.

I chuckled, twisting the crystals again, now only one more touch, and my daggers would do my bidding. "Pretty, huh? You didn't have to throw me out to let me know you fancied a fuck."

"At him, lads!" Aaron yelled and his men — plucking daggers and knives from their pockets and belts — came at me.

My index finger pushed down on my bracelet and my daggers jumped from my belt, hovering in the air on my sides. Their grips, adorned with green crystals — Doran — twinkled in the dim streetlights. Flinging out my hands, I let them soar. Four slices and wet sounds later, his men stood rooted to the spot, staring at me as blood gushed from their opened throats. With gargling, stricken sounds, they fell, their blood flowing freely and seeping into the ground.

I curled my fingers and my daggers zipped back to me, rotating to shake off the blood, before settling in mid-air at my sides.

Cries and shouts erupted as the patrons fled. Back into the bar, down the street, away from me and Aaron.

Aaron stood, his face whitening as he stared at me open-mouthed. "How... Who are you?"

"I'll tell you, Baldy. Remember the last time you were in Leozar? You raided a village by the name of Gish. But it wasn't a raid, was it?" I shook my head, a mirthless chuckle leaving my lips. "You were ordered there." I flexed my index finger and one of the daggers flew toward him. He tried to duck away, tried to swipe at it, but the blade soon met his neck. He stumbled back until his shoulders hit the wooden wall of the bar. My dagger pressed against his pulse, slicing into his skin just a little, enough to bring forth a tear of blood.

I strode up to him, careful not to get too close. "What I want to know, Baldy, is who sent you there? Who ordered you to raid Gish?" My voice grew hoarse with anger and I drew back my hood. "And who ordered you to kill Lady Odette? My mother?"

Aaron gasped, his pea-green eyes resting on my face. "The bastard Prince," he whimpered.

"Talk. Now," I snarled.

"Please. I had nothing to do with the attack on Lady Odette! Spare me, Prince."

"Aaron, I have been looking for you for some time now. And while I know you are the one..." I had to swallow at the bile rising from my stomach. The hate I felt and the anger coursing through me culminated into a frothing, feral maelstrom. "You are the one who carried out the killing blow. I know that for a fact, you can cease lying. I want to know who sent you. If you tell me, I will make your death a quick one. If not… You know who I am, so you have heard of my feats. Choose.”

More whimpering and stuttering. “I-I-I I had nothing… Oh Goddess! Please. I can’t tell you.”

“Fine.” I raised my palms, curling in the ring finger on either side. My remaining dagger flitted to his crotch, giving him a little poke.

“No! Please, I-I will tell you.”

“I am listening.”

His eyes nearly popped from his head as he glanced down his body at the dagger about to nick his nut sack. Sweat beaded on his forehead and he wheezed.

I had to steady my breathing, or I would kill him on the spot for what he did. But he had merely been a sadistic weapon, in a grander scheme of things. I had to be patient now. Just a few more minutes.

“His name is…” He pressed his lids shut, clearly afraid of saying the name. I didn’t care. With the flick of a finger, I made the lower blade slide up a bit.

Aaron yelped in pain. “Biron, his name is Biron. Tall, thin fellow. Dark-brown hair with almost black eyes.”

“Where do I find him?”

“I don’t know. Really! H-he came here, to Hem and hired me and my men. Then he left.”

My jaw clamped up with effort, as I tried to tamp down on the need to open him up from bottom to top. “You know something. Tell me!”

His features lit up. “Y-yes, there is something. I-I saw his traveling bracelet when he gave me the money. He had to be nobility, his crystals – they were many and most of them red, but not the red of Illain, it was different… Deeper, darker, almost black, but with a red shine. I have never seen any gems like it before. M-maybe he was from Chardour?"

I had a name and a description, there were only so many people outside of royalty who could afford red crystals. And even less who had more than one. This would do. "Goodbye, Baldy," I said, closing my right fist. The dagger at his throat swiped from right to left, making blood gush from his throat. He palmed his wound, stumbling forward, his eyes shimmering with tears. I felt nothing when he fell to my feet, bleeding out.

Flicking both my hands up, I called my daggers, who followed behind me as I strode away. They sank into their sheathes and I walked on, the burning hatred inside of me not doused. *Biron.* I would find him, just as I found Aaron, then maybe, my mother would be fully avenged.

****

The next three days I traveled to the Foudan of Midden, where I stepped into the stone circle and reappeared in Leozar. Home. Getting to Sif would take two more days and I bought a horse from the village of Ranne, close to our Foudan.

Using Foudans always had me nauseous for a day or two, but I forced my body to pull through and my horse to be quick. She was a fine mare and we made good time. I was careful to let the animal rest enough, though.

Finally, dusty, hungry, and tired, I saw it. Floating above the Crushed Mountains. A large piece of land, sharp edged and hovering. What looked like small and larger parts of stone floated beneath and around Sif. Broken pieces of land, belonging to nothing but the magic holding it between the ground and the sky. Ivey, the Witchgoddess was the only one holding sway over this kind of magic, which was different than the inherent magic of our continent – the crystals.

Right at the foot of the mountain, crystal powered docks took me and my new horse up.

Flea, the name I had given my new mare, did not like heights and I stroked her gently, telling her everything would be fine. She seemed to believe me, but snorted and threw up her head from time to time. Once we arrived at the landing platforms, she jumped from wooden deck and pulled me with her.

"Prince Hamon," one of the guards greeted me. He didn't smile, his bow was curt and not really low, and his gaze didn't meet mine. I was used to all of it. People feared me, yet felt disdain, as I was only the bastard son of the king. Not true royalty. And most of Sif let me know it.

My father and my half-siblings, never let me feel anything but welcomed though, even if I hadn't been home a lot these past few years. Their continued support was what had kept me going after finding my mother dead amongst the rest of Gish. Burned to a crisp. Houses and people. My stepmother Beata was another matter. She had never been unfriendly or unwelcoming toward me, but I knew she liked it better when I was away.

I led Flea through the streets leading up to the palace sitting between two fortresses. The walls were dark gray, meant to intimidate. When I had seen them for the first time as a child, stumbling along my mother's side wide-eyed, it was daunting. Finding out who I was, and that I had to live there for some time each year, had seemed unreal at the time. Now, I had mixed feelings. Sif had never really been home. Not like Gish. But feelings of home shouldn't concern me right now. I was here for a reason. To find out more about Biron and red crystals. And to ask my father if he would allow me to travel to Chardour. Even as a prince – whose travels were not limited like those of common folk – Chardour was strict. It was better carrying the letter of a king with me if I wanted to go there. And I needed to speak with my sister, Leigh, who was deep into crystal lore and their abilities. I would ask her first, it could save me a trip.

Flea and my steps echoed off the walls when we walked through the stone-gate leading to the castle. I frowned when I looked at the banner of our house fly at half-mast. A sing of mourning. Fear sliced into me and I hurried on, falling into a jog. Had something happened to anyone in my family?

I bit down on my cheek, hoping it was something else.

When I arrived at the front entrance, a servant walked up to take Flea off my hands.

"Take good care of her," I rasped, before handing him her reins.

"Of course, Prince Hamon, it is good you are home," the man answered and bowed.

Taking two steps at a time, I hopped up the stairs and entered the castle of the House of Belenet. The entrance hall was filled with people, chaotic chatter reigned supreme, and I made my way through the masses, getting more agitated by the second. It wasn't as though the castle was open to the public at all times. It meant something bad had happened.

I spotted my brother, Marcus, and headed in his direction. When he saw me, a small smile flashed across his features, only to vanish again swiftly. He came my way and we clasped hands.

"Home again, at last?" he asked. "Any luck?"

Marcus was one of the few people in my life who knew what I had been up to this past year. Younger than me by a year, but still the crown-prince because he wasn't a bastard like me.

We shared the same charcoal hair color, tall physique, and tanned skin. But that was where our similarities ended. He had a full, groomed beard, hazel eyes, as opposed to my blue ones. My brother was upstanding and just, if not known for his mercy when it came to battle, or the plight of others. His loyalty in regard to family and the House of Belenet was absolute and I was sure he'd make a fine king one day.

"I found the one who killed her," I said.

He nodded, his eyes narrowing. I didn't have to tell him what had happened to the murderer of my mother, he knew. And he understood. "Good. I am glad you did. What else?"

"Later. What is going on? Why are the flags at half-mast, what are all these people doing here?"

"Come, brother," he said and clamped a hand down on my shoulder. "I'll tell you everything. Knowing you, you are ravenous as always. Kitchen?"

I knew my brother and he didn't seem distraught as he would have been if something would have happened to our family, so I nodded. "Kitchen."

We exited the grand entrance hall and headed to the east-wing and into the kitchen.

The moment I entered the room, it was loud, and something came sailing my way. I stepped to the side and a ladle clattered against the stone wall behind me. Along with the missile, yelling came our way.

"You good-for-nothing heap of waste! I said a log of wood every half hour," Kiria screamed at some unfortunate kitchen boy who ducked away from her as she threw more things. "Now look what you have done."

She heaved a platter with roast onto the table. It was black. "The work of half a day, gone! I should throw you into the next chasm. Pea-brained imbecile!"

The guy was close to tears, and I walked into the middle of the kitchen and leaned on the table with a smile. "You missed, Kiria."

The curvy woman glared at me. "Pity. It wouldn't have struck an innocent." She breathed in deeply and waved her hand at the boy. "Get out of my sight for the rest of the day, Rupert, or I will stick you into the oven and serve you instead." The lad didn't have to be told twice, he raced from the kitchen as though the fires of the deep were after him.

"Good to see you, too," I said.

"Sit over there, I know you're hungry," Kiria said and pointed to a little table in the corner, underneath an assortment of pots and spoons hanging from the wall.

While the rest of the kitchen staff bowed at us as we traversed through the large room, Kiria didn't care for such things. We had known her growing up, so we never felt the need for formalities between us. Besides, the kitchen was her kingdom, she ruled over every pot, pan, and person in here.

Marcus and I sat down, and Kiria soon brought two plates filled with bread, cheese, wine, and roasted chicken. It was cold, but smelled delicious. She tapped my shoulder before leaving. "It is good to have you back, Kay."

"Thank you, Kiria."

She inclined her head, then looked at Marcus, her face turned sad for a second, then she strode off, barking orders as she went.

"So, what did I miss?" I asked, ripping off a piece of bread and stuffing my face with it.

Marcus was silent for a moment, seemingly lost in thought. "Uhm… Father drummed up an alliance with Chardour. I was to marry the princess and join our kingdoms."

My brows rose. What a happy coincidence. I swallowed my mouthful, relishing the taste of freshly baked bread. It was still a little warm. "Chardour? Not bad, everyone and their mother has been trying to get their hands on their riches. How did Father manage it?"

"The looming war? They need allies," Marcus said.

I cut off a piece of cheese. "Marriage, really? I recollect that the beauty of the Vaster sisters is well-known. Though one hears things about the younger one."

"None of that matters now," he said, his voice strange. "The Vasters were on their way here. King Edrick, Queen Mauve, Prince Reagan, and my wife-to-be, Pavette, when their whole entourage was slain, mere half a day before they would have reached Sif. They left Princess Fabienne at home, so I think she is still safe."

My outstretched hand stopped mid-air on the way to another piece of cheese. "What? In our kingdom?"

Marcus nodded, his face dark. "We should have been married tomorrow. Now most of their family is dead. Except for–"

"The youngest sister." I sank back in my chair, the old rickety thing creaking under my weight. "Goddess. I can't even imagine. Poor girl."

Marcus scowled at the table. "It is a tragedy. Father has already put together a searching party to find out what happened and who did it, but they came back with nothing to report. No tracks, no nothing. It is unacceptable, we owe Princess Fabienne an explanation, and the bodies of her family, so she can grieve and bury them properly. Father and Mother are dealing with preparations and sending the guests home."

"I'm sorry, brother."

Marcus shrugged. "I didn't know Pavette, or her family. But I did look forward to meeting her. I'm sure we would have been a fine match."

I laced my fingers and placed them on the table, pushing my plate to the side as I did. My appetite had curiously disappeared from one second to the next. "It makes no sense. Who would want to kill them, and on our land, no less?"

"That's what we still have to find out." My brother's hazel eyes narrowed, his expression grim.

Chapter Eleven
Rayla

She was like a fire against me. Her lips branding me, searching, delectably soft. I couldn't help myself. My hands sank into her hair and I pulled her close, answering her kiss with abandon.

I couldn't deny the need I had for her any longer. Being this close to her the past day and night… It was exquisite torture. The feeling of using her grief to be close to her had taken leave upon her words. I would be what she needed. Right now. Whatever happened after was not important.

Eliza groaned when I cradled her head in my hands, deepening our kiss. Her hands came up to my shoulders and she tore at my armor. I stepped back a bit, without losing contact to her lips, ripping at the leather clasps to shrug off my chest plate. With a clatter, it fell to the floor, followed by my weapons and lower armor.

Eliza stroked over my shoulders, her palms snaking beneath the shirt I wore under my armor. Her skin on mine sent shivers over every part of my being, rattling me to my very core. How could a simple touch burn, tingle, and spark at once?

Her tongue slid over my lower lip and I nearly sank to my knees at the feeling of the silken softness. Heat, alive and scorching, sang through me when our tongues met and I drew both arms around her, done with my armor.

Her skin was soft and still wet from the bath, my hands slid down her back slowly, until I cupped her butt, squeezing the plump flesh I found.

A sigh broke from her lips, then she lifted my shirt. Even the small space of time it took for her to pull it over my head was too long. I would never get enough of her lips.

We clashed back together, my chest now naked, meeting hers. I gasped at the feel of her body sliding against mine with nothing between us. Tremors of lust sparked down my spine and I nudged her back until she hit the windowsill next to the tub. It was broad enough for her to sit on and I plucked her up, seating her on the tiles.

She yelped from the feel of the cold, but groaned a second later, when I wedged myself between her legs.

"You are divine," I rasped, kissing and licking a path down her jaw and throat. Her hands tangled in my hair – which I had not yet braided again – and my lids slid shut at the feel.

Her breaths came in harsh bursts and I pulled back a little to savor her. Green eyes looked at me, filled with the same wonder and heat I felt, cheeks blushed and lips slightly opened. I looked down and swallowed. She was more than perfect. Creamy white skin, with golden freckles, her breasts small and lovely, with pink tips. Her body soft, but surprisingly firm. Even though she lived a life of bodily comfort, she was active, and it showed in her toned legs. Those long legs. My palms ran over her thighs, digging into the silkiness.

"You…are not fair," Eliza said. "I want to see all of you, too."

I smiled and undid the band tying up my pants. It fell down and I stepped from them. Even if all I wanted to do was set down on her, taste her, love her, I held still, my skin warming under her perusal.

Her hand shook when she reached for me, running her palm over my toned stomach and up. "You are so beautiful, Rayla. I could look at you forever." Her legs hooked around me and she yanked me against her. Her still traveling hand cupped my breast and she kissed me again, this time sucking my lower lip into her mouth, then nibbling softly.

"But I want to taste you, too," she rasped. "All of you."

I smiled and cupped her chin, then pulled back to look at her. "Not before I have explored you."

She swallowed visibly.

Bending down, I kissed my way across her collarbone, then lower. While need devoured me, I did my best to slow down, running my palms down her throat and to her breasts. Cupping both, I groaned, sinking my lips to one peak. Kissing, licking, and sucking a path around it, before giving it my undivided attention.

Eliza whimpered, her nails digging into my shoulders. The little sharp pricks felt amazing and I switched to the other side. Crouching to my knees, I slid both arms around her breathing in the scent of her skin, kissing her stomach, her sides, her hips. Softly, I nibbled on her hipbone, before pulling my arms back to stroke my hands up the inside of her thighs. Opening her before me. I glanced up at her, seeing her biting her lower lip, looking a bit self-conscious. "You are perfect. In every way."

Bringing my face close to her center I breathed in, relishing her intimate scent, before kissing her thighs, working my way to the middle.

Eliza's hands shook on my head, the sounds she made shattering my resolve. The first taste of her had me gasping, and her yelping. She shook when I dragged my tongue up, circling.

"Goddess," she groaned, her voice hoarse and beyond sexy.

"I agree," I rasped, latching onto her center.

"Oh! Oh my!" Eliza trembled, her legs shaking next to my cheeks. I slid one arm around her, holding her flush against my face, while I ran my other hand up beneath my tongue, sliding a finger into her. Sliding heat. Silky warmth.

A sharp gasp tore from her and she undulated against my face and fingers. "Oh, don't stop. Don't…"

I flicked my tongue repeatedly and she ground against me. Then a series of tremors went through her, prompting me to hold her in place as I savored each spasm, every flex, and every whimper.

****

Eliza

Shiver after shiver raked me, my body lifting and releasing in waves of pleasure. Madness consumed me with each one as Rayla made me ride out every nuance of it, holding me in place and devouring me. I had never known this feeling could be amplified by about a million times. She glanced at me, and the sight of her between my thighs was unbelievable.

"Rayla," I gasped, threading my fingers through her curly hair.

She kissed me softly, then pulled back, her smile radiant. Had I not sat down, my knees would have buckled. As I was busy coming down from the waves of high, I cupped her face, drawing her up to me. Our lips met and I tasted me. "My turn," I said.

Rayla pecked my lips and swung one of her incredible legs past my knee, so each of us had the leg of the other between their thighs. When her thigh hit my sensitive spot, I let out a sharp breath, hugging her to me. She moved in the most sensual and smooth way, curling her hips into mine.

I placed one hand to her throat, letting it slide down and pushing her torso back but keeping our bodies joined below. I got lost in the sound of her breath, her scent of lilies, and the feel of her skin under my palms. Cupping her breasts with my hands, I thumbed the tips lazily, watching her eyes grow darker and her lids droop. Leaning forward, I took a taste of her skin, making my way around her breasts, then to the center of one, then the other. She was the most beautiful woman I had ever seen, curves and muscle, firm softness. My hand ran down her rippling stomach, circled her navel, then dipped between us. Parting, sinking, searching. She was gliding heat, and her moans grew hoarse, as her hips curled faster, adding friction. She rubbed herself against my hand, and I pressed my hand lower, curling a finger into her.

"Fuck," Rayla ground out, her forehead meeting mine. We stared at each other, breath short, hearts hammering. I moved my fingers faster, tilting my chin up to take her mouth. The kiss was sloppy, coupled with moans and passion. I entered her mouth with my tongue in sync with my fingers below, running my thumb up in circles.

"Oh, Liz," Rayla gasped into my mouth. "My Liz."

Her movements grew frantic, fast, and harsh. Then she blurted out a yell, shaking from head to toe. Her body convulsed in the most beautiful way, her face drawn into a mask of absolute passion. I watched her climax for me, stunned by the perfection of her and how she made me feel. Steady and tethered, in a world were nothing else was.

Her legs shook and she sank against me, her head coming to rest on my chest. I pulled my hand free and hugged her, squeezing her to me, never wanting this moment to end. I wanted her to be mine, like I wanted to be hers. In this very moment I was. I would have given her everything, body, heart, and soul, if she would have me.

We stayed as we were, clutching each other until our breathing got back to normal. I felt her heartbeat slow and she kissed me between my breasts. "You are unbelievable."

"As are you."

When she wanted to pull away, I held on, not allowing it. "Let us stay like this for a little longer, please."

She brought her face to mine, kissing me sweetly. Slow and loving. "I would stay forever, if you wished it, but we can't."

"A little longer."

"Fine." Another slow kiss. "Just a few more minutes." Our lips met once more, making my insides melt. It conveyed so much without either of us saying a word. Desperate to cling to her, I didn't stop, holding her, not wanting to go back to my reality.

Finally, Rayla pulled away, stroking my cheeks with a thumb. "You'll catch your death, Liz. Let's wash up and get dressed." She looked strange, a crease appearing between her brows. "And let's hope that Marie hasn't heard us."

Her worry made a chill rise through me and I shivered. Hopping from the sill, goosebumps covered me. We quickly washed, standing over the now lukewarm tub and Rayla's features closed up, as if her thoughts were miles away from this room, from us. I shouldn't be surprised, she had told me in no unsure terms that a fling wasn't what she wanted. But her distant features made me crash back to reality brutally, as if we hadn't just loved each other. As if she hadn't just turned my world upside down.

I pulled on the new undergarments Marie had laid out, wondering if Rayla had only done it to help me. The same as sleeping in my bed, comforting me, consoling me. The fabric of my clothes felt heavy and scratchy after her touch.

In the grand scheme of things, it seemed trivial to be held up by such thoughts, but they distracted, as well as deeply moved me. When Rayla tied her boots, stroking back a strand of black tickling her face, I couldn't take it any longer.

"Do you regret what just happened?" I asked.

Her steel-gray eyes latched onto me. "Why would ask such a thing?"

I drew the light-blue dress over my head which hung over a stool. "You seem like you regret it. Worried that Marie heard, and you look…distant."

A frown appeared on her face while she donned her armor and fastened it. "I worry about Marie, because if she did hear and tells anyone about it, it will reflect badly on you, which is something you can't afford right now."

I drew my brows together and Rayla circled me, starting to lace up the back of my dress with swift fingers. "And if I seem distant, it's because I have no idea how to start telling you what I must. Especially after what you have been through." Her fingers landed on my shoulders, then her arms came around me from behind. "When all I really want to do is take you away from here and run." Her breath next to my ear made my lids slide shut.

I reached up, taking her hands in mine and leaning back against her plated chest. "What do you have to tell me?" I asked, not wanting to know the answer.

"It is more of a decision you have to make very soon. And it troubles me." Rayla kissed my neck, directly beneath my ear, making warmth fan down my spine. "I wish we could vanish, stay together locked up in our own little word, but we can't – you can't. You will have to decide whether or not you want to rule in your parents' stead, and you will have to take some steps…accordingly."

The mention of my parents made me swallow at rising tears. I shouldn't have asked. "I…I don't know."

Rayla hugged me, then let her arms drop. "You will have to figure it out, and soon, or the decision will be made for you."

I turned, coming to face her worried features. "What do you mean?"

"I will fell anyone who dares to come too close, who dares to attack you, but I can't protect you from politics. The senate will question your capability to rule, as will half the population, especially the nobility. Many will sense their chance to take the throne from you. Just yesterday I…" She took a deep breath and scowled. "Yesterday, I followed a maid who was searching for information about how you were doing. I couldn't see her master, only hear him, and I have no clue as to why he wanted to know, but I have a feeling his intentions aren't noble, whoever he is."

I swallowed again. "That is a lot to take in." No wonder she had looked miles away.

"There is more. If you decide to rule, the laws of your kingdom dictate that you–"

"Marry. I know." The truth and all its magnitude hit me like a punch to the gut. Just the thought of marrying anyone was laughable, especially after I met Rayla. After knowing what it was like to be in her arms, to feel her passion and how she ignited my body, heart, and soul.

When I looked into her eyes, I saw anger and frustration, but she blinked and the feelings seemed to vanish. "Please don't make your decision with me in mind, Liz." She brought her forehead to mine. "As much as we enjoy each other," she smiled, "we would never work out. I am beneath you, and while the general population accepts same gender relationships, we both know royalty is different. Which is why I care whether or not Marie has heard. If anyone gets wind of us, they will use it against you, to take what is yours, to take your right to rule."

She was right. And as much as it pained me, I would have to distance myself if I wanted to continue my parents' legacy. But was it truly so? Did I want to rule? "I have to think on this. On all of it."

"Of course. Do you want to go somewhere?"

"My parents' study. And I have to be alone, or I will take you into consideration."

Rayla nodded. "I understand. I will accompany you and wait outside."

****

No matter how much time I spent pondering my situation and what I had to decide, as I stood at the windows in my parents' study, looking out at the gardens, I couldn't reach a final choice. The weather outside was dreary, dark clouds hovered in the sky, letting rain pour down and beat against the windows. I breathed in deeply, loving the scent of rain, and watched the trees and bushes dance in bouts of wind.

Was I fit to rule? Did the senate have a point in questioning my abilities? I bit down on my lower lip. Reagan was the one who should have stayed back, no one would have questioned him or his right. He had been groomed for the throne his entire life. I was the wild one, the one who questioned things. The one who people talked about as strange and too headstrong. The one who was too honest in social situations.

None of it truly mattered, though. I would have to take the throne. Because of what my father had written to me. I had to protect the White Peak. For whatever reason, it had been important enough for him to insist upon it.

I could become fit, I could learn to rule, to be a worthy queen for my people. The rain got heavier and I blew out a breath. I wanted none of this. I wanted my family back. Agonizing yearning for them assaulted me. It was astounding how many tears one person could cry, surely by now, mine should have dried up. But as they fell, my insides mirroring the storm outside, I was helpless against the grief overwhelming me.

It took me the better part of an hour to regain hold over myself. Rayla said I had to make a decision, I wanted to. Yet, she was the reason why I hesitated, unable to put myself behind my convictions. Remembering her touch, the feelings I had when she was close... How could I deny what I knew was happening? I was falling in love with my guard.

I snorted, wiping away the residue of my tears. It wasn't as though many marriages in my circle were love matches. Marrying for love was a commoners' prerogative. Most royals married for alliances, or power, or wealth. The thought of having to do so was frightening. I wasn't my sister, who would have been a good wife and queen to anyone lucky enough. And I would have to find a king who wasn't needed in his own kingdom, so no first-born.

Still, how could I promise myself to someone when my heart would never be theirs? How could I – I gasped. I was being very selfish. It might very well be that Rayla didn't care, or that she had just indulged me, while doing her duty to be close to me and protect me. What of her feelings? Were they the same as mine? Could I marry someone else if they were?

I straightened and called her name. The door opened and she entered. My pulse quickened at the sight of her and I felt blood rush to my cheeks. Had we truly loved one another only hours ago? The memory of her body against mine, the sounds she'd made, her scent, the taste of her lips… It floored me, and made my heart ache with something other than grief.

"I have tried to come to a decision. It is obvious what I should do, but I have to ask you something first."

Rayla closed the door behind her and came to my side, keeping a regrettable distance between us. On instinct, I wanted to reach for her, but forced myself not to. Her presence was still like a flame, dangerously exciting and raw.

"What is this, between us?" I asked.

Rayla crossed her arms. "I don't know, Liz. It is whatever you need it to be."

"Why were you with me? Because I asked?" Afraid of her answer, I looked straight out of the window without seeing a thing.

"Partly. I would have left if you had let me. But to be honest, I wanted you from the moment I first saw you, sitting in a marshal's station, dressed as a man. Not even your costume could hide the truth of what you are."

I raised a brow, still staring ahead. "A woman?"

"No. Exceptional."

I turned to her and she looked as earnest as ever. "Liz, what I feel and don't feel should not matter to you when it comes to your decision. You know even if you stepped aside – especially on my behalf – you'd regret it. You are royalty. This is your birthright and you'd be better at ruling than anyone I can imagine."

"You'd be fine with me marrying someone else?"

Rayla gave me a sad smile. "We don't even know if we would fit, we only know what we feel now. It is so new, it could change at any time. Don't hesitate because you think you might have strong feelings for me, or I for you. Because we don't know yet if that would even be the case. And you can always send me away."

I glared at her and she chuckled. "You are insufferable. Who would beat up guys on my behalf in dark alleys if I did?" I asked. "Well, it seems I have decided, then. Will you call Stefan? I think I have to speak with him now."

Chapter Twelve
Rayla

I lied. I knew exactly what I felt and I knew it would tear me apart to see her with another, no matter how planned and clinical it would be. I should call on one of my brethren to protect her and head back to Xilum. To protect my stupid, infatuated heart.

A dry huff escaped me as I traversed the castle, asking around if anyone had seen Stefan. As if I could leave her, as if I ever wanted to. I would stay at her side as long as she would have me, no matter who she chose to be with, or what it would do to me.

I found the steward in the entrance hall, busy conversing with one of the senate, a man I didn't know. He had been quiet during the judgement and even now, seemed soft-spoken. He had honest eyes though.

"Dovani," Stefan said upon seeing me. "Is everything in order? How is Princess Fabienne doing?"

"She is ready to see you," I said with a short bow.

"Right. We will pick this up at a later time, Senator Ferton."

Ferton and his honest eyes stayed beneath the painting of King Edrick while I brought Stefan back to Eliza. She was still alone in her parents' study, standing at the window the same way as I left her. I wasn't comfortable leaving her alone with someone, but I waited outside, spreading out my senses to listen whether or not the conversation would turn south. I didn't think it would, but I was prepared, nonetheless.

"Your Highness, I wanted to tell you how deeply I regret what happened to your family," Stefan said.

"Thank you, Stefan. What will be done about it?"

"Pardon?"

"I want to know who did it and why. I want the murderers of my family brought before me. What will be done to achieve that?"

"Your Highness, I can mobilize a troupe of capable men who will travel to Leozar and look into it. But I must tell you, I have little hope of success."

"Why?" Eliza snapped.

"Because by now, the trail will have gone cold. I-I will send them nonetheless, of course, Your Highness."

I just knew she had unpacked that impressive glare of hers by the sound of his voice.

"Capable troupe… I'd rather…" Eliza cleared her throat. "Leave it, Stefan, you are right. I have a different plan. Regarding the future, I loath to think about it, but we must address it. I have decided to rule and you will teach me everything I need to know to do so."

"As you wish, Your Highness. But there is the matter of–"

"Me not being married. I know. You will write a letter to me, for the Belents. They have the bodies of my family in Sif?"

"I believe so, Your Highness." A chair slid back and creaked beneath weight. "What do you want me to write?"

"I need a husband. Apparently. And Leozar was my father's choice for an alliance. The family is large enough, if they can spare a Prince, he'll do."

It was silent for a few heartbeats. "I-I can't write that, Your Highness."

"Then find better words." Liz sighed. "I apologize, Stefan. This whole deal aggravates me. Please ask them if they would still be interested in an alliance through marriage, obviously not to Marcus, as he will inherit the throne of Sif."

"No worries, Princess. I understand this is hard, and a big decision. I will find the appropriate words." The sound of a quill scratching on parchment reached me.

"I'll ask Rayla to carry my message and oversee the return of my family when she comes back."

I gasped softly, surprised by her wish.

"Your Highness? The Dovani? But she is your guard. We could send anyone."

"I don't trust anyone. If this is a plot to break the alliance before it even manifests, the messenger will never reach Sif. Rayla will."

I hadn't thought of it, but Liz was right. It was dangerous to leave her unprotected though. Because clearly, she would be in danger too, especially in this perilous time when she wasn't yet queen.

Stefan seemed to have thought the same thing. "What about you, Your Highness? If this is truly a plot, and not some robbery gone wrong, you will be in danger too, not to mention many will question your ability to rule. There is no telling how far any of them will go. Your Dovani will deter any direct attempts on your life."

Damn right I would.

"I have decided, Stefan. And if you are worried about an attack, I will take measures to assure my protection."

"If you don't mind me asking, Princess. How? Castle guards?"

"No. I will ask someone I trust. Our guards are great, but I will need someone who can't be bought and who has my best interest at heart."

I grabbed hold of my scythes, then let go. It was her choice and I shouldn't feel any type of way toward people she trusted with her safety. I would make damned sure they were up for the task though. If she truly meant to send me to Leozar.

"There is another matter to discuss," Stefan said.

"Which is?"

"Will you be moving into the main wing?"

Silence followed.

"I…I don't know. Not now. I'll decide when we get word from Leozar. I can't very well stay in my wing when I marry." Her voice was heavy with sorrow and it tore at me.

"As you wish, your Grace." The scratching continued for a moment. "May I say that I am humbled at your decision? It is a great deal of responsibility and will not be easy. Even now, I had many people come up to me, questioning…"

"My ability to rule. I can imagine. I question myself too, but I will have to grow into it. There is no other choice."

While I was proud of her, I wondered why she said it that way. Eliza wasn't the type to want to rule, even if she would be a great queen. Did she feel obligated because of her family, or was it something else? The thing moving me even more was that she had asked me about us. As if she would have given up her reign for me. Even though she clearly decided to take her throne. I wasn't sure what I felt at that, but the familiar heavy nervousness made an appearance.

Paper rustled. "Thank you, Stefan. I will read through it and sign, seal, and ask Rayla to do my bidding."

"Your Highness." The chair scraped over the wooden floor once more. "I am honored to be at your side at this time. Whatever you might need, I will provide."

"Thank you. I will ask for one thing from you. Which is honesty. I do not care for compliments or opinions warped in order to placate me. Please tell me what you think at all times, truthfully, and I will take your advice into account."

"I will, Your Highness."

"And one more thing. When we speak in private, you can drop the whole highness and majesty crap. I loathe it already. Call me Fabienne, if we are to do this together, we will need to be able to speak harsh truths from time to time. I don't want you to feel like you can't say what is on your mind because I will be your queen."

"Understood…Fabienne. It will take some getting used to, but I will heed your wishes."

"Thank you, Stefan, you may send in my Dovani."

I breathed in, pulling my senses back when the door opened. "Princess Fabienne is asking for you," Stefan said, his face looking curiously pale.

I nodded, waited until he had shuffled around the next corner, then entered the study. Eliza's shoulders sank and she plopped down into one of the armchairs with a dull sound. Her hand shook when she threaded a strand of her dark-red hair around an index finger. Her breathing was short when she glanced at me.

"Did you hear some of our conversation?" she asked.

I sat down on the plush armrest of a chair next to hers. "I heard all of it."

Her lips trembled into an unsure smile. "I-I hope I was steadfast enough."

"You sounded it." I jerked my chin at the letter in her free hand. "Is that the message you want me to bring to Sif?" I decided not to add the 'to ask for a man you can marry' that was in my head. It would have sounded accusatory.

"Yes. Will you go?"

"If it is your wish."

"I'm scared, Rayla. If it truly was no accident what happened to my family…I need you to find out as much as you can, and bring them back to me. If you can, find whoever did this, and why. I truly believe you are the only one I can entrust with this. Where it any other way, I would never ask you to leave me."

"I understand, Liz. You don't have to explain yourself to me."

"But I want to." Eliza tugged on the strand of hair in her fingers. "I feel brittle, like I'm about to fall into pieces at any second. And yet, I have to go on, even when you are gone. Guess I'll find out if you are the glue holding me together."

She looked so small, her normally so intense eyes staring into the distance. Lightning struck outside, painting her face in light and shadows. I fought the urge to kneel at her chair and take her into my arms. If she knew how I truly felt, she would likely give up what she believed was right. I could not allow that.

"Don't be afraid. You are strong, and you will prevail, no matter what comes at you. I believe that. I will go to Leozar and get your family, and if I can, I will bring back information. But, Liz… Who will protect you while I'm gone?"

"Someone who probably won't want to, like you in the beginning." This time her smile was a tad firmer.

"I never–"

"You never wanted to come here, it wasn't hard to see." She sat up, let go of her hair and folded the letter neatly on her lap. "I am glad you were sent."

"As am I."

****

"The marshal? Really?" I asked, walking at Liz's side through the city, heading toward the marshal station where I had first met her. Wind and rain billowed around us, soaking our clothes to the skin.

Liz had put on a long cloak and hood, tying her hair back and drawing the hood deep into her face. "Yes. He knows me, and he will make an excellent addition to the castle guards."

"What if he says no?"

Green eyes glanced at me. "He will not."

It turned out she was wrong. As we stood in marshal Jentz's office, and Liz asked her question, he pursed his lips, making his beard bunch up. "No. Absolutely not. I am far too old and slow to be of any use to you, besides, I only have a few years left of work."

"But Jentz," Liz said, drops of water falling from her cloak to the floor with soft plops. "You have been my unofficial protector for years now."

"Not willingly, Princess, I can tell you that."

"And during all those times you got me out of tight spots and helped, during our chats and the odd game of Trice, you never revealed to anyone who I truly was. You are a good man and I trust you. I need someone I can trust if I am to take the throne."

Jentz crinkled his nose, scratched his chin, then folded his hands over his rather large belly. "I am honored, Princess. But what do you expect? Even your Dovani is skeptical of this idea."

Liz and Jentz both looked at me. One reproachfully and one amused. I had to work on my face, it was clearly showing too much of my inner thoughts.

"He is right, Liz. Jentz is old – no offence, I'm sure you are a capable leader of this station – and if you are attacked, he won't be able to stop it."

"None taken." Jentz waved me off with a grin.

"I think you misunderstand," Eliza said. "I don't want you to be my guard, I want you to be the captain of the castle guards. My head of safety."

The grin melted right off the old man's face, his bushy brows rose, ready to jump from his forehead. "E-excuse me?"

"You heard me."

"Captain of the guard? Are you – what of the current one?" Jentz asked, his voice rising.

"As I said, I need people I can trust. If that means I have to make changes in certain areas, I will." Eliza drew up her hood. "You will be given free reign of the guards, a great salary, and a dashing uniform. I expect you in the throne room tomorrow morning."

A stricken noise erupted from him.

"Good day, Jentz. Don't be late." With that, Liz turned from him and walked out of his office.

I stared, shrugged at Jentz, then jogged to catch up. "You can be tough as nails, you know that?" I asked when we crossed the station and traversed the steps down, into the streets. Liz had dark spots of red on her cheeks, looking shaken. "It does take some getting used to, I'll tell you that. Speaking with authority isn't half as easy as one would think."

I was impressed. "You do it well."

She blew out a breath through puffed up cheeks and waved at me to follow her. "It feels…exhilarating and frightening all at once. As if at any time my front will shatter into a million parts and everyone will see what I truly am. Unsure and inexperienced."

Something surged inside of me, making me instinctually reach out for her. I let my hand sink before she noticed. This was neither the time nor the place. But pride made my heart jump as we headed back to the castle.

****

I was to leave in the morning, and I couldn't stand being close to her without touching her. So, I had spent the day watching over her from further away, always catching her glances and smiling encouragingly. Eliza had done a lot during the day, other than recruiting a new head of guards, and I felt she was trying to distract herself as much as she needed to get things done. In small moments, I saw her shoulders sag when no one was watching, and her eyes would water, or she would blush, or stare off into the distance, and it pained me. But at any time she dealt with others, she was confident and assertive, something I admired endlessly, knowing how she really felt about all of it. I could only hope she would endure.

When the night came, I withdrew to my room, keeping my senses sharp to listen to her. While I sat on my bed, armor in one corner and bags packed, I sharpened my scythes, preparing to leave in the morning.

Eliza and Marie chatted next door while the handmaid tidied up, turned on the warming crystals, and fluffed up Eliza's bed with audible puffs. I didn't listen to their conversation, only the tone of their voices. It was amiable and there was no indication Marie had heard us in the morning. I bet she would have asked, or sounded different, if it were the case.

Sudden silence and a closing door had me look up from my curved blade. Marie had left apparently. I let my head sink again, continuing with my weapons. They were a thing of beauty, the curved blades sharp as razors,

147

gleaming in the light coming from the crystal lamp on my nightstand. The handles had some crystals and empty settings, waiting for more gems once I could afford them. As they were now, they moved faster than normal weapons, making me able to wield them with deadly speed and precision.

Would I need them in Leozar?

A soft knock at the door made my breath short and a tingle erupt in my chest. "Yes."

Eliza stuck her head through the door. "I-I know it is… Can I come it?" She bit her lower lip, looking so far from how she had appeared the entire day, I swallowed and nodded.

"Of course."

Liz slowly walked up to me, her face showing a lot of feelings at once, so many I couldn't discern what I was seeing.

"I, ah…" She sat down at my side, without touching me. "What I decided today was hard on me. I have no idea if it is hard on you as well, and if it is, I am sorry and I will go. But I…" She chuckled shakily. "I can't stand being far away from you. I understand why you retreated today, but it eats at me. All I want to do is lock us away and be with you, forget everything else."

Her words hit my heart without warning and it took me a few moments to be able to form a coherent answer that did not include grabbing her and kissing her. Slowly, I placed my scythes on the bedside table. I had to be smart about this. "I want you." Wow. Not smart. Truthful, but not smart.

Eliza blinked at me. "Then take me."

Unable to deny the pull I felt, I pounced on her, my lips finding hers as if we had kissed a thousand times. Her taste was just as I remembered. Uniquely her. Madness burned through me, heating my body as every touch sparked, every kiss was singeing, branding, searing. The fear I felt at leaving her, at not knowing what I would come back to made me desperate. Clothes tore under searching hands, moans formed under heated lips and skin shivered beneath caressing palms.

I loved her with everything my body was capable of, sending her over the edge again and again. Frenzy, dark and heavy, consumed us both, as we were too afraid to truly voice what we were feeling. Some things could not be taken back once said, so we let our bodies do the talking, clutching and devouring each other until deep into the night. Eventually, we collapsed in a heap of limps, pants and sweat, still holding each other tight.

Sleep descended on us before our breath returned to normal, while the storm still raged outside.

Chapter Thirteen
Kay

Two days after arriving in Sif, I leafed through book after book in the library, piling tomes into towers on the desk I had chosen. They leaned precariously and I nudged them straighter, or I would reap the anger of my sister Leigh. She loved books and any mistreatment of them resulted in a scolding that made one feel five years old.

Leigh was hanging from one of the ladders, her foot hooked into one of the rungs, while she leaned right, stretching her arm out to grab one of the books. It looked dangerous, but she did spend most of her days in here, and were I to say something, or dared to hold the ladder to help, she would remind me of that fact in no uncertain words.

"Why are we looking for this again?" she asked, finally snatching a large tome from the shelf. It was huge and dropped, making her sway a bit and my heart sink to my stomach. But before I could run to her rescue, Leigh had steadied and traipsed down the ladder.

I let out the breath I had held. "Because it's important to me."

My sister reached the ground and skipped up to me, the tome cradled to her chest. "If you told me why – I mean the truth – maybe I could help you better." Her amber colored eyes narrowed at me. "Instead of just mumbling vague things about deep, dark-red crystal."

I bristled. "It is important, that's the truth."

She rolled her eyes. "Yeah, yeah, important. Whatever." Leigh set the book down on the table, giving me a side-long glance when my built-up towers swayed. It was all she needed to do for me to rearrange them swiftly.

"Here we go, The Gems of Old." She blew some dust from the book and opened it. The pages were yellowed with frayed edges. "I haven't read this bad boy for years."

"Looks like no one has."

Leigh didn't answer and searched through the pages. "Aha! Here we go." She slid the tome to me, opened on a list of stones, their names, and powers.

> *Clear – Sinu = to control water*
> *Clear with yellow tint – Sinusai = to capture light*
> *Yellow – Micra = to warm*
> *Brown – Rigna = to travel*

I placed an index finger on the page and drew it down, skimming the colors. Past '*Leaf-green – Doran = to control metal*' which was what my bracelet was made of and what my daggers were embedded with. I got to the reds and frowned.

> *Blood-red – Sangus = to mend wounds*
> *Cherry-red – Illain = to travel – multiple people and objects*
> *Dark-red – Krais = to lift heavy loads*
> *Light-red – Krias = to add weight to objects*

"How original," I muttered and turned the page over.

> *Violet – Rani = to taste sounds*

"Wait a minute. Where is the rest of the reds?" I flicked back and forth.

"What do you mean?" Leigh asked, tugging the book over to her. "What exactly are you looking for?"

"Dark-red, as I said, but I don't believe it is uncommon to get Krais. Half the staff uses it. He said something about a nearly black with a red shine."

"Who said?"

"Never mind."

Leigh slammed the book shut, with my finger still inside. "Ouch! Are you crazy?"

She pushed me back and I shook out my squished finger. My movements slowed when I saw the thunderstorm raging on her face. "Hamon Kay Belenet, you will tell me everything. Right now!"

My sister was a small woman, but the sound of her voice could border on dangerous, as could her glare. She had the distinct talent to make one feel tiny compared to her by just a look and a word. It was how she survived growing up as the only girl with three brothers.

"Fine. You harridan."

Her features didn't loosen, her face as hard as ever.

"It's the crystal that was in the bracelet of the man giving the order to raze Gish."

Leigh raised a brow. "You are not seriously thinking of pursuing him? Are you?"

"Of course I am, Leigh. He ordered to kill my mother."

Her face softened. "Kay, listen to me. If what you are talking about is what I think it is…you have to stay away as far as you can."

"Wha – why?"

Leigh sighed and opened the tome once more, she flipped past the reds, oranges, and to the very last of the list. Black. Tapping her finger to a paragraph below the black, she clicked her tongue. "Read."

I bent over the tome.

Black-red – Obsidian = the stone of war

Obsidian has long-since been lost, hidden, or destroyed. As it has led to the great war, breaking the world. Not much is known from that time, but it is said that gem-wielders of Obsidian created the acidic sea between Iyune and all the other continents. Uncrossable, unsailable, and not survivable. The power of this crystal is past the control of anyone but the Nera.

"The Nera? Who or what is a Nera?" I asked.

"That is what sticks with you about all of this?" Leigh asked. "I don't know. I never heard of that word, other than reading it here. But did you read about how it created the acidic sea? And how it broke the world?"

"And? Ivey broke Iyune, and some say she crossed the acidic sea. All without any crystal powers."

"Ivey is a Witchgoddes. *The* Witchgoddes. Her magic is different. I heard it comes from sound and song." Leigh shook her head. "But that is beside the point. There is no such thing a gem-wielder anymore, and no such thing as a Nera. How anyone would come by Obsidian reveals one thing. Danger. Wealth and power. You can't get involved."

"I have to know. I need…"

"Revenge?" Leigh touched my shoulder and I looked at her. "It won't bring her back, Kay. And it won't make things better for you. It does not solve anything, but hardens you until you break. Do not go down this path. Please."

I remembered the bloody path that had led me to Aaron and a bitter smile settled on my lips. "Too late, Leigh, I've already come too far."

"It is never too late. Please. Stay with us, take your place at our court. You know you have one."

"A place? No. Just because Father wills it so, does not mean people accept it. They never will. I will always be the bastard, the scary one, the son of a whore, the outcast."

My sister shook her head. "You are not scary, your mother was a lady, and none of us ever called you a bastard."

"You haven't, enough others have. I see it in their faces, Leigh. The aristocracy, the guards, the servants, even people I meet on the streets of Sif, once they realize who I am." I huffed out a mirthless chuckle. "There is no place for me here. No matter how much I wish there was."

"We are your family. Never forget that." Leigh's warm smile was tinged with sadness and what looked like guilt.

I hated that look on her face and cleared my throat. "So. You know you can't stop me, only help. Where would one get Obsidian from?"

My sister glanced down, then elbowed me out of the way to get to the stacks of books I had put up. "You are incorrigible." Her short, slender fingers skimmed the backs of the books and she nibbled on her lower lip. "Hah!" She gently pulled one of the books out, careful not to topple the rest, and opened it on top of the tome with the list. "Well, it says here that Chardour has the largest concentration of Rigna and Illain, but we knew that already. Not many other kingdoms have mines. Midden has a small one that unearths a decent amount of Sangus and Sinu, Pasha and Espen have…Doran and

Krais…Chardour again…Sinusai, Krias, Doran…and so on and so forth… Nothing about Obsidian. But if I were to look anywhere, it would be Chardour. It just makes sense, as it has the largest mines in all of Iyune."

As I thought. Not a great lead, but what other choice did I have?

"Right," I said. "Chardour it is. Thank you, Leigh." I just wanted to leave when my sister shouted, "Hey! You put the books away first, mister. I'm not here to pick up after you. And leave your daggers with me, I have some new ideas."

I laid my blades out on the table, then gathered my findings and sorted them back. Meanwhile, Leigh scrutinized my daggers from every angle, pressing down on the crystals here and there. She had made them for me, or rather, gemmed them, but other than me, no one knew about this secret passion of hers.

"Hmm. No, this won't work yet," she murmured.

"Can I have them back, then?" I asked.

"No. I'm not done. You go ahead, I will give them back later, need to sketch and plan first. When you come back, I'll have something new for you."

I left her, deeply in though, humming a false tune to herself, drawing something on a blank piece of paper, while measuring my daggers.

****

"Leigh tells us you plan to leave again," Queen Beata said. "How long will you stay with us?"

My stepmother attempted a kind smile across the dining table, but it was shaky. She had never been unkind to me, but I knew she was happier with me gone.

I cut off a piece of roast on my plate. "Not long. I plan to leave tomorrow."

156

"We could use you here," my father said. "With this business of the Vasters… We need to find out what happened and who is at fault." His eyebrows drew together, creasing his forehead. "You could join the third regiment as captain."

"Oh yes, they will certainly respect a new captain because he is the king's son," I said, grabbing my goblet of wine and taking a swig.

My father sighed. "There is no need for sarcasm, son. I just thought it would be something that interested you."

"Or you could simply stay here," Leigh said.

"Or not," Rickard, my youngest brother offered with a grin. "It's always so nice and quiet when you're gone."

He received glares from Marcus and Leigh, but shrugged them off. "What? It's true."

"Just because he will beat your sorry behind in every sparring match and none of the ladies look at you twice if he is here, doesn't make it 'nice and quiet,' jerk," Leigh spat.

"Leigh…" our father chided.

"He doesn't beat me – every time. Kay never fights fair in the first place." Rickard jerked his chin at me, his face a mask of reproach.

Marcus grunted. "Kay earned his daggers, why shouldn't he use them?"

"In a sparring session?" Rickard snorted. "Now tell me again how that is fair."

"I'd beat you with a wooden stick, little brother. Your form leaves much to be desired," I said and took a bite off my fork.

Rickard scoffed. "Right. You know we could find out right after dinner if you wanted."

We grinned at each other. "Deal," I said. Rickard was always trying to push my buttons and I knew that deep down, he wanted to best me in all I did. It was unnecessary, but I indulged him.

"Now, now," Queen Beata said. "There is no need for competition."

"Let them, Beata," my father said. "It builds character."

Before any of us could answer, the door to the dining hall opened and Gerard, our manservant hastened inside, his aghast expression and short breath very uncharacteristic. "Apologies, Your Majesties, but you have a visitor."

"Tell them to wait in the library," my father said. "We are almost done."

Gerard teetered back and forth anxiously. "That will not be possible, my King."

"Why not?" my stepmother asked.

"Because the visitor demanded to see you straight away," Gerard said, his voice rising.

"We are the House of Belenet, no one demands to see us, they inquire an audience," Marcus growled. "Which we then might or might not grant."

Gerard looked stricken. "Not this time, Your Highness. This can't wait."

"Then for chasm's sake, bring them in," Leigh snapped. "I, for one, am curious who dares to demand to see us – during family dinner, no less."

Gerard looked at our father, and after he received his nod, waved at another servant standing in the door. "Bring her in."

Now even I was intrigued. Her?

The servant vanished and moments later, the sound of boots, squeaking on the polished floor got louder, and a woman entered the dining room. She was a sight to behold, tall and proud, her black hair plated in intricate braids, two scythes catching the light of candles on her belt. She moved with almost unnatural grace, a feat, given she was wearing matte black, gray edged armor. A Dovani. Her eyes, intimidating and stern, swiped over us to rest on the king, and she halted halfway down the table, then bowed.

"My apologies, Majesties, I come from Chardour, with a message from Princess Fabienne Eliza Vaster." Her voice. It was warm and of a certain coarseness, reminding me of a summer's day. I shook my head. Where had that thought come from?

At least Gerard's hurry made sense now. A Dovani as messenger from the princess of Chardour. A bold move, or a desperate one.

My father stood and nodded at her to approach him. "Be welcome, Dovani. We were all shocked when the news came to us. How does Princess Fabienne fair?"

Slowly, and with that daunting grace, the Dovani walked closer to my father, plucking a letter from a satchel she had at her side. "As one would expect, Your Majesty. She sent me to bring you this." The Dovani offered the letter to my father, who took it immediately. He was a full head taller than the Dovani, and had always been an intimidating man, but I had the sudden urge to stand up and put myself between them. There was danger in the air around her, a feeling I could almost grab and hold on to.

"And Princess Fabienne asked me to bring her the bodies of her family, so that she might bury them." The Dovani looked to my stepmother who gasped. "Apologies, your Majesty. I should have not said such words while you are sat in front of your dinner."

My stepmother waved air at her face with a palm, blushing. "Oh, no need to apologize." Her tone indicated that she *did* think it appropriate to apologize, however.

The Dovani showed nothing, only her eyes narrowed a fraction. "Furthermore, my charge has asked me to inquire as to what exactly happened. I would ask of you, Your Majesty, to grant me passage and authority to search the space and surrounding where the murders took place. I intend to bring Princess Fabienne answers."

"Of course. Any of my sons will happily escort you to make sure your search isn't hindered."

"We are?" Rickard asked, frowning. "We did send out an investigation, but it yielded nothing so far. No tracks, no indication of what exactly happened. I don't think you'll find anything."

"I could take you," I said, making everyone gape at me.

The Dovani arched a brow, her gray eyes searing into mine. Chasms and gems, that look was formidable. She glanced back at my father a second later and I felt like I could breathe again.

"My princess asks a big favor of you, Majesty," the Dovani nodded at the letter in his hand. "But she has put that into her own words. I apologize for interrupting your dinner," she glanced at my stepmother before continuing. "Might someone tell me where I can find Princess Fabienne's family? I would like to take a closer look."

Marcus rose from his seat. "Of course," my brother said.

"May I take my leave, Mother?" Marcus asked, and while my stepmother opened and closed her mouth a few times, her expression not happy, she finally said, "Of course."

Not needed to be told twice, Marcus quickly walked up to the Dovani, ready to lead her below, to where the Vasters had been placed before they could be moved back home. I stood too, uncomfortable with Marcus being alone with the warrior. I couldn't tell whether it was because I found her extremely intriguing, or because I sensed she was dangerous. Maybe a bit of both. The Dovani bowed, then followed the two of us from the dining hall.

Marcus, dashing fellow that he was, tried to strike up a conversation immediately, which hit me as odd. Even stranger was that her answers were short and to the point, leaving him flustered as women usually found him quite charming.

Soon, more footfalls followed us and when I looked around, I saw Rickard and Leigh catching up.

"What do you want?" I asked them.

"We're coming with you," our younger brother said, while Leigh threw strange glances at the Dovani, walking ahead, next to Marcus. "I have never seen one before, only read of them," Leigh said. "And a woman? I need to get her view on being a warrioress. How intriguing."

"She is not your field-study, Leigh," I whispered.

To my surprise, the Dovani turned while Marcus droned on about something then stopped, confused as to what had happened.

"I will gladly answer your questions, Princess," the Dovani said. "Once I have seen the Vasters."

Leigh grinned at me, shot past us, hooked her arm through the Dovani's and led her off.

Marcus stared after them. "What just happened?"

Rickard sniggered. "You got out-done by our sister, that's what."

Marcus snorted. "Not possible. I do know something you lot don't. Her name."

"And?" Rickard asked. "What is it?"

"Rayla," I said, having listened to their short conversation. I received a glare from my brother and shrugged. "Oh, you wanted to dangle that nugget over our heads, did you? Pity."

He elbowed me in the ribs and we continued after the two women.

Leigh chatted happily, receiving much more detailed and warm answers than Marcus had.

"Something is very wrong here," Marcus said. "This isn't normal."

"Maybe you're just not her type," I offered.

"Impossible. I am everybody's type."

Rickard chuckled, promptly receiving a smack on the back of his head. "Ouch!" He rubbed his head, glaring at his older brother. "Jerk."

"Moron."

"Cut it out, will you?" I sighed. "Aren't you too old for this? Also, why are you following them again? Leigh can lead her to the bodies, they don't need all of us."

"I want to see what she does," Rickard said. "I have heard the Dovani know more about death and killing than anyone else."

"What he said," Marcus added. "What about you?"

"I'm not letting Leigh go into the catacombs alone."

Rickard and Marcus looked at me funny, but I ignored them both.

Besides my reasoning, my brother was right, it would be interesting to see if the Dovani could gather more than our physicians had, which hadn't been much to begin with. From what I heard, the causes of death were simple, stabs of swordblades, daggers to the throat etc… I wondered if there even was more to garner.

To my relief, Leigh did not enter the deeper underground, but stayed at the top of the stairs. "They are down there," she said, pointing into the cold darkness.

The Dovani nodded her thanks, then plucked one of the crystal torches from one of the metal hooks in the wall. She twisted the metal ring containing smaller gems beneath the big crystal to align them and a diffuse, yellow light flickered to life in the top stone. She descended the stairs and was out of sight in seconds.

Marcus and Rickard followed closely, after taking their own torches each. I smiled at Leigh when passing her, making my own way down.

Chapter Fourteen
Rayla

My heart beat fast as the light in my hand chased shadows across the walls and down the stairs I was taking. I was uncomfortable, seeing as this would be my first time examining dead on my own. I had learned all I could, or I would have never made my trials, but this was no test, this was reality. Furthermore, these were people I had known. Not that I hadn't seen dead comrades before, but for the most part, I had been present during the fight that killed them.

I breathed in and out deeply, placing my steps with care in the uneven stairs. This was for Liz. I had better do a good job.

The steps behind me were another thing bothering me. Why would the princes all want to be present? I didn't need an audience, it made me even more nervous.

Marcus, I could understand, as he had been trying to chat me up – even if I was the messenger his would-be sister in-law had sent. Which struck me as weird. The younger brother would be just curious, but what about the other one? The one with the brooding eyes. He looked much like Marcus. Same hair and skin-color, but that was where any similarities ended. His eyes were ice-blue and he was more…intense. As if he had seen more, lived more, endured more. I knew he had to be the bastard prince, the one other kingdoms talked about none too favorably. He was known to be a rake, an unwanted part of the Belenets, which could not be true when seeing him with them. They seemed very comfortable and fond of him, if their body language was any indication. As in so many cases, the rumors seemed unfounded. He was obviously different from them, though. Not as trusting, and by far more on edge. He was uncomfortable with me alone with any of his family. It was obvious from his tone of voice when asked why he had come along. It had been too strained, and his sister had not come down the stairs, but he had. I heard three sets of shuffling steps behind me.

My feet met even ground and I raised my torch to shine light on my surrounding. It was cool down here but dry, a good place to keep corpses from decaying. Pushing at my nervousness, I strode into a large open space. Big square bricks made up the walls and spanned the high ceiling. Columns of the same stone supported the ceiling, making our steps echo back to us.

Before us, slabs of stone rose. Many of them. The first four held the Vasters, those behind, the entourage they had traveled with.

I had to swallow repeatedly when seeing Pavette. Her kind face was waxen and pale, her delicate throat slit. I placed the torch in the chain dangling from the ceiling above her slab. Each slab had a corresponding chain to place a light, probably for examination, or to ready the bodies for burial. Places like this were not uncommon in castles or keeps and I was used to the smell of decay mixed with cold stone. I heard huffing and retching behind me, indicating one of the brothers was not. Hasty steps back to the stairs and up told of a prince leaving. My guess was the youngest, it would be likely he hadn't seen or smelled anything similar before.

I placed a gloved hand on Pavette's pale one, then rounded her and looked for more wounds. It looked like her jewelry had been taken, the lobe of her left ear was ripped open. I frowned when seeing a ring left on her finger. It was valuable. Not something a robber would have missed. She also had no bruises or cuts from defending herself.

I placed a palm on her forehead, remembering her voice and presence, and the night she had laughed with Liz, while the two of them walked before me to Liz's wing. The day she had spent with her sister in the gardens, just talking and being sisters. It was unfair that her life was cut so unnaturally short. Sadness sank into me, different from when one of my comrades had died, because I knew of the sorrow it had brought Liz.

"See anything?" Marcus asked, stepping up at my side. His face was drawn into a mask of angry sadness when he looked at is dead betrothed. So, he did seem to have feelings about it. My opinion of him rose slightly.

"Not yet." I left Pavette's side and took a look at Reagan. Much of the same, no defending wounds, and his left pocket carried a pouch of gold. I carried on to the king and my breath hitched. He was different. His face was beaten beyond recognition, indicating wrath. Personal. King Edrick also had cuts on his forearms and hands, his knuckles were bruised and cracked. He had fought. His torso and stomach showed multiple stabwounds, but like his children, a cut across the throat had killed him. The more I looked at him, the more my stomach went queasy. This was the important body. The one telling the story.

The queen was the same as Pavette and Reagan. I balled my fists, then relaxed them. It was hard being clinical about any of this, but I had no choice.

"I don't think it was a robber's ambush," the tall, quiet brother said. He was right, but I crossed my arms and tilted my head, looking at him, waiting for him to go on.

"If it were, all the valuables would be gone."

"True. And it was personal, at least when it comes to the king," I said.

He rounded the slab of King Edrick. "How so?"

"He fought, his family didn't."

Marcus frowned. "Maybe he wanted to protect them."

"No. He was forced to fight, while his family was held down, blades to their throat."

"How do you know?" the taller brother asked.

"They have multiple smaller cuts around the deep one that killed them, all their knees are dirty, and what is more – the king was forced to watch them die before he was killed."

The bastard prince huffed out a humorless laugh. "And how could you possibly know that?"

I placed a hand on King Edrick's knee. "He fell down, shattering his knees."

"He could have just fallen during the fight," Marcus suggested.

"Maybe. But straight down to prompt the shattering of both kneecaps? Unlikely." I picked up the king's hand showing the two princes his palms and the crescent shaped wounds his nails had made on his flesh. "There is also this. He clenched his fists so hard, he drew blood." I gently placed his hand down. "No. This was no robbery gone wrong. This was calculated, carried out by professionals and most notably of all, it was personal." The certainty of knowing that made me uneasy.

Someone with a vendetta against the king of Chardour had killed this family and their guards and I had left Liz behind. Defended by an old man. I had to get back as soon as possible.

"I agree," the older brother said. "You'll need to see the scene where it happened as soon as possible.

Anything of note will only stay visible for a short while." He clicked his tongue. "I doubt there will be much left to see anyway. If you want, I will take you as soon as you want."

I was surprised by his offer, as he had struck me as closed off and distrusting.

Marcus looked from him to me, his face darkening a tad, but he said nothing.

"That would be much appreciated," I told him.

"Yeah, Kay was going to leave tomorrow anyway," Marcus said, his voice strange.

Kay. What a curious name for a prince, I thought. His grave eyes met mine and he nodded slowly, then took his torch from above Reagan's slab and walked off in the direction of the stairs. Leaving me and Marcus alone.

"Is there anything else to see?" Marcus asked.

"I doubt it. The guards and servants were killed quickly, it looks like it was done by arrows." I plucked my torch from above Pavette and we made our way up together.

Once appearing from the catacombs, the youngest brother still waited for us, his face pale. He did smile at me winningly, though. "Got what you were looking for?"

"In parts. Is there any chance one of you could take me to the servants' wing? I'd like to inquire from the manservant if he has lodgings for me. The day was long and I will retire soon, if I am to travel again tomorrow."

"O-Of course, but I don't think…" Rickard straightened, pulling his shoulders back. "I will lead you to the guest wing. You are a messenger from Princess Vaster, you will have lodgings according to that."

"Really," Marcus said, looking from me to his brother and back. "Seems like you should show her the way then, little brother."

Rickard ducked away when his brother reached out to ruffle his hair and glared at him. "Oh, I will," he said.

Marcus chuckled, nodded at me and turned to take his leave.

"You ready?" Rickard asked.

"If you are. Thank you, Your Highness." I bowed at him and he looked like he wanted to wave me off, then thought better about it.

"Let us go then."

"After you, Your Majesty."

****

While Prince Rickard led me through the Belenet castle – which was a lot gloomier and darker than the one in Chardour – I spread out my senses, listening closely to any and all conversations I could catch.

I doubted the Belenets had orchestrated the attack on the Vasters, but maybe someone else in the castle knew something.

There was nothing of note, so I said yes when Rickard asked if I wanted to see more of the castle before he showed me to my room. He seemed glad and smiled from time to time, telling me about some of the Belenet history and customs. Over time, he walked closer to me, leaving no guess as to what he truly wanted from me. I found his behavior funny, especially after his brother had tried his luck earlier.

The castle itself had little use of gems, most light came from candlesticks or fireplaces. Only in some of the grander halls did I notice chandeliers with crystals in them. And the walls were bare, making me long for the reliefs in Chardour. There, every wall told a story, here it only made our steps echo with their emptiness. It seemed like a cold place in many ways, if a lot bigger than the palace in Dearn.

I ignored all the advances the prince threw at me, staying detached and aloof. It only spurred him on, so I was relieved when we came by the library and I saw Princess Leigh sitting at one of the tables, tomes opened all around her.

"Excuse me, Your Highness, but I promised your sister she could ask me some more questions. Might we join her?" I asked, watching his face morph into a frown. He was unable to come up with a reason not to, so we strolled toward the princess, who looked up from her books and beamed when she saw me.

"Princess Leigh, you had more questions for me," I said.

She glanced from me to her brother, a sly smirk on her lips. "Oh yes, thank you for remembering. Please, sit."

About five minutes into us chatting about trivial things, Rickard fidgeted, then took his leave, saying he needed to see his parents about something.

Leigh watched him leave the library and chuckled, falling back into her chair. "Oh my, was it that bad?"

"I have no idea what you are talking about, Your Highness," I said.

She laughed. "Right. Did he give you the tour? Told you all about how grand and fierce the Belenets are – him in particular?"

"The topic might have come up," I said.

"I don't doubt it." She drummed her fingers on one of the books in front of her. "Please don't think bad of him. He acts this way when his brothers show interest in a woman, it is exhausting. And it has everything to do with the three of them and nothing with you. You are beautiful and a curiosity to all of us. That does it for my brothers."

"What do you mean? Why does it have anything to do with…your oldest brother?"

Princess Leigh looked at me for a moment before speaking. "Kay is our half-brother, as you no doubt know. Our father's first son, but illegitimate. He will never have the throne, and he will never have the true love and acceptance of our people. We love him regardless, but he has always felt like he didn't belong. Something about the broodiness and his woe-is-me demeanor makes all the ladies go crazy over him. No matter if royal, peasant, or servant, Kay could always have his pick of affairs and naughty thrills. Since Marcus has come into his own as the crown prince, so does he. Rickard feels left out, or left behind, I guess. So, he tries to one-up Kay and Marcus when it comes to conquests. It is boyish and stupid, but he can't seem to help himself."

I raised a brow. "Curious. And rather senseless."

"Right. But it is true." She stared into the distance for a second. "I had hoped Marcus would find love with Princess Pavette. I had hoped to find a sister. It is tragic what happened. And even though he acts like he doesn't care, I know Marcus was looking forward to meeting her and building a life with her."

I remembered his face when we stood in front of Pavette below. He had seemed sad, and angry.

"Thank you."

"For what?" Princess Leigh asked.

"You had no more questions for me, but played along."

Leigh smiled, she had a pretty smile and it seemed to come easy to her. A nice trait. One Liz shared. At least she had, before everything happened.

"You looked desperate. I had to help."

"I did?"

"Positively. Plus, had I not intervened, Rickard would have shown you around until you sank into his arms from exhaustion."

We both chuckled at that, then spoke of other things. Princess Leigh was bright and interested in almost everything. She asked about my training and Chardour. About what Princess Pavette was like and whether I had seen the mines. Her eyes sparkled with longing when she spoke of them, as if she wanted nothing more than to see them one day.

"Oh, and the cutters and inventors? I would love to talk to them one on one. I have so many questions, and tinker with inventions myself." Princess Leigh giggled. "Until now, I have only had small victories." She twisted a green crystal on her bracelet and one of the small, round metal tables took off from the floor and hovered toward us. I stared as she moved her hands, setting it down at our side, pouring us a drink from the glasses and carafes placed on it.

"That is…quite the feat," I said, accepting a glass of wine from her.

"Yeah… I try. I dabble in weapon-gemming as well. My brother Kay carries daggers I made for him. He tells everyone he won them in a sparring match, so my parents won't know." She leaned forward. "Please don't tell anyone."

I smiled. "Your secret is safe with me, Princess. But I must ask, why would you tell me about this in the first place? It is a rather big secret."

"Hmm. I don't know. Maybe because you are the first person I met that is coming from Chardour. Someone who would understand the importance of gems and their properties."

I nodded, deciding not to tell her how short my stay in Chardour had been up to this point.

It was a strange interest for a princess, but I didn't mind. And when she asked more questions, I kept my answers truthful, but short, not overly sharing anything. It became clear that Leigh would have become fast friends with Pavette, even more so with Liz. I could clearly see the two meeting, no one else would ever get a word in.

The thought made me smile. I hoped they would though, one day. No matter how draining the two would be, not to mention the shenanigans they would come up with, they would certainly have fun together.

Chapter Fifteen
Kay

"She what?" Rickard asked, his face a mask of shock.

Father scowled at him and my brother closed his mouth. We all sat back in one of our sunrooms, a place we all came together during the end of the evening to talk and spend time together. This time, our father had called for us.

Marcus and Rickard sat on one of the couches, while I stood next to the piano, which was placed in front of the door leading to a terrace. With one elbow, I leaned against it, earning a frown from my stepmother, who sat next to Father, both in their respective armchairs. Leigh was in the library, no doubt, but this conversation did not concern her, so Father had not called on her.

"Princess Fabienne wishes to continue relations between our kingdoms. In order to rule, she needs a king. She has asked if one of my sons would consider marrying her." Father said.

My stepmother wriggled in her seat, looking as excited as I had ever seen her. "This is a chance, boys. Another chance to merge with Chardour, and an even better one if you ask me. As king, you would hold much more sway over the exports than as the son in-law of the king."

I swirled the brandy sitting in my glass, then took a sip." Mother, her entire family was killed."

I had been asked to call her mother ever since setting a foot in this castle, it had never been a label of comfort for me.

"Whatever do you mean, Kay?" she asked, looking confused.

"I mean, it seems a bit distasteful being so happy about all of this," I said.

My stepmother gasped, glancing at my father. "I-I never…that you would think… Say something!" She nudged our father's arm.

"That is no way to talk to your mother, Kay," my father said. "But he is not wrong, Beata. The poor girl has lost all and is forced to look for a match to even be eligible to her own throne. I can't imagine what it must have cost her to write these words."

My stepmother placed her hands in her lap, looking sheepish. "I didn't mean it like that."

"We know, Mother," Marcus said, drawing a palm through his beard. "Well, I certainly can't marry her. It would mean moving to Chardour and become king. Unless…"

"No." Father shook his head. "You'll be king of Leozar once I die, and you have been groomed to pick up the crown all your life."

Rickard swallowed visibly, his Addam's Apple bobbing. "I-I don't want to get married. I'm only eighteen."

"But Rickard," Beata said. "You would be king. Think of the possibilities."

His hands grabbed the armrest to his left, his knuckles turning white. "Please don't make me, Mother."

He looked so young and vulnerable in that moment, I felt like my heart was being squeezed together. I downed my brandy. "I'll do it."

All eyes flashed to me. My stepmother positively gawked, while Rickard looked like he was deflating from the inside out with relief.

"You? Marry?" Marcus asked, then chortled. "The poor girl just lost her family, don't you think she's been through enough grief?"

"Outrageous," my stepmother said. "You have never learned how to rule, you travel around like a…a vagabond, and you are not of pure royal blood. Who is to say she would even accept you? Rickard is much more suited for an allegiance."

"And why is that?" I asked. "Because he would do anything you'd suggest and I won't?" I placed my glass on the piano, instantly regretting my words. "I apologize, Mother. I know it's not the reason – or at least not all of it. Yes, I may not have gotten the exact same education as my siblings, but I have had my share, thanks to you and Father. And I don't think Princess Fabienne can be fastidious about this. Rickard is too young to marry. I am not. And even if I travel around like a vagabond, my loyalty has always been to Leozar and Sif."

"No one doubts that, son," Father said. "And I think you'd do us proud. But are you sure?" His face turned sad. "I know you have suffered because of your heritage, and it is my fault. I'd loathe to think the people of Chardour would treat you badly because of…" He trailed off, never having been able to put into words what I was.

"Because I'm a bastard."

My father jerked in his chair as if I had lashed out.

"I know, Father, but I do not care. If the princess will have me, I'll be her king. It solves everything." I did not mention that I had been looking for a reason to visit Chardour anyway, because of the man carrying

Obsidian. Biron. This was the perfect opportunity. While I had no ambitions to become any kind of king – and the princess would certainly find me lacking in many ways, on this my stepmother was right – proposing to her would give me plenty reason to be in Chardour. And it meant I didn't have to ask Father for a letter of approval. He would never have to know why I wanted to go to Chardour. It was genius. All I had to do was join her Dovani, ask the princess for her hand, she would decline, and then I'd be free to search for the man who had ordered to kill my mother. The House of Belenet would have offered a prince, not damaging the relations my father had built with Princess Fabienne's father and all would be well. She might be desperate, but no princess would choose me as her king. It was simply unthinkable. The look my stepmother was giving me was all the proof I needed.

"We can't be sure the princess will agree," Beata said. "And if she does not, we will have lost our chance with Chardour."

I sighed. "If I do not live up to her expectations, you can still send Rickard."

My younger brother looked stricken and I winked at him. "But how would she be able to resist?"

Marcus snorted, then laughed. "By all means, go and try to become king, Kay. You could use a little humility."

"Look who's talking."

"Marcus, Kay, enough," our father said. "If this is truly your wish, you have my blessing to go. I will write to the princess and you can leave with her Dovani in the morning."

"So soon?" Rickard asked, still looking relieved, but seemingly aghast at how fast things were moving.

"That will have to be some letter," my stepmother said, then she glared at me. "You better be on your best behavior, son. We can't have you being…" She looked at a loss for words.

"Myself?" I suggested. "Don't worry. I'll be as charming as I can."

Marcus slapped his thighs and got up. "Then we have nothing to worry about. You are known for your charm, first and foremost after all." The sarcastic tone in his statement wasn't lost on me.

****

During the night, I lay awake. The need to find the sucker who had leveled my home was a live, burning flame in my chest. No matter where he was, I would find him, and I would end him. Maybe that would snuff out the raging anger I felt all the time. Maybe after my vengeance, I could turn back to what was left of the life I had. Hope. It was a fickle thing, and for the first time since my mother died, I felt it. And I hated it. Hope meant having something to lose. I wasn't sure I was ready for that. If I didn't find him… No. I would. There was no other acceptable outcome. I would avenge the lives of the people I had grown up with, the ones who had never treated me differently from the next person, because they had known me. The man needed to die.

At the far corner of my mind, a laughable small voice asked what I would do if the princess did say yes. What if this whole idea went south and I became king? What then? I wasn't king material, not in the least. I knew it, and the people telling me so all my life knew it as well.

I turned and pulled the blanket between my legs. It wasn't likely. She would have heard of me and as unwilling as Rickard was to marry, I was pretty sure I was incapable of marriage. Just the thought of loving someone, to be afraid of losing them… It made me anxious. But marriage didn't mean love, and proposing didn't mean the other person would say yes. She'd be a fool to choose me as her king.

With that happy little nugget of wisdom, I silenced the voice in my head and resumed to plan my vengeance until the sun lit up the horizon and I rose from my bed without an ounce of sleep.

Time to get ready.

****

"This is the place?" Rayla asked, looking around. The Dovani and I halted, while the escort carrying the bodies of Princess Fabienne's family had taken another way. We would meet them at the Foudan later on.

"So, I have been told." I stopped Flea and took in the part of road before us. From a waylaying point of view, it was perfect. Thick bushes covered the sides of the road, growing into tall trees further in. The road itself led up to this small hill, and one could see it curve and twist down, knowing who came this way long before they actually did.

Rayla slid from her steed, which was larger than Flea by quite a bit. He was black as the night and looked fearsome. The warhorses of the Dovani were meant to strike fear into the hearts of anyone they met. Flea had no such qualms, as she flattened her ears when he took a few steps in our direction. Her neck elongated and she opened her mouth to nick him. I reigned her in and pulled her to the side, then slid off the saddle and fastened her to a nearby log covered in moss and mushrooms. A good distance away from the warhorse.

Rayla was already walking around, studying the patches of blood in the sand. When she heard her horse move behind her, as he seemed as interested in Flea as she took a dislike to him. She said a word I didn't recognize and he stilled on the spot, only looking at my mare.

"You sure he'll stay there? Cause Flea looks like she will kick him if he comes closer."

"I'm sure," was all she said.

I walked over to where the Dovani was crouching, careful not to step on any footprints or blood.

She picked an arrowhead from the gravelly road and inspected it. "Hmm." Rayla flicked the head with a gloved finger and held it to her ear.

"What are you doing?" I asked.

"Doran," she said. "This arrow has a splinter of it in the head. They sound different than normal ones."

I twisted the bracelet on my wrist, feeling my daggers hum at my side in answer. "Really? I have heard of arrows and weapons being used that way."

She glanced at me, her gray eyes darkening. "Do not play coy with me, Prince Hamon, I know of your weapons using the same gem. You take me for a fool?"

"Absolutely not. I just—"

"I do not mind you lying to me, frankly, I don't care, but if you lie to my mistress, or try and harm her in any way, I will end you. Prince or no prince." The way she said it left no room for interpretation. She meant every word she said. It angered as well as impressed me.

"I did not lie to you, I am not comfortable sharing certain things with a stranger, that is all."

Rayla stood, dropping the arrowhead in the sand. She slightly placed one foot in front of the other, adapting a subtle stance. What was happening? For a moment, I thought she'd attack me. On reflex, I reached for my bracelet, and one of my daggers zinged from my belt and hovered in mid-air next to me.

The Dovani watched my dagger, then pulled her scythes from both sides. She took a step in my direction and I – still not knowing what happened – let my dagger fly at her to stop her.

With a swift movement, Rayla swatted at my dagger, trapping the blade in the space between the hilt and curved blade of her own weapon.

My dagger vibrated and shook, but she held it steady, looking thoroughly unimpressed. "So, you use this often? Doran, I mean. Happen to come this way lately?"

My jaw dropped, as did my hands. The dagger clattered to the path, bereft of any crystal magic. "Y-you think this was me?" I asked, waving my hands around the entire surrounding. "What would make you say that? What exactly would I have to gain?"

Rayla stuck her scythes back into their sheaths and fastened them, then she bent over and collected my dagger from the ground. She took a few steps in my direction and handed me my weapon. It was dusty and left her black gloves with patches of near-white. She dusted her glove off, her eyes not leaving mine for a second.

"Doran is only used by some, for a plethora of reasons. One being that it is extremely hard to control, another that it is expensive. You might know how to steer your blade, but you are by far not good enough to control an arrowhead. So no, I don't think you did it. But I had to be sure. I was not going to allow a man in the vicinity of my charge – possibly even into her bed – if he killed her family. Makes sense?"

I weighed my dagger in a palm, then swiped off the dust before placing it back in its sheath. Her tirade made a multitude of feelings sweep through me, some of which made sense. Most of them didn't. Her thinking – even for a second – I would be able to kill an entire family, plus escort, was a hard pill to swallow. Then I remembered what I had been doing this past year and suddenly, the accusation wasn't as baseless. I had changed. I had no right to get upset about anyone stating the truth of what I was. But the fact that she deemed me 'not good enough' to be a threat made me bristle. Granted, I had only begun using the daggers and the Doran about two years ago, but I was sufficiently deadly.

"It makes sense, but what would I have to gain by harming the princess, or any of the Vasters for that matter?"

The Dovani raised one of her arched brows. "Really? You are the bastard son of a king, you will never rule your own kingdom, lest you marry a princess who has her own kingdom. Does that sound familiar in any way?"

Her words snapped something inside of me, most likely better reasoning, and I yelled: "I don't even want to be king!"

"Huh. Now *that* is interesting." Rayla bent over and picked up the arrowhead, she threw it up and caught it again. "Then why are you here? Mind you, I will not accept any more lies."

"Your princess needs a king, Marcus can't marry her, he has to rule over Leozar one day, and Rickard begged his mother not to make him. He is only eighteen." I shrugged. "Who else was there?" Admittedly, it was only half of the truth, but maybe it would suffice.

Rayla narrowed her eyes at me, throwing up the arrowhead once more. Something about her posture, her glare, and her presence called to me. In a very disconcerting way. I wasn't sure whether it meant I wanted to fight her – just to see who would win – or fuck her. Probably both. I was under no illusion that she wouldn't kill me in the blink of an eye if I tried either of those things. I had never seen anyone move with such speed and precision as she had when rendering my dagger useless. It called to my competitive side. Always a dangerous thing. I was often unable to quell that part of me. I would have to make an exception in this case, though.

"You want me to believe you are doing this out of the goodness of your heart? Because you love your little brother?" she asked, that brow still raised skeptically.

"I don't care if you believe me or not. It's the truth. If your princess will have me, I'll be her king, if not, then I have tried to be of service to my family. End of story." I kicked at a pebble on the gravel-road. "By the way, don't you have a job to do here? Find out who actually did this?"

"I know who didn't," she said, eyeing me up and down until I was tempted to roll my eyes. Curious, normally only Marcus was able to get me to do that.

Rayla stuck the arrowhead into a pocket, then she turned and walked across the road, marked with dark, dried patches, and long tracks where the bodies had been dragged to the wagons bringing them to Sif. "Huh," she said, then dashed away and into the bushes covering the right side of the road. I heard her moving around, leaves rustling and branches cracking. Then the sound of metal clanking and chainmail swooshing sounded from the brush. Rayla suddenly became visible as she climbed one of the tall trees at breakneck speed. My eyes widened at the sight. She had removed her armor, sporting what looked like a black body suit, tailored to fit her body perfectly. Her braids danced on her back, while she climbed higher and higher, making me crane my neck to keep her in my sights.

"Please don't fall," escaped me.

She chuckled drily. "I have no intentions of falling, but it warms my heart knowing you care."

"I don't mind the falling, but I'd have to mop you from the ground and then go and explain it to my parents. Not something I'm keen on."

This time a curt laugh came from above. "You seem like a very caring individual, makes the story of you doing this for you little brother so much more likely."

"And you don't seem to like me all that much."

A branch cracked and I flinched when she slid down a bit, but she caught herself and continued as if nothing happened. "I don't have to like you. I only have to take you to my charge."

"You are very loyal to her, where does that come from? As far as I know, you haven't been her guard all that long."

Rayla swung one leg over a thick branch and scraped at something in the bark before her. "I am a Dovani. Our loyalty is absolute."

"Hmm. It does seem to be personal to you, though."

Rayla frowned at the branch, then swung off it and looked around. "Threatening to kill someone who might have ill intend toward a charge is not unheard of." She sniffed, then began her decent. Almost as fast as she had climbed up, she slid down. I heard her chainmail and her armor clanking a few seconds later. Then she emerged from the bush, her cheeks flushed a little, making her look charming. Not something I associated her with.

"Besides, I am as entitled to like and dislike people as the next person. You are trouble."

I crossed my arms and laughed. "How do you figure that?"

"Experience." She whistled once and her horse came prancing our way. She caught the reins and patted the horse's shoulder. "You feel like you don't belong because most people have made you feel that way. It made you angry and bitter. Also makes the ladies in your life flock to you, thinking they can change you if only you'd be nurtured by love…" Her gray eyes looked at me mockingly. "They are wrong, and you leave them broken-hearted. But you don't care, because as much as you feel like you don't fit in, you still feel entitled to fuck everyone willing to do so, perhaps promising stuff you never plan on delivering." She smiled widely, making a charming dimple appear on her cheek. "Or you 'decide simply not to share some things.' It's not your fault if they believe what they want to believe, right? Well, it's not, but it is not nice on your part. Which is why you are trouble, and I don't like you. And it is the reason I will not take my eyes off you. Because my charge has been through enough. And if you so much as send one cruel word her way, I will be there to place a few knots in your spine." She jumped onto her horse and left me standing there, bug-eyed and shocked.

"Come along, trouble, or we'll never reach the Foudan before dark," the Dovani called over her shoulder.

Chapter Sixteen
Eliza

The days were hard, but the nights topped everything. I missed my Dovani, even as my heart pained with knowing I would probably never wake up next to her again. It was one more thing that ripped at my insides.

While I was able to distract myself during the day, with Stefan droning on about the obligations and liabilities the throne brought on, I could focus on nothing during my nights. Sometimes, the pain grew so bad, I fled into memories of Rayla. In the bath. In her bed. I often snuck into her room to lie down there, smelling her and closing my eyes, I'd imagine her still next to me. It hurt, but it was bearable, compared to memories of my family.

I pressed my face into Rayla's pillow, breathing in deeply to catch her scent of lilies. Wondering where she was right now and whether she was on her way back. Had she found out what had happened? Was she coming back alone or with a prince at her side? As much as it should, the prospect of marrying some unwitting man didn't frighten me, I was more concerned with duping him. I needed a king, and that was all he'd ever be to me. If he came looking for a wife…I would be a sore disappointment. Poor guy.

But that was only if the Belenets actually had someone they could send, and who was willing to marry the opinionated, wild child of Chardour.

I sniffed again, pressing my face deeper into the pillow. Goddess, I missed her. In moments like this, when I was left to my own dark thoughts, I wished I had given in to my wish and run away with her. But Rayla was right, I could not give up my throne for something we both didn't understand and hadn't even fully defined yet.

A sound made me sit up. The squeak of my door in the next room. I'd know that sound anywhere, as I had cursed it on multiple occasions when sneaking out, thinking it would announce my intent. Who was it?

Sitting as still as I could, I listened. Then one of the floorboards creaked. Someone was in my room. Silently, I slid from Rayla's bed and snuck to the door separating our rooms. I had left it ajar to come back later, once exhaustion would settle in. Glimpsing through the gap of the door, I saw a hooded figure creeping up to my bed. Moonlight threw shadows on their dark cloak and the curtains billowed in the wind. The figure pivoted at the movement, and the moonlight reflected on a dagger in their hand.

I placed a palm over my mouth to stifle a gasp. My heart raced as the figure continued closer to my empty bed, raised the dagger to plunge it down, before noticing that my bed was indeed empty.

They pulled the covers away and a whispered curse floated my way, then their hooded face turned toward the door I was spying through. Fear paralyzed me as the figure slowly moved toward me, dagger in hand.

My breath hitched and I told my legs to move, but nothing happened. It felt like my entire body was stuck inside a block of ice. Immovable. Even as the figure stopped in front of the door, reaching out a free hand to push it open, I could not see their face, because the hood prevented any kind of light to hit their features.

Just before a black-gloved hand reached the door to push, I stumbled back, letting out a scream. My foot caught on the edge of the rug and I fell flat on my ass.

The door swung open and the figure rushed through, finding me sprawled on the floor like an offering. I yelled some more, then scuttled backward until my head hit the bed post. Turning around, I pushed myself up and rounded the bed. The figure cut me off by jumping on the mattress. They grabbed my throat and surged forward, pinning me against the cupboard. The air was knocked from my lungs when my back hit the wood, the impact making the cupboard door to my left open slightly. I stuck a hand inside the cupboard, feeling around, while my attacker held me in place, swinging one arm back to skewer me like a roast-pig.

My fingers closed around something made of metal and I pulled. Clattering and banging followed when I freed a gauntlet from the depths of Rayla's cupboard. It was heavy and made of the same metal as the rest of her armor. Something sliced into my side and I cried out, but didn't let go of my new weapon. With all the strength I could muster, I slammed the metal glove into the side of my attacker, who made a curious 'hmpff' sound, and bent forward. The dagger was pulled from my side and I quickly thumped them over the head with my deadly gauntlet, then kicked at them, making them stumble away, falling onto the bed. I raised my gauntlet high, with both hands, ignoring the fire in my side and looked at my attacker threateningly.

"Get out, you filthy slimeball!" I yelled.

The figure rolled over with lightning speed and stood up at the other side of the bed, again the dagger in their hand caught the moonlight, blinking as my blood dripped from the blade.

Noise and shouting erupted from outside my rooms, and running feet sounded through the hallway outside. The figure looked at me, then the door, before hurrying toward the balcony and leaping into the night.

I sank against the cupboard, letting the gauntlet sink down, then I cupped my side, feeling warmth drip over my fingers.

Doors flew open and people poured inside. Marshal Jentz, Marie, and a couple of guards surrounded me in the blink of an eye.

"What happened?" Jentz asked, his face drawn and worried.

I pointed at the balcony. "They left that way."

My new guard-captain yelled a few orders, while Marie rushed to my side, gasping when she saw the blood flowing over my fingers and down my side. "Call a healer!" she cried. "Now!"

My legs started to give out and I slid down the cupboard until my butt hit the floor. "I showed them, Marie," I said with a soft smile. "Clonked them on the head with my deadly gauntlet."

"What is she saying?" Jentz asked.

"I have no idea," Marie said. "Maybe she is delusional from the blood loss."

I cradled my gauntlet in my lap with one hand, refusing to let go of it, as the world went hazy and my lids felt like they were made of stone. It became harder to keep them open. The last thing I saw was people running in and out of Rayla's room and Marie's worried face, before darkness pulled its curtain around me.

****

I woke to sunlight tickling my nose and a dull pain in my right side. With a grunt, I came to, opening my eyes, then hissed when I was blinded by light. My hand flew to my side but was caught before it could reach my wound.

"The healer says not to touch for a couple of hours, your Grace," Marie said.

"Marie?"

"I'm right here." She squeezed my hand gently.

I blinked a few times and finally adjusted to the glaring light. This was not my bed. And I was not in my rooms. As a matter of fact, I wasn't even in my wing, but in the large bed of my parents.

"What am I doing here?" I asked.

Marie patted my hand, her smile much too cheerful. I knew my friend, something was wrong.

"Why am I in my parents' chambers, Marie?"

"Well…" She sighed. "They didn't find whoever attacked you and since you would have to move into the main wing eventually, and it can be protected better – and the windows are higher up – Jentz made the decision to move you here." She crinkled her nose. "I'm sorry, Eliza."

I looked around and swallowed. How often had I played hide and seek in this room, vanishing behind the heavy red curtains, or climbing into the dark-brown box at the foot of the bed? The scent filling everything around me was unique to my parents and tears brimmed my eyes. "I-I can't be here. Please…please take me back."

"Jentz says we can't risk it."

"I do not give damn what he says. I will go. Now." I grunted as I tried to get up from the bed, my side burning as if someone was holding a gleaming knife to it. "What is this? Why am I in so much pain? Didn't a healer see to me?"

"The blade used on you was poisoned. The healer said it will take a while until all of it is out of your body."

"Well, color me intrigued," I gasped and wriggled to the side of the bed. "Crafty little pissant."

"Princess, you have to stay," Jentz said, walking into the room, his face much paler than I remembered. "I-I am inconsolable about what happened. We didn't find anything, and we searched the entire garden and all of the castle last night."

"I do not blame you, but I will not stay here."

"You can't move while you still have poison in you. The healer said it could do irreversible damage if you did. Plus, the royal wing has defenses your old one does not. I am not taking any chances."

I stilled and sank back. "Fine." I breathed through my mouth, not wanting to smell what was all around me and trigger another bout of memories. "But please put me in one of the other chambers. One that doesn't have all their things in them. One that doesn't…smell like them." Fighting for composure, I felt tears brim my lids and I swallowed.

Jentz's eyes got big and he blanched even further. "Oh my. I hadn't thought of… I am so sorry, Princess."

"I told you to not put her in here," Marie hissed. "But no one listens to a mere handmaid." She looked at him with an anger I had rarely seen on her face and in that moment, I felt deep gratitude for her swallow me up.

"As soon as the healer says it is safe, we will take you to another chamber. I am afraid I must insist on you staying in this wing, though." He looked straight at me, his expression remorseful. "I am very sorry about this, Princess. Maybe you'd want to reconsider putting me in this position and find a more suitable captain of your guard."

"Jentz, you could not have stopped that idiot trying to kill me, unless you had slept under my bed, and I doubt your wife would be fine with that. I would have moved into this wing eventually, after marrying, so it's no big deal. I just…It was surprising and caught me off guard to wake here. They are still…" I thumped a fist to my chest to counter the pain lodged there, radiating to every part of my body.

"I understand, Your Highness," Jentz said. "And from now on, I will listen more closely at what Miss Marie has to say."

"That would be good," I said. "Now do me a favor and get another room prepped for me. I will leave as soon as I can."

"Certainly, Princess," Jentz said, bowed, and left.

"I will see to it myself, Eliza," Marie said, patting my shoulder softly. "Unless you want company to distract yourself."

"No, thank you, Marie." My voice cracked on her name. I was close to coming apart. Keeping it together this long was taking a toll. "You can leave."

"We will be quick," she said and rushed out, closing the door behind her.

I blew out a shaky breath and looked around, my vision swimming with tears as soon as I heard the double doors close. I tried very hard not to sink back into the depths of sorrow, but I lost that fight after a few seconds. Tears streaming down my face, grabbing hold of the sheets around me with both hands – sheets they had slept in last – I sobbed and sank ever deeper into despair and memories.

Their presence was still very much here. The warmth of my mother, who could be so stern she bordered on scary, but she seldom used that trait. The fair nature of my father, who loved so deeply and unconditionally, he had room in his heart for an entire kingdom.

"I miss you," I whispered. "I miss you so much. How can I ever go on without you? What am I even doing, thinking I can carry on your legacy?" Doubt, heavy and sticky, mixed with the sorrow, adding weight to it and making it unbearable.

I turned my face and pressed my nose into the pillow, breathing in deeply. The scent of home, safety, of family and acceptance, surrounded me. Only memories now. Gone. They only lived in my heart.

The fact that I was nearly killed last night paled in face of what I felt. There was no room for fear, no room for even thinking it might happen again. I was focused on my grief. Drowning in it. And a very small part of me could not help but hope. Hope that it had been a misunderstanding, that Rayla would come back with my family still alive and well. It was stupid and made no sense, but it was a smidge of delusional hope I clung to with all my might as I wept and wished for things to be different.

****

In a way, being forced to lie in my parents' bed and feel them around me, reliving many memories and wallowing in them, helped. For the first time since the news of their death, I slept soundly. After crying so long, I fell asleep, it was dreamless and left me rested.

It felt like I had been able to say goodbye to them in their space.

I was able to limp into the room Marie and a few other servants had set up for me with a little help. The healer was happy with my progress and said I'd be up and about in two days.

The room was on the other side of the wing, and one none of us had spent much time in. Marie had seen to it that all my belongings had been moved and she had outdone herself with making the space mine, without replicating my old bedroom.

The bed was large and made of dark wood, sitting directly opposite the door. A heavy dresser, painted white and gold, now held my toiletries and my old ceramic dolls. It also had a large, round mirror sitting atop it, decorated with an intricate frame, housing several crystals. None of them had powers, but it looked stunning.

The bathroom was across the hall and had two large tubs. The room itself also had two cupboards. Two of each. Like my parents'. It reminded me that it had been likely furnished with the possibility in mind that this would become the royal suite.

I shuddered at the thought and concentrated on the wallpaper. Golden leaves on a cream background, surrounded by thin lines of gold. It looked very royal and elegant. And I missed my old room dearly. It had been a lot simpler. This was too much. It also seemed as though my staff had doubled. Miss Grant herself visited to tell me who was to care for me now. Three handmaids. One to help me choose clothing and dress, one to do my hair and face, and another who would be in charge of my bathing.

She looked as though she had bitten into a lime when I told her that I was fine with just Marie.

"When you are queen, you will need the extra servants," she told me.

I disagreed, but when I told her this and the lime turned into gleaming coals, I demanded that we at least keep it as it was until I really was queen.

It was a compromise she seemed to be able to make, as she nodded once, curtsied and stormed off – her three servants in tow.

I had Marie bring me letters from Stefan, about the goings on in general and stately affairs. I signed off on a few, put my thoughts down on others and made it work. It wasn't like I could invite the man into my bedroom, to speak politics. He did send me a lot of reading material, which I hated. It was dry and heavy reading, but I devoured it. Each word helped me learn more about leading, about Chardour and its cities. I was especially happy he included a book on Leozar, Sif, and the House of Belenet. Learning about them was a good idea. When I got to the family tree, however, a bookmark fell out. It was a dove, made of rare, white wood, hanging on a silken thread. Pavette's. I had quickly closed the book and was now left staring at the wallpaper. Focusing hard. The golden leaves were hand painted, each one unique. And they fell in different directions. It bothered me slightly to see them chaotically float and fall. Random. Like real leaves.

I frowned and placed the book on my nightstand. I was not ready to look at it again yet. With a little effort, and a jabbing in my side, I heaved myself off the bed and stumbled through the room. I plucked Tina from the row of dolls and looked inside her. The letter was still where I had left it.

"Chin up, Tina," I told her when sitting her back down. "We'll get through this."

Looking for something to do, I opened my closet. A neat line of dresses, undergarments and shoes greeted me. A long box sat in the right corner and I groaned when crouching down to open it. A small "hah," slipped from me when I saw Marie had gathered my costumes for nightly excursions inside. As well as my Trice pieces. I was helpless against the smile tugging at the corners of my lips. I closed the box, fought myself to a stand and opened the door of the other closet. It was empty. Anxiety crept up on me at the sight. If Rayla did bring along a prince, these shelves would soon fill. As would the left side of the bed.

I swallowed at the sudden discomfort. No matter who she brought – if she brought someone – I would marry him. There was no other choice. As to the fact of her bringing back my family, so we could put them to rest… I would cross the bridge of seeing them unmoving and cold when I got to it.

Without a knock, my door burst open, banged into the wallpapered wall, making me jump. Pain seared through my side, and I blinked at Marie who stood in the doorframe, her face anxious.

"Eliza, you have to come. Something strange is going on," she said, her voice shaky.

"What do you mean?"

"The senate. They have gathered in the throne room, along with a bunch of nobles. I just heard some maids talking about it. You have to hurry, I think they… They are up to something."

My heart dropped to my stomach. "What? Find Stefan and tell him to meet me there."

Marie's face fell. "Eliza…Stefan is already with them."

Now my heart jumped back up and it felt like it was stuck in my throat. "My coat," I rasped. Marie quickly helped me into it and brought me a pair of shoes. All of it took too long and I cursed while fighting my feet into the shoes with Marie's help. She steadied me on the way and my thoughts ran rampant. Fear, surprise, and the feeling of betrayal coursed through me, but as we hobbled through the castle it culminated into something else entirely. Wrath. If this was really about outvoting me, they had another thing coming.

Chapter Seventeen
Rayla

The prince aggravated me. Part of it was his lazy arrogance, coupled with his strangely magnetic, brooding, demeanor. It was a small part, though. What really gnawed on me, as we rode toward the Foudan, where we would meet up with the rest of his entourage and the carriages containing the Vasters, was the reason he came along. Oh, and not to forget the way he looked at me from time to time. The possibility of Liz marrying him enraged me to no end, add in how his gaze felt way too intense when it brushed me, and I was a few heartbeats away from punching him from his mare.

As I had told him before, he was nothing but trouble in my eyes. The handsome kind, sure, charismatic even, but trouble, nonetheless.

I finally snapped when I felt him look at me once again. "What? Should I draw you a picture? It will last longer."

A dark chuckle floated my way as the path ahead turned and vanished in a line of tall trees. "Are you always this…abrasive?"

"No. You are special."

He chuckled some more and I was barely able to stop myself from rolling my eyes. We entered the forest and the air grew cooler immediately. The smells changed. Moss and damp bark. Moist earth and resin. Birds chirped close by and wind whooshed through the tall trees.

"I wanted to ask, what have you learned from the place the Vasters were ambushed?" he asked, his tone void of all teasing.

"However bad it looked, the attackers were few. Two or three at most, I would say."

"What?" he sounded genuinely perplexed. "That makes no sense."

I pulled the arrowhead from the satchel hanging behind me. "We have already concluded that they had someone there who could wield this. We found no other arrows, neither back there nor with the dead. The entourage was killed by one person. The one able to control this arrowhead. The royal family is another deal. Which is why I think it had to have been two to three people."

"One person killed that many people? That is a concerning thought."

I snorted. "Concerning isn't the word I would use. They would have to be highly trained to pull it off, though. Talent and an affinity for crystal magic only takes one so far."

He was quiet for a while and I threw out my senses, listening to a family of foxes hiding from us in their burrow a few paces to the right, and a stream, gargling along further away. All was well. We were alone. It still was sensible to check every now and then.

"Have you ever heard of a crystal called Obsidian?" Prince Hamon asked.

What felt like an icicle piercing my lower stomach made me jerk in my saddle. Gintac, my horse, noticed and huffed. He kept on going at the same pace, but I felt him stiffen below me. Reaching out a hand, I patted his shoulder reassuringly. "What?" I asked, unsure about what had just happened.

"Obsidian?"

The icicle took a stab at me again.

"Ever heard of it?"

I concentrated on a few long breaths and the feeling vanished as quickly as it had come. Could it be the word itself I was reacting to? If so, it was highly unusual. "Can't say I have," I told the prince truthfully.

"It's a form of magic crystal. Supposed to be the most powerful one."

I turned my head to look at him, confused by his question. The prince shrugged and didn't meet my eyes. "My sister is really into magical crystals, when she heard I would be going to Chardour she told me about it. I'd love to bring her one someday."

I raised a brow, saying nothing. Something about his behavior felt strange. But why would he lie about something so trivial? Except my reaction to it, it seemed perfectly normal for him to inquire about something his sister was interested in. And the way I had gotten to know Leigh, it made sense. She loved crystal lore and all that had anything to do with it.

"I have not been in Chardour that long, but I have never heard of...Obsidian before." This time, I was prepared as the feeling returned. It was definitely the word itself. Curious.

Gintac suddenly stopped short and shook his head snorting. Alarmed at his behavior, I looked around, then threw out my senses again. I barely heard the twang of a bowstring before I ducked, feeling something swish over me.

"Ambush!" I yelled and slid from Gintac, simultaneously grabbing both my scythes.

To my surprise, the prince was at my side in a second, his daggers floating next to him as he twisted the bracelet on his left arm.

"Hide!" I yelled, just as three men broke from the tree line, armed with swords. Rage boiled inside of me when I beheld them. They looked too well armed and armored to be robbers. This was a planned attack.

Placing myself in front of the prince, who had decided not to heed my words, I took a stance when I heard the twang again. This time, I was ready and threw out my right arm, deflecting the arrow aimed at the prince. I warded off two more closely following the first.

"Hide," I snarled over my shoulder.

The prince finally dashed away, vanishing in a few bushes to the left of the road.

With a roar, the men charged me, their blades raised. I stood still, flexing my fingers on the grips of my weapons. A smirk flashed across my lips. Idiots. I pressed down on the crystals in my grips, feeling my scythes hum with power.

The first strike thrown at me, I dodged, then I brought one scythe up and cleaved through the sword of the second man. He looked dumbstruck for a moment too long, in which I turned and swiped my other scythe at his neck. His head hit the forest floor before his body did, both collecting leaves as they rolled from the path and down into the forest.

Pivoting, I blocked an attack from the third man, then sank my right scythe into his chest. With a yell, I pushed up and forward, lifting him from the ground and throwing him from me. My weapon left a large cleft in his chest. He landed on his back with a huff, blood pouring from his open chest. His rattling breath would soon subside, but I already faced the first man who had attacked me. He glanced at his two companions and licked his lips nervously, his grip tightening on his sword.

"Who sent you?" I asked.

He roared and swiped at me. I deflected the blow to the side and down, then kicked his wrist. His sword sailed from his hand and plopped to the ground. "Who?" I placed a scythe to his neck, pushing him back until his shoulders hit a broad tree.

He grunted, then spat at me. The sound of another arrow made me swipe up my left scythe to swat it away without looking. The man in my grasp swallowed past my scythe, blanching.

"Don't make me ask again," I said.

A zing sounded through the air behind me. Seconds later, metal sliced into skin further away and arrows clattered to the ground, along with a body. The prince had just finished off the archer with one of his daggers. Nice of him, but unnecessary.

A hiss erupted from the direction the attackers had come and impossibly soft steps – not human – reached my senses. I frowned, not knowing what to make of it.

"Attack!" a sharp voice rasped.

A growling roar was all the warning I got, then teeth sank into my shoulder and ripped me from the man in front of me. The world went dizzy as I was thrown around like a puppet. The teeth released me, and I landed in a heap of leaves, rolling over, springing to my feet. I turned to face black eyes, and a snarling maw. A Sauvey. Its scaled skin glinted in the specs of sunlight filtering through the canopy of leaves above. Sleek and deadly, it rounded me, hissing and growling. Each time the scales around its face would stand and rustle, adding depth and danger to the growl itself. The large cat-like creature carried a collar around its neck. A crystal I didn't know was embedded inside, glowing in an amber color.

Not far away, a robed woman stood, turning a ring with the same color on one finger. She winked at me. "Attack," she hissed again.

I was fast, swiping at the Sauvey when it lunged, but my scythes didn't penetrate its skin, they didn't even reach it, bouncing off something. It was as though a magic field shielded it from my blades. Without my weapons, I was taken to the ground fairly quickly. I dropped my weapons and held the snapping mouth from my neck with my arms. I screamed when talons scraped at my armor, one slicing into the space between the front and back plate. My skin ripped from my ribs to my hipbone. It wasn't deep, but burned like fire.

Huge teeth clicked above me, hot breath fanning over my face, smelling of death. Saliva dropped onto my face and I grunted with the effort of keeping the deadly teeth away from my throat.

A yell sounded from beyond, sounding like the prince, then a scuffle ensued. The idiot was probably fighting the woman who had turned the Sauvey loose on me.

The growling cat suddenly froze atop me, then was punched clean off its feet. Gintac jumped over me, turned and kicked at the downed cat. Landing gruesome sounding hits. The Sauvey wailed and dashed off into the forest, no amount of calling from his mistress able to get it to return.

Her calls were cut short and I struggled to my feet, seeing one of Prince Hamon's daggers sink into her throat. He got up himself, breathing heavy as he twisted his bracelet, calling back his weapon. Gintac nudged my shoulder and I patted his cheek. "Thank you," I said, receiving a short whinny in answer.

I held my side and looked around. The prince had done a lot of work while I was downed. The man I had questioned looked as though had been nailed to the tree by his daggers.

With some effort, I bent over and scooped up my scythes, cleaning them of leaves sticking to the bloody blades before wiping them clean on my pants and returning them to their holsters.

Prince Hamon breathed heavily, sporting a split lower lip and a cut on his left brow. He dropped down on a fallen, mossy tree and twisted his bracelet, making his daggers spin through the air, cleaning them. "What in all the chasms was that?" he asked.

"Stupid, that's what," I said, walking toward him with Gintac in tow. "Did you have to kill all of them?"

His ice-blue eyes found me and he scowled. "Excuse me?"

"The armor they are wearing? A tame Sauvey? Not to mention the weird shield surrounding the Sauvey? No robbers I know of travel around like that. They were lying in wait for us. We should have questioned them. What if they knew something? What if they were part of the plot?"

"I just saved your life," he said, grabbing one of his daggers from the air and pointing it at his chest. "A 'thank you' would be nice."

"Please, I had it under control."

"Yeah. Sure looked like it. You had a fucking cat atop your chest, about to bite off your face."

"Gintac took care of that," I said.

The prince snorted mirthlessly. "You are truly something."

"It doesn't matter," I said. "If I am correct and this attack is connected to the one killing the Vasters, someone is trying really hard to thwart the Vasters from ruling. Which means they were here for you. We have to go. The faster we get to the Foudan, the sooner we are in Chardour."

I reached a hand out to him and pulled him to a stand. "Are you hurt, Prince Hamon?"

He swiped at his brow and shook his head. "No. But you are bleeding." He pointed at my side. "Let me take a look."

"No need. I will be fine."

He scowled, tucking his daggers into their sheaths. Thrusting his left arm at me, he presented his bracelet. It was a beautiful piece of art. A silver band adorned with Doran and other crystals.

"You want me to have it, is that it?" I asked.

"No, of course not. I am showing you that there is more on my bracelet than Doran." He tapped to a red stone. "Sangus." Now let me have a look at that wound and mend it."

"You can use Sangus?" I asked a tad surprised.

"Yes. I can. It comes in handy to be able to heal oneself." He drew closer and flicked a finger against my chest plate. "Off with that and let me see."

I looked at the path ahead, then him. It would hinder me if I rode with this wound. And even if Sangus only healed superficially, it would stop the bleeding. "Fine," I said and undid the leather straps holding my armor in place. I shrugged from my chest plate and turned my injured side to him.

He was careful as he parted the frayed edges of my under suit, then he pressed a thumb to the Sangus crystal and his free palm over my wound. I gasped when his hand touched my skin, keeping myself in place by force of will. It didn't hurt, but felt strange. A sense of pulling pinched in my wound, then warmth seeped into it and radiated across my entire side.

I watched with bated breath when my skin knitted together. A red scar was left as his palm traveled up my wound and toward my ribs. It looked delicate and the pain didn't leave. I would have to be careful, it was prone to rip open under pressure.

"Thank you," I said when he reached the top and closed it.

His hand lingered a few seconds, his face close enough to mine for me to feel his breath on my cheek. I stepped back.

"Don't mention it," he said, his ice-blue eyes finding mine for a moment before he turned and strode up toward the path to collect his mare.

Gingerly, I slid my chest plate back on and fastened it. Gintac snorted and I led him up to the road and carefully mounted him.

I waited until Prince Hamon rode my way, then let Gintac fall into step at his side. "It will get dark soon, we have to hurry."

"I agree, but be careful, the wound is still too fresh."

I huffed and clicked my tongue. Gintac burst into a gallop immediately and I stood in the stirrups, buffering his movements with my knees.

Prince Hamon caught up to me, his face dark. He said nothing, but his lips were a grim line.

Curiously, his dismay amused me and I almost smiled.

Together we raced along the road, making good time. Still, the sun was down when we reached the Foudan and the rest of the Prince's convoy.

My side thrummed with pain, but the scar held together. Traveling here would have taken me considerably longer if the prince had not healed me. I was wondering where he had learned how to do it. Sangus was not easy to use, and short of studied healers, I hadn't met anyone who could.

Prince Hamon greeted his convoy and the small, bald convoy leader – who looked relieved to see us –

told him that we would be able to pass in a few moments, if we were ready.

The prince looked at me inquisitively.

"Ready," I said.

The Foudan before us was large circle of stones. Old and mossy, the grey rocks stood taller than two men on each other's shoulders. Each one had a big crystal imbedded in its middle. Rigna and Illain alternated on each stone.

Our entire convoy entered the circle together while the bald man ticked off each person, horse and carriage in a book he cradled to his chest. It was gigantic and he teetered a bit carrying it.

"Stay inside the circle," he said, then walked from it himself to hand the manifest to a woman, before coming back to us.

The woman vanished in a small house next to the circle and emerged a moment later with two staffs. Each one held a crystal the size of a fist in an intricate setting. One Rigna, and one Illain.

She bounced the crystals against one another, eliciting a humming sound, then touched them both to two large stones on either side of her.

The humming sound grew into a buzz, until the stones around us seemed to sing with it. The horses whinnied fearfully and the prince slid from his mare to calm her down. Gintac stood still as a statue, making me the only one seated in a saddle when the stones lifted from the ground and started to circle us. Faster and faster they went, until they became invisible and the buzzing hum rose steadily to an almost unbearable sound. A thrum went through me and my stomach sank when we were propelled through space.

Chapter Eighteen
Kay

The moment the spinning subsided, I heard retching and groaning around me. I related and held a hand to my stomach in order to quiet it. Travelling through a Foudan was never nice. Whereas it hadn't been fully dark in Leozar, here the stars blinked in the sky already, only a pale stripe on the horizon told of early evening. For a moment, I wished it to be day, so I could see the surrounding we landed in more clearly. It helped with orientation. And I was curious. Chardour. Many stories surrounded this rather small kingdom, shrouding it in mystery.

As it was now, all I could see was the circle of the Foudan, filled with the people who had come with us, and a lit pathway leading from it toward a few houses. More and more lights lit up as I watched, and the few houses grew into a city. The lights were crystals. Of course. It was Chardour, they would have an entire city – nope, what looked like an entire garrison lit up – alight with gems.

Flea nudged me and I dug into a pocket absentmindedly to give her a treat. "You've done good," I told her.

Rayla rode past me on her huge black horse, the only person to have not vacated her saddle during travelling. The woman was unbelievable. I had never met anyone who outright told me what they thought of me to my face, no one who had warded off a Sauvey with bare hands, and shrugged off being sliced up by one as a mere inconvenience. My respect for her had only increased during the past day and a small part of me wished I could throw my plans to the wind and beg her to elope with me. Not that I thought we would fit, or be happy, but she called to something in me. She was not afraid of me, didn't care about my reputation or station, and there was a grave calmness to her. She kept a distance toward others which I understood.

"Coming?" she asked over her shoulder.

I shook off my stupid thoughts and led Flea from the circle. The whole convoy filed from the Foudan, more or less slowly. Some of our people lingered here and there, breathing heavily.

When we all finally made our way up the lit path and into the city, I noticed a lot of guards around. They patrolled in pairs, or stood watch at many of the houses, most of which were inns catering to travelers from other kingdoms.

Our convoy garnered much attention. People came from the inns and houses, openly staring at our little procession, windows opened and men, women, and children hung out of them to watch us. Whispers rose around us, their gazes glued to the large carriage carrying the Vaster family. To my utter surprise, many of them looked stricken. The guards all bowed silently while we passed, and the whispers subsided, swapped for a grave quiet.

"We'll stay here for the night," Henry, the small, bald convoy leader said, his voice carrying through the thick silence uncomfortably. He didn't seem to notice and waved at the servants, guards, and carriers to follow him to the grandest inn. His talking had broken the silent reverence and a woman stepped from one of the porches and into the street. She raised a palm to run it along the black lacquered coach carrying the royal family. Others followed and soon our convoy slowed to a snail-pace.

Our little leader turned, probably wondering what was happening and his eyes popped. "What the… Hey! Stop that! Guards!"

The guards who had come with us started to square off at the people, trying to get them away from the coach. Immediately the village guards unsheathed their weapons, taking a stance directed at our guards. This would get out of hand in a second.

"Leave them," I said, my voice carrying over the ensuing commotion. "Stand down." Our guards immediately left the people alone, many looked at me with reproach, but they did listen. Simultaneously, the village guards resheathed their weapons.

"These people are only paying their respects, Henry," I said. "Let them."

Our convoy leader frowned, but nodded at me before continuing on. It took us a while to reach our destination as more and more people emerged from everywhere, paying quiet respect to their ruling family. They had obviously been loved by their people. What astounded me was how the guards had immediately stood up for their citizens, without question. They knew where we came from and who we were, but still, they had not flinched. Also, they seemed especially hit by their royals rolling by. I caught some of them even lowering their heads and placing two fingers to their foreheads, a sign of deep respect, usually saved for a fallen comrade.

"They loved their queen," Rayla explained, obviously seeing my confusion. "Eliza told me she had a high standing with the military."

"Eliza?" I asked.

The Dovani jumped in her saddle, making her horse prance to the side a bit. "Princess Fabienne," she said.

She didn't look at me but the back of her neck reddened. I didn't ask, but found it very strange she would call her charge by her second given name. It was a very intimate gesture, mostly only reserved for family members and close friends. No one but my family called me Kay. Rayla's slipup had to stem from habit, so the princess had either asked her to call her Eliza, or she was doing so in her head. Both options were unusual, to say the least. I decided to not think any further on it, once I saw the two interacting it would make sense, I guessed.

We eventually passed all the people and reached the inn. Rayla told the guards who stood at the sides of the inn to get a few men and protect the coach. The man she was talking to assured her that they would work in shifts to guarantee the safety of the Vasters.

Rayla nodded and watched him hurry off with an unreadable expression on her face. She slid from her saddle and only approached the stable boys standing at the ready when the coach was surrounded by guards and brought around to the side of the inn.

I was about to hand Flea's reins to one of the stable boys when Rayla got into a small argument with the one wanting to take the reins of her horse. By argument I mean he tried to take the horse from her and she told him no in a firm voice. The poor guy seemed flustered, obviously not knowing what to do with her denying him.

His curly, dark-blond hair fell into his face and hid big eyes that widened even more as he looked around to understand what was now expected of him.

"I will take care of Gintac myself," Rayla told him. "You may show me the stables."

"Of course, miss…grace…majesty?" he stammered, blushing profusely.

Rayla smiled at him, which stopped the stammering but furthered the blushing even more. "What's your name?"

"Oren."

"I am neither a miss, nor a grace, and definitely not a majesty, Oren. You can call me Rayla. Now, will you show me the stables?" The tone of her voice was similar to when she had spoken to my sister Leigh, soft and warm.

The stable boy nodded, still flushed, and led her away. I smirked and handed the boy in front of me Flea's reins. "Take good care of her, will you?" I asked.

"Yes, sir," he said and was off. Just as I wanted to follow the rest of my entourage into the inn, I felt as if someone was watching me. The hair on the back of my neck stood and I subtly scanned the area around us. There was no one and I entered the inn, but the feeling didn't leave me and it continued to make me uncomfortable.

I tried to get rid of the feeling, as there was still no one to be seen, and looked around the entrance. The inn was built with large wooden logs. From the walls to the floor, the ceiling, the chairs and tables filling half of the room, to the reception, was made of the same colored wood. The smell was warm and agreeable, mixed with the scent of roasted meat drifting from the kitchen, which seemed to be to the left.

"We will need accommodation for our convoy," Henry said at the reception, standing on his toes to lean his elbows on the desk. A tall woman stood behind it, glancing down at him. Her thin lips smiled, softening her face. "Of course, sir," she said. "Thank you for choosing the Wayward as your home for the night. How many people are you? And how long will you be staying? Breakfast as well?" Golden earrings caught the light of the crystal lamps set on the desk in front of her.

"Fifteen commoners, twelve guards, one Dovani, myself and our prince of course," Henry said. "We'll stay one night, and yes, breakfast would be nice, thank you." He unhooked a leather pouch from his belt and placed it on the counter, the coins inside jingling audibly.

The woman blinked at him, then his coins, and back to Henry. "Your prince? Y-y-you mean…"

"Prince Belenet is joining us on our way to Dearn," Henry explained and waved at me.

I cursed underneath my breath when the patrons seated at the tables of the other half of the room got up to bow, remaining low. The innkeeper shot from behind her desk to sink to my feet, making her long blond hair sway, gushing out some words of reverence and adoration.

I quickly reached for her upper arm and pulled her to her feet. "Please, stand everybody," I said, severely uncomfortable with their behavior. "Do not be bothered by my presence, we only want to stay the night and travel on."

"Of course, forgive me," the innkeeper said, beaming at me. "You have a long journey behind you. I am afraid that not even our best room will live up to your expectations, Your Majesty, and I apologize. But there is still none better to be found in all of Khoras."

"It will be sufficient, I am sure," I told her.

She bowed again. "My name is Cynthia. Welcome to the Wayward, Your Highness. You honor us by being here." She shuffled back, bowing as she went. "A real prince, in our little inn," she crooned at Henry, as if she was telling him something new. "I can't believe it." Cynthia snapped her fingers at a silent boy I hadn't noticed before. "Trevor, rooms ten, fifteen, eight, and six for the guards, five, eleven, two, and nine for the commoners." The boy hurried to her side, nodding along at her words, looking like he was memorizing what she said.

He rounded the desk and led away the bulk of our convoy, some of whom threw me strange looks at the way I was treated. They weren't used to it, neither was I. Had it been any of my brothers or Leigh, they would have behaved differently to begin with, but it was only me, so no one had given me much attention since we left Sif. It was the way all of us were most comfortable with.

"I will take you to your room personally, Your Highness," the innkeeper said, leaving Henry to stand at her desk looking aghast.

"What about me?" he asked in a small voice when she bowed at me before tugging at the duffel bag I was carrying.

"You wait your turn, sir," Cynthia said over her shoulder. "The prince has to be exhausted."

As uncomfortable as I was with her fawning over me, I couldn't help being amused at Henry's ensuing stammering and gawking.

The innkeeper managed to tug the duffle bag from me, gasped when the full weight came down on her, and smiled at me as she heaved it on her shoulder and asked me to follow her.

I waved at Henry and weaved past the other patrons, who bowed when I passed, and caught up to Cynthia at a staircase.

The wood creaked under our feet and the innkeeper chatted incessantly, asking all manner of questions which I answered in a few words. Cynthia did not seem to care about my short answers, but changed the topic and told me about the inn itself. When it had been built, how it was state-of-the-art when it came to crystal magic, and how she had bought it a few years back.

We went up two landings and walked down a corridor. She opened the door to a rather big room, which looked cozy but not very special.

Cynthia placed my bag down in one of the wooden chairs with utmost care, then she shuffled over to the only thing made from stone, the fireplace. She reached for a handle next to it. A small crystal was imbedded in the handle and fire roared to life in the hearth. State-of-the-art indeed. Fire crystals were expensive and hard to get, and normally only palaces and mansions of nobility had those. Inns did not. What was more, most crystal magic worked in pairs, which meant for every one crystal to work, one needed another it could bind with. There had to be another fire gem inside the hearth for it to be able to light.

Cynthia rubbed her hands together, a proud expression on her face. "Twist the handle next to the tub to fill it with water. It will be warm until midnight. If you need anything, press the crystal on your nightstand and I will be here immediately. She fiddled with the pendant of her necklace, revealing a summoning crystal on it.

"Is there anything I can do for you now, your Highness?" she asked. "We have nobility coming through here from time to time and the House of Vaster was here before…" She swallowed, her face grim for a second, then she conjured up a smile. "Well, they didn't stay, of course, but went on to Leozar as soon as they came. What I'm trying to say, is…" She trailed off, looking at a loss for words.

"Everything is perfect, Cynthia, thank you," I said.

She beamed once more, apparently genuinely happy to have me there. "Then I shall see to your little convoy leader now." Cynthia curtsied and was halfway to the door when she turned. "He said you have a Dovani with you, is he to be placed with the guards, Your Highness?"

"She will have an extra room, if you have one."

Cynthia gaped at me. "Oh, certainly, Your Highness. Certainly."

Thankfully, she left after that and closed the door. I was left alone and explored my room a bit more, curious as to what else was imbued with crystal magic around here. Leigh would have been already taking things apart to see how they worked. To my surprise, I found quite a few places. Apart from the fireplace and the tub, there were summoning crystals for the innkeeper, the kitchen staff, the stable, carriers, and something described as "recreational company." I smirked when seeing it, wondering how long it would take for any "recreational company" to arrive once that crystal was pressed.

The lights all worked with gem-magic and there was even a latch next to the door that would render it impenetrable when turned. I was impressed.

I eyed the tub and decided to take a bath. After today, it seemed like a sensible idea, I would travel to Dearn tomorrow, meeting Princess Vaster, after all.

I reached for the gemmed knob on top of the copper tub. Sure enough, heated water gargled forth from a pipe moments later. "Huh, amazing." I undressed while the water rose, thinking of how rich Chardour had to be if even an inn such as this could afford this amount of crystals.

With a sigh, I slid into the warm water, letting the day pass in my memory.

Searching for signs on the road, having my head verbally torn off by a Dovani, riding directly into a trap, fighting off said trap, traveling to another kingdom after.

What stuck out was the fact that if Rayla was right, someone didn't want me to reach Dearn. The feeling from earlier came to me then, the sensation of being watched. Did it mean danger? Even here?

I scooped up water to wash my face. It made no sense guessing. I would have to be vigilant and ready at all times. Swiping water from my eyes and blinking, I looked at my bracelet. Upon touching it my daggers clattered softly on the table I had set them down on. As long as I had this, I should be safe.

The door flew open, startling me. Water sloshed over the sides of the tub and I reached for my bracelet quickly, until I saw Rayla barging inside my room. She looked positively livid.

"Get out of that immediately," she snarled and threw the door shut behind her. "We have to leave right now!"

I spluttered and cupped myself from her view. "What are you doing here? And what are you talking about?"

"No time for modesty." She stomped toward the windows and glanced outside. "We must leave, now!"

"What is going on, Rayla?" I asked, springing from the tub and drying off.

"They are waiting for us," she said, her eyes still roaming the streets outside.

"I don't understand. Who was waiting? *What is going on?*" Confused, I reached for my pants when she turned, zeroing in on me. I was very much naked, stretched to gather my pants and stilled.

She crossed her arms, not acknowledging my current state in any way. "I was attacked in the stables by an unknown man. Unlucky for him, my initial cut warding him off was too deep, but he did elude to there being others who would succeed where he failed. They are here for you, Prince Hamon." For a split-second her gaze dipped, then flew back up. It could have been a trick of the light, but it looked like her eyes had widened for moment. "Pants. Now. I'll pack anything else you have lying around." With that, Rayla began stuffing my belongings back into my duffle bag.

I slid into my pants, struggling to pull them up my barely dry legs. A clean shirt flew my way, followed by my boots.

"Hey." I caught one and smacked the other one down before it hit my stomach. "Will you cut that out?" The only answer I got was a dark look before she stuffed my old shirt into the bag and closed it.

"Keep you daggers close," Rayla instructed.

I hopped around on one foot, trying to pull on my boot as fast as possible. Then the other. Quickly, I swiped my daggers – still in their sheaths and attached to my belt – from the table and wound the belt around my hips. Walking over to Rayla, who listened at the door, I closed it.

"Shh," Rayla held a finger to her lips and slowly opened the door. She peeked out, left, then right, then waved at me to follow. We snuck through the lit hallway – the opposite way Cynthia had brought me up. Turned out there were steps in the back of the corridor, too. We snuck down and when the floor of the second landing leveled with my head, I saw movement at the other side of the corridor. I narrowed my eyes and sure enough, a group of darkly dressed people rounded my door.

As fast and noiselessly as I could, I dashed down the stairs, following Rayla, when a crash sounded from above. Shouts grew louder, and doors opened. We ran down the stairs of the first landing, and some of our guards spilled from the rooms down here.

"Intruders, above," Rayla called and they sprang into action. I glimpsed one of them – dressed in nothing but his underpants and boots – brandish a sword as they stormed up the stairs on both sides, just as we continued down. The clattering of weapons soon sounded our way, paired with yells and a strange zinging sound. The foreign sound was always followed by a short scream.

"Shouldn't we help them?" I asked. "They are only a few people."

"They will not hold them for long," Rayla grumbled, hurrying past the kitchen and out the back door. "Remember the Doran arrowhead? The sound you hear is one. We would both die if we went up. Quickly now." Our feet met crunchy gravel and we ran around the house, to the side the coach had been brought to. There it stood, Oren on the coachman's seat, holding the reins of Flea and Gintac. I gasped when I saw a heap of bodies not far away, the Chardour guards who had watched over the coach. All dead.

"They killed them... Why would they–"

"Later. Now we have to be quick, or we'll be next." Rayla threw my bag at Oren, who let the reins fall to catch it, and was nearly taken down the other side of the coach by it.

I snatched up Flea's reins, who pranced back, her ears flat. Forcing my voice to be calm and soft, I told her it was only me and that we had to go now. She snorted, but one ear rose, then she sniffed at me and let me pat her face.

"Good girl," I said, stroking her neck before pulling myself up and into the saddle.

Rayla was already seated atop Gintac. "Oren, you go first, we will protect the coach as best we can, but you have to be fast."

The boy nodded grimly. "I will, Miss Rayla." He clicked his tongue and soon had the two horses pulling the coach thunder past a few trees leading them onto the road out of the village.

Chapter Nineteen
Eliza

My wrath had morphed into an outright murderous rage by the time we reached the throne room. Leaning heavily on Marie, I waved at the guards to open the door. They obliged, clearly surprised to see me and sure enough, we walked into what looked like a heated discussion.

"All of you should be ashamed," Stefan shouted, standing from his seat, far from being the collected and stoic man I knew. "The princess has just lost her entire family and you try to stir up this…this… What exactly is this meeting supposed to be? A vote? You can't do that!"

The feeling of betrayal left me in a rush, swapped out with an intense knot of guilt. Stefan hadn't joined them to conspire, but to stick up for me. I was an idiot for thinking otherwise.

"She has not made a claim yet," Senator Gilles said. "She hasn't even addressed the public and announced the death of our king and queen formally. That is not the behavior of a leader. She has shut herself away when what we needed was leadership and a strong hand."

"And I suppose you think of electing that strong hand, or even maybe become it yourself, Senator Gilles?" I asked, walking toward them with Marie's help.

"Your Highness," Gilles said, his face whitening. "What are you—"

"Surely you are not asking me what I am doing in my own castle, joining a meeting I have every right to be part of?" I asked, glaring at him.

The senator stammered without really saying anything.

"Princess, you should be resting," Stefan said, hurrying to my side and taking my free arm. Marie sighed softly when most of my weight shifted off her.

"My throne, Stefan," I said. The whole senate and aristocracy watched with bated breath as Marie and Stefan helped me up the stairs and into my seat. The journey had taken much from me and I gasped when my butt finally met the cushion. I breathed deeply for a few moments, feeling sweat pearl on my forehead.

"Now, you wanted to talk about me. I am present. Tell me, Senator Gilles, what exactly is this about?"

The senator I'd addressed rose from his chair, straightened his shoulders and pulled at the lapels of his coat. "Your Highness, it is as I said. You are not fit to rule this kingdom, the past few days have shown it. Shutting yourself away from the senate and the public? We understand a grieving process, but why have you neither declared your intentions, nor the death of your family?"

He did not meet my eyes when asking, but his chin jerked up arrogantly. I had the unprincessly urge to punch it.

"Not that I owe you any kind of explanation, Senator Gilles, but I will indulge your silly questions."

He opened his mouth to fire an answer at me, looking angry, but I held up my palm. "I have not announced my claim to you because I haven't yet addressed the people of Chardour. And while you may think you have a right to know before them what my intentions are, you do not. You are all citizens of this great kingdom," I said, letting my gaze sweep over the people around the room. "I wanted to address all of you at the same time. The reason as to why I have not, why I have "shut myself away" is because I was attacked a few nights ago."

Whispers rose, most looked shocked, a few unsurprised. Gilles was one of the latter.

"In my own home. In my room. But it looks as though some of you knew that already. What I don't understand, is why you thought it was a good idea to call a meeting knowing full well why I was incapable of doing any of my duties, while making it seem like it was a failure on my part. Senator Gilles? Do you care to elaborate on that and end my confusion?"

The senator cleared his throat. "You could have made an announcement before that…unfortunate incident."

"I truly hope that is not your explanation," I said. I grabbed hold of my armrests to pull myself forward. "The Steward addressed the people of Dearn on the same day we got the message from King Onis. I lost my family. *My entire family*. In one day. I do not wish anything of the like on my worst enemy, certainly not on you, Senator Gilles. As someone who called himself a friend of my brother, I thought you mourned as well. I see now nothing could be further from the truth. At the first opportunity you pounced."

"I have every right to call a meeting. We hadn't seen or heard from Your Highness in days," Gilles said, bristling.

"No." I shook my head. "You knew full well I was attacked and healing. Don't try to deny it, my explanation did not surprise you. I find it despicable how you would use my absence to stage a coup."

"A coup? Your Highness, I have every right to question your capability of ruling or inquire as to what your future plans entail."

"Certainly. But you could have just asked me. Once I was healed and met with all of you. We have just established that you knew, have we not?"

Some chuckles rose here and there, making Gilles' face redden considerably. He pumped out his chest, about to say something, when Senator Margaret rose, touching his arm. Gilles looked at her and she whispered something at him that made him plop into his chair.

"Your Highness," Senator Margaret said. "I apologize for my fellow senator's behavior, he has only the good of the kingdom on his mind. He meant no harm." She smiled at me. It looked like a grimace. "But since we are together and able to address you, what is you plan? Do you intend to rule? If so, we will have to launch a formal inquisition as to what makes you capable of doing so. You are young, unmarried, and have no knowledge of politics or leadership. Those are serious concerns." She sat back down while a murmur rose around the room, one that seemed to agree with her.

"Thank you for addressing your concerns directly," I said. "Although, I imagine, you would have done so with or without me present."

Margaret scowled, but again chuckles rose around the room.

"I do intend to take my throne, as it was passed down to me by my parents. As for what makes me fit to rule, you would never ask the same questions had my brother sat here instead of me. No. Had he been in my stead, you would all fawn over him, trying to get on his good side. So, in a way, I am glad to be here right now, seeing firsthand who opposes me and who does not."

Half the senate looked sheepish at my words.

"Alas, you do raise valid points. Why am I fit to rule? I have spent every waking moment before and *after* the attack on my life learning how to. Our kind Steward has tutored me and will continue to do so. All I can do is learn and grow into the leader Chardour deserves, but I do think I will live up to the task ahead. Does that address your doubts in me?"

Senator Margaret raised a brow, her lips pulled down in a frown. "Many others would be ready by now. We could just as easily pick a rightful successor to the throne."

Shouts and voices grew loud, mingling and echoing through the grand hall. Many of the noblemen yelled their names, bringing on a headache.

I raised my hands and slowly the shouts ebbed away. "This kingdom, this throne," I banged a fist on the armrest for emphasis, "has been under the House of Vaster rule for centuries. My family has steered Chardour true and firm. My grandmother and my father built up Chardour after the Breaking, making it one of the richest in all of Iyune. You all reap the benefits. I am a Vaster. No one is more capable of ruling than me."

"You are unmarried," Senator Ferton said in a calm voice. "Our laws are clear, Princess Fabienne. Were you to marry, my vote would be yours."

"Indeed. In this regard, the laws of our kingdom are antiquated. My Dovani is on her way to bring back the bodies of my family, and if Leozar has deemed it wise, a prince from their family who will become my king. If they are unable or unwilling to do so, I will find another kingdom to form an alliance with through marriage."

The silence following my words was absolute.

"I hope that addresses all your concerns, senate, lords, and ladies. If no one has any other questions, I call this meeting done as I still have some recovering to do from the poisonous blade that struck me."

A few of the ladies fanned themselves and many lords looked outraged. I had no idea whether it was on my behalf or because of what I had said. I was sure a princess was not to reveal the gruesome details of her being attacked. There surely was a way to talk about these things that was acceptable. I did not care, however.

On the bright side, no one raised a voice and they all stood to file from the hall. Once the door closed, I sank back in my seat exhausted. "Goddess, I hate this," I murmured. Anxiety, anger and confusion raced through me like a pack of wolves. But I had done it. I had addressed the entire court and held my own.

"You did very well, Fabienne," Stefan said, coming up to my throne. "I didn't call you because I was worried. Had I known…"

"It is not your fault, Stefan. These vultures were waiting for an opportune moment to gather while thinking I would stay absent."

"You told them, though," Marie said, a warm smile on her face.

"I tried." I shrugged and grimaced when looking at the distance to the doors. "Now let's get me back to my new chambers. I think I have to lie down."

Stefan and Marie both laughed, helped me to stand and steadied me on the way back. My insides felt raw, feeling something else than sorrow was welcome, but not something like this. More than anything, the thought of standing my ground again and again unnerved me. This surely wasn't the last time. I could only hope to get better at it.

At the door, we met a very angry Jentz. His bushy brows enhanced the glare he threw at me. "You should not be up and about, Princess. I can't do my job if you traipse around without calling me or a guard to escort you."

"Apologies, dear Jentz. My rule was questioned and I was in a bit of a hurry." I tried my best at a charming smile.

His brows jumped up. "They did what? Those conniving lowlifes!"

"It is taken care of, Jentz, but you could swap places with Marie, if you wouldn't mind. She has practically carried me all the way from my chambers."

"Of course," Jentz said and took my arm from Marie.

"Captain!" someone called out from our left. A guard came running from the entrance, his lapels flying with each step. "Captain!"

"What is it, Jacob?" Jentz asked when the guard skidded to a halt, bowing with a strangled huff when seeing me.

"Th-the alarms for Khoras have gone off. Something is happening at the garrison close to the Foudan," Jacob gasped out.

"Send soldiers immediately," I said, my heart skipping a beat.

"There are four regiments stationed in Khoras," Jacob said.

"And would they send an alarm if they didn't need help?" Jentz asked. "No. They would deal with it and then send a messenger. Now get me the captain of the regiments stationed here."

Jacob bowed again and sprinted off.

"Apologies, Your Highness, I have to go and—"

"No need, Jentz," I interrupted him. "See to it that we send them help. Find out what happened as soon as you can. Report back to me, no matter the hour."

"Certainly, Your Highness. He gave my arm back to Marie and followed after Jacob, muttering something about early retirement.

****

I was unable to rest. My thoughts hanging on Rayla. Had she made it through to Chardour? Was she in the middle of whatever happened at the Foudan? Gruesome scenarios played in my head while I tossed and turned during the night. If anything happened to my Dovani – no. Rayla could take care of herself. She was a Dovani. Whatever happened, she would be fine. She had to be. I would not allow any thoughts of the contrary. Worry ate at me steadily, I would not be able to go on if I had sent her to her death.

230

Chapter Twenty
Rayla

Prince Hamon and I galloped side by side through the night, the coach ahead of us. Too soon, I heard hoof beats behind us. Twisting in my saddle, I saw three riders catching up to us. The coach ahead was slower than a mere rider, and we had adjusted our pace to it. They would be on us in no time.

I ordered Gintac to follow the coach, then swung around in the saddle so I sat in reverse. Quickly, I grabbed hold of my scythes and pressed the embedded crystals on the hilt. It wasn't a moment too soon, as one of those gemmed arrowheads came zinging my way. I swatted it to the side, but it rose again, this time aiming for Prince Hamon. I yelled "left" and Gintac turned as instructed. This time I cut the arrowhead in half and the pieces fell to the ground, getting lost on the path in a blur. An angry shout reached me and the riders following us sped up even more.

"Protect the coach and get to safety," I yelled at the prince, who nodded grimly and rushed on with his mare, leaving me behind.

Holding my weapons tight, I waited for the attackers to reach me, ready for them. The two in front parted and rode up on either side of me, their swords drawn. I deflected their blows with both hands, my swipes powerful enough to cut their blades in half. Of course, my gemmed scythes did most of the work, but it was satisfying seeing their surprised faces.

The surprise didn't last and they unsheathed daggers, made from stronger steel, striking at me again.

I warded them off, then kicked up my right leg, hitting one of them under his elbow. He teetered to the side under the blow and fell from his horse. Something whistled past me from behind, striking the second guy in the chest. A dagger of Prince Hamon. The man gasped, his hands flying to his chest, just as the dagger twisted and was pulled from him to fly back to its owner.

The horse slowed down with its wounded rider, making way for the last attacker. This one had no weapons visible to me, but as they got closer, I saw their hands were adorned with multiple gemmed rings. The figure spread their fingers, pointing at me and two more arrowheads barreled my way. Quickly, I swatted one away, but the second went through my defenses, tearing into my shoulder.

"Faster!" I yelled, and Gintac sped up, leaving the figure behind. The arrowhead ripped from me and I grunted, feeling my fingers around my weapon loosen. Before it fell, I resheathed it and concentrated on my good arm.

"Slower!" I commanded and my horse slowed once again. The rider caught up once more, sending their arrowheads at me, and I focused. With two quick slashes, I cut them to pieces, eliciting another frustrated roar from my follower.

This time, they turned both hands into fists and yelled something. It was the same feeling I got when the word 'Obsidian' was used, and I steeled myself. An orb of black grew from nothing, between the figure's fists, until it was the size of a head. Then they hurled it at me. I wanted to deflect it, but my scythe sailed right through it, as if it was thin air.

Before the orb of black hit my chest, silver light exploded before me, shattering the sphere into a million pieces.

"No!" the figure cried as the pieces fell to the ground, searing into it as though melting through it. The figure yanked at the reins of their horse but as the ground cracked open, the horse stumbled and fell into it, out of my sight.

To my horror, the cracks grew, and the ground trembled with a deafening roar. Gintac snorted and Flea whinnied somewhere at my back.

I gasped and turned in the saddle, bending low over Gintac's neck. "Faster," I rasped, clutching my bleeding shoulder. My heart almost burst from my chest when the coach ahead swayed precariously. In no time at all, I had caught up with them.

"What was that?" Hamon bellowed over the sound and the beating of our horses' hooves.

"The ground is cracking. We have to keep going."

He gave me a curt nod and we raced on.

Tremor after tremor shook the ground and more than once our horses stumbled. Cracks reached us, parts of the ground sliding away, while rocks the size of men lifted from the ground. Was this still because of the orb? Or was the Witchgoddes near?

Having grown up in a floating city, I knew what remnants of her magic looked like and they were nothing like this. Her magic had a smell that would grow into a taste the closer one got to the edge of a floating city or country. It was sharp and leaden. All I could smell now was rock and fresh earth. There was no relief to be found in that fact, as we dodged sudden rising rocks, or our horses jumped over forming cracks.

I glimpsed over my shoulder and my breath left me in a rush. The earth was falling away behind us. A gigantic hole of darkness swallowed up everything. The forest, the hills of grass, houses, people, and animals…everything. Strange was, how some patches of surface seemed to hover higher, but most of it fell.

Flea, who was smaller than my warhorse, was also faster. Her neck elongated, ears flat, she propelled forward at breakneck speed, leaving us in her dust. Gintac did his best to try and keep up, but he was a heavy boy. His hooves soon slipped on some of the cracks.

"You got this. Take us home, Gintac," I said to him, bending even lower over his neck and holding on for dear life.

Flea and Hamon were already next to the carriage, the ground around them free of cracks. Gintac and I fought our way forward. At every jump I thought we would slide back and fall into the darkness, but he did it. He raced on and eventually, his hooves met even road. The cracking and crashing behind us grew quieter but I was not taking any chances.

I waved at the prince and Oren to go on when they slowed to wait for me. Even when the rumble vanished entirely, followed by an eerie silence, it felt like waiting for something worse. And it came.

The sound. The one I had been afraid of. Earth falling into water. Chardour was a floating kingdom, but it didn't float as high as some others, meaning the acidic sea had washed into the depth it had left when rising up.

A hissing sound followed soon and a misty spray rose from the hole killing everything it touched. I looked back and watched in terror as an entire tree looked like it was being eaten away by nothing before my very eyes. It just fell in on itself, leaving nothing behind but white ash.

"Run!" I screamed, squeezing my thighs to spur Gintac on. He seemed to smell the same thing I did then – the burning acid that was the sea – and he flew forward, away from the source.

What felt like hours, but could only have been minutes, we raced away from devastation, and eventually cleared it. The smell of the sea was gone, nothing else turned to white ash, and the hooves of our animals sounded steady on the road.

We didn't talk as we fell into step next to each other, on the left side of the coach. Hamon looked horrified and Oren stared into the distance seeing nothing. There was nothing to say at what we had just witnessed. Nothing to encompass the otherworldliness of it. Had this been what my grandparents had felt after seeing the world break? This empty terror? It was unlike anything I had ever felt. How far back had the cracks gone? I hoped it had not reached Khoras. What had that thing been, that orb of black?

I pointed at a small clearing between trees, next to the road. "We sh-should rest for a bit," I suggested. I had no idea if the guys heard me, because neither answered, but after a few moments, they both turned in the direction and off the road.

I slid off my horse and hugged him for a while, whispering to him how good he had done and thanking him, then I took off his saddle and reins. From jiggly-snoot to back-hoof, I examined him, making sure he was not hurt anywhere. His left hind leg had a cut, as did his front knees. Probably from slipping on the cracks. The wounds were superficial though and nothing to worry about. I got out a tincture from my pouch and was about to smear it on his wounds when Prince Hamon approached.

"Let me," he said in a low voice, rubbing his bracelet. He crouched down and closed Gintac's wounds as he had done with mine the previous day. I watched, not understanding why I felt tears welling in my eyes.

"Thank you," I said when he was done.

The prince nodded at me once, then walked over to the coach and helped Oren with the horses. They were fine, as was the boy, but he was very quiet. Taking a bracing breath, I opened the coach door and peeked inside. As if by miracle, the caskets of the Vaster family had stayed neatly stacked and fastened. Relieved, I closed the door and sat down on its side, leaning my back against the wheel.

"Rayla?" Prince Hamon stood over me, his eyes glued to my side. "You are bleeding."

I looked at my shoulder and shrugged. "Yeah, one of those arrowheads found me," I said.

"Not only that, your wound reopened," he said, pointing at my other side. I glanced down, patting my side and my gloves came away bloodied. I chuckled, not knowing what else to do. "Would you look at that. I never even noticed." With trembling fingers, I tried to open my armor but the leather strap would slip from me time and again. I cursed and once more, felt tears brim my eyes.

The prince knelt at my side, gently pushing my hands out of the way, and unclasped my chest plate. He peeled back my under suit and looked at the wound. "It is only a small tear," he said, then placed his palm on my skin to heal me. The sensation was as before, but this time I actually felt his hand on me. It was warm and comforting. His face, drawn and unrevealing, was very close to mine. So close, I felt his warmth fan over me, battling the crisp night air.

"What happened?" he asked.

Dread filled me and chased away any qualms I had about him being so close to me. "There was an orb of black. It came at me but my scythes did nothing to ward it off. Before it flew into my chest, it met something

236

mid-air and shattered. The pieces melted right through the ground, forming the cracks.”

A muscle in his jaw jumped. “Obsidian.”

The icy feeling, I associated with the word, spread through my stomach again. “Yes. I think you are right.”

“It is the only thing that makes sense. Leigh showed me a book on the crystals and their uses. Obsidian can’t be wielded by anyone but a Nera. Now, I have no idea who or what a Nera is, but I am guessing if anyone were to try and use it, disaster as we have just seen, would be the outcome.”

“The one following us did use it, directing it right at me,” I said.

Prince Hamon switched from my side to my shoulder, pulling at the fabric covering it gently. The same strange pulling sensation knitted through my wound.

“Why didn’t the orb reach me?” I asked. “And why did it shatter?”

“I have no idea,” he rumbled.

For a few heartbeats, we sat there looking at one another. I couldn’t say what shifted between us in that moment, but I saw my own fear mirrored in him.

He leaned closer, the warmth of his skin fanning across my cheek. “Rayla, I–”

“I don’t think you should bring your sister back some Obsidian,” I said, already knowing the cold rushing through my belly would come. “If this is what it causes, it’s way too dangerous.”

A crease appeared between his brows and he leaned back. “What do you – oh, yes. No, I don’t think I will.”

Prince Hamon circled his bracelet around his wrist and stood. He held out his hand to me, but I waved him off. “I think I’ll just rest for a bit. Thank you.”

He inclined his head and wandered off, his low voice floating my way when he spoke to Oren. The boy looked white as a sheet, his hands trembling as he got an apple from a burlap sack on his lap. I wanted to go over and ask him how he was doing, but felt like I couldn't move. Glancing down at my side, I discovered that my entire leg was soaked with blood. I must have lost a lot of it during our escape.

Rest. I needed rest.

My heart warmed when I saw Hamon getting out one of his daggers to slice Oren's apple to pieces. They shared the fruit, talking softly. And with each word, the boy got back a little color in his cheeks. The prince himself even managed a smile on the boy's behalf here and there.

As tired and strung out as I was, it was good to see something right with the world after what had just happened. After what I had possibly caused.

****

Sure enough, the sun did rise despite what transpired during the night. And it was beautiful. Golden light drew frames around puffy clouds, the heavens a vision of pastel colors, right before the sun peaked over the horizon. I lost myself in the beauty, feeling Gintac's movements beneath me as I swayed with them. We had packed up early and rode on, wanting to reach Dearn soon.

It was still half a day of traveling when I saw an entire regiment of soldiers ride our way.

Their captain, a man with a very long, thin face and an even longer and thinner mustache cantered toward us and bowed in his saddle when he recognized my armor.

"Dovani, I am Captain Richard, of the ninth regiment. We got an alarm from Khoras last night. What happened?"

"The ground fell out from beneath our feet, that's what happened," Prince Hamon said. "We barely escaped."

"What? That can't be right. You are, sir...?" Captain Richard asked, eying the prince up and down with a raised brow.

"This is Prince Hamon Kay Belenet, Captain Richard," I said.

The captain swallowed hard. "I-I apologize, Your Majesty. I had no idea. You are on your way to Dearn to..." The whole truth dawned on him then and he spluttered a few words without stringing a sentence together.

"Let me help you a bit, Captain Richard." Prince Hamon made his mare step up closer to the captain. "We arrived from Leozar yesterday, with an entire convoy of people. My entourage, and the coach containing the Vaster family," he jerked his head at the coach. Oren waved from his seat.

"We are on our way to return the Vaster family home. Last night, we were attacked and fled. Shortly after, the earth opened up, swallowing the entire place. We don't know how far the damage reaches, but if you continue toward Khoras, you can't miss it. That is all I know so far."

With each of Prince Hamon's words, Captain Richard's long face grew paler, and his lower lip sank, until he was outright gaping at us. After the prince was done, he cleared his throat, shook himself and said, "Prince Belenet, I would offer you an escort to the palace, but after what I just heard, we have to ride on as fast as we can to see what we can do to help."

"Of course you do," Prince Hamon said. "And we have to reach Dearn with news of what happened."

The captain bowed again, then turned toward his men. "Let them through!"

We rode on, the sea of soldiers parting to let us through them, while they followed their captain onward. I couldn't begin to imagine what they would find. I didn't want to. Unease paired with guilt swam in the pit of my gut as I watched the faces of the men riding into the unknown.

"Why didn't you tell them the truth?" I asked when we had passed the soldiers.

"Because the truth is dangerous right now. Obsidian isn't known widely, and somehow you destroyed a direct attack of the stuff on yourself. What would he have done with that kind of information?" Prince Hamon said.

His reasoning was sound and I was partly grateful for his story, but guilt squirmed in my gut.

"I will tell the princess, though," I said.

Prince Hamon threw a sidelong glance. "That is entirely up to you."

The rest of our journey was uneventful and we reached Dearn in the afternoon. No one paid us any mind as we entered the city and the normality of life going on seemed alien to me. People milled about, working, traveling, shopping and just living their daily life. While I was burdened with a sense of foreboding, fear, and guilt, everything around us was devastatingly normal.

I felt my anxiety flare the closer we got to the castle, hoping Eliza was safe. My worry should be for naught, as surely Captain Richard would have said something if anything had happened to her. Still, I urged Gintac on faster the closer we got.

Finally, we entered the gates of the castle. The guards took one look at me and opened the gates to let us in.

Prince Hamon looked around with wide eyes. "It is…"

"Quaint?" I offered.

"Yes. Quaint. And filled with so much light."

Oren stared as well, not able to take his gaze off the meticulous garden and then the white palace before us.

I felt my lips part to a smile at their wonder, and got down from Gintac in front of the entrance doors.

Stable hands, dressed in their dapper uniform took our horses.

"The coach stays here," I said to one of them. Oren nodded, settling back down in his seat.

"Come along, Oren. We'll find you a place to stay and some food," I said.

The boy looked a bit shocked, but climbed down from the coach and joined Prince Hamon and me as we ascended the stairs to the entrance.

The two guys seemed stunned at the entrance hall, especially Oren. I had to nudge him on from time to time when he stopped to gawk at the paintings, the reliefs, or the large chandelier covered in gems.

"Dovani!" a familiar voice shouted and I couldn't help a smile when Jentz came strutting our way, swiping at his bushy beard with one hand.

"Jentz, great to see you."

"Thank the Goddess you are back," he said, his stern face clamped with worry. "We feared the worst when the alarm from Khoras reached us. What happened?"

"Prince Belenet and Oren here will explain what we saw," I said. "I have to see the princess immediately. Is she in her chambers?"

Jentz bristled a bit and looked like he didn't know what to do first, bow to the prince or answer my question. He decided to do both. "She is in the royal chambers. Welcome Prince Belenet, may I offer you refreshments in one of our sunrooms while your luggage is brought to one of the guest wings? Hold on, where is your luggage? And where is the rest of your entourage?"

I only half-listened to Hamon answer in his low and calm tone, when I saw her. She stood on top of the stairs, looking as beautiful as ever, her eyes solely on me. The world fell out of focus and dropped from existence as she started to descend the stairs, one arm leaning on Marie.

My breath left me in a rush and my heart hammered like mad. All I wanted to do was rush to her, take her in my arms and kiss her. In that moment, the nervous heaviness was back full force. It grew into something akin to warm pain, thrumming with each beat of my heart. Love. I loved her. I knew it in that instant.

Her green eyes were still on me, a radiant smile lighting up her porcelain face. But something was wrong, she had to be steadied by Marie and took one step at a time.

I couldn't help myself and dashed toward her. Taking two steps at a time, I reached her and forced myself to stop. To not pull her into my arms and kiss her.

"Rayla, you're back," she said, tears shimmering in her eyes. Her breath came in bursts, as if she had run all the way here.

"What happened?" I asked.

"Nothing much. I just need to–"

"Nothing much?" Marie interrupted her. "Nothing much, she says…" The handmaid shook her head, glaring at Liz. "The princess got attacked a few nights

242

ago. The blade was poisoned so the healing is taking its sweet time."

"Marie," Liz said and I felt red-hot rage descend over me.

"Now, you know what you ought to, and my deed is done. It's good to see you Rayla," Marie said. "You can steady the princess from here, Miss Grant has laden me with additional chores today." The handmaid winked at me and I got the distinct impression she used an excuse to give me and Eliza some time together. However brief.

I reached out a hand to my charge when her handmaid curtsied and left, quickly pulling off my glove before I did so. Eliza gave me her hand and I nearly melted at our touch. It was all I could do for the moment.

"Are you–"

"Fine. I am fine, Rayla. Better now that you are here," she said. She squeezed my palm in little bursts, her gaze fixated on mine. "I missed you."

I wanted nothing more than to hug her, hold her, then look to make sure she really was fine, but I could not. "I missed you," I said.

She wound her arm through mine and smiled. "I can't believe you are here. I-I was afraid… After the alarm from Khoras… Goddess, Rayla, I was so scared." Her smile faltered and her lips trembled.

"I brought all you asked of me," I said. "The coach with your family is outside and down there is the prince."

Eliza still didn't look away from me. "I'm not ready," she said. "Rayla, I want to…"

"Yes. Me too. But we can't vanish right now. You have to meet him." I swallowed. "He is a good man from what I can tell. Troubled in some areas, but compassionate."

Eliza blew out a shaky breath, then nodded at me. "Let's get it over with."

Chapter Twenty-One
Eliza

I never wanted to let go of her. Ever. Just feeling her by my side, her arm in mine to steady me, I pressed my body against hers, wanting to touch more of her. To hold on and know she was there. It tore at me knowing I could not. The moment I had seen her stand in the entrance hall, my heart had beaten so fast as though it was about to jump from my body and fly toward her. My Dovani. My Rayla. She was alive and safe.

Step by step, we walked down the rest of the stairs and yet, I could not bring myself to look at anything or anyone but her. It was dangerous, but right then, I didn't care.

"Liz, you have to stop," Rayla whispered. "He is right there."

I tore my gaze from her and finally looked at the prince she had brought me. The one with troubles who was compassionate. I didn't care.

He looked…handsome. In a dark and brooding way. His dark hair brushed his shoulders and his ice-blue eyes stood out in contrast. He was tall. Taller than Rayla. With broad shoulders and a strange intensity around him. Had I met him on any given day, he would have been the kind of man Pavette and I would have giggled and swooned about. But he was not Rayla. And my heart bled because of it.

"Princess Fabienne Eliza Vaster," Rayla said, her voice only a tad shaky. "May I introduce Prince Hamon Kay Belenet of Leozar."

He inclined his head at me. "Princess Fabienne. I am charmed to meet you." His voice was as dark and warm as his appearance suggested.

"Prince Hamon, I am elated to greet you in my home and my kingdom." My gaze fell on a teenage boy next to him, ogling me. "And who might you be, young man?"

Prince Hamon smiled and clapped a hand to the boy's back. "This is Oren, he helped us escape from Khoras. He is an excellent stable boy and coach-driver."

Oren sank into a bow. "Your Majesty."

"Rise, Oren. Thank you for helping my Dovani and Prince Belenet reach us." I immediately wanted to know what had happened warranting them needing to escape, but it had to wait. Marie seemed to have told the staff who had just arrived, because manservants and maids soon lined the hall, ready to be called upon.

"Regine?" I addressed a maid, knowing she was kindhearted and always smiled. "Will you take our young friend to the kitchen and see he gets something to eat?"

"Absolutely," Regine said waved at the boy to follow her.

"Please, let us sit and discuss your journey," I said.

"Allow me," Prince Hamon said and offered his arm.

Rayla looked like she was about to growl at him, but then stepped back. I hooked my arm through hers once more, offering my other to the prince. "I am healing from poison right now. I can use all the support I get."

Prince Hamon looked from me to Rayla, then took my free arm.

"Call Stefan, he will want to be part of this conversation," I said to Jentz.

The sun had set by the time Rayla and the prince had told Jentz, Stefan, and me about their journey and what had happened last night. Neither of us knew what to say to any of it.

"We can only wait and see what news Captain Richard brings once he gets back," I said, close to tears. "If the damage has reached Khoras and maybe even the Foudan, we will have lost countless lives."

"Not to mention means of travel, several regiments of soldiers and our only way of export," Stefan mused. "It sounds unreal."

"I bet the people fifty years ago thought the world breaking before their eyes was unreal," Rayla said.

A heavy silence followed her words.

"How could it happen? I mean would one crystal really be able to cause such a thing?" Jentz asked. "And who were these people?"

Prince Hamon, who looked tired sitting opposite me in an armchair, spoke. "We have no idea, but they attacked us twice so far if I am not mistaken." He took a sip of tea and placed the cup down on the table between us.

"You look exhausted, Prince Hamon," I said. "Maybe we should pick this up in the morning? It's not as though we will solve this entire mystery by just talking about it. We will need information on how bad the situation is before we can take any more action."

He nodded and sent a small smile my way. "Thank you, Princess Fabienne. I would love some rest."

****

It took me some time to sneak through the castle while having to steady myself along the walls. But eventually I made it all the way to my old wing, without being seen. It was quite the feat and I was very proud of myself when I knocked on a certain powder-blue door.

Rayla had requested to stay closer to the royal wing so she might intervene if anyone broke in again, but none of the rooms were ready yet, so I surmised she would be back here.

The door opened, revealing her steel-gray eyes and undone black hair.

We reached for each other the second I slipped through the door. I held her to me, feeling her heart beat against mine. Strong and steady.

"You shouldn't have come, Liz," she whispered into my hair. "This is far too dangerous. If anyone finds out…"

I pulled back and silenced her with a kiss. She groaned against my lips and I would have melted to a puddle on the spot if she hadn't held onto me. My hands searched her, slipping under her chemise and up her back, until I dug my nails into her shoulders.

We stumbled to the bed, ripping each other's clothes off as we went. Breathless, I sank into the softness, pulling her on top of me.

"Rayla. My Rayla," I whispered against her lips. Our kisses turned deep and branding, every touch burned and sizzled across my skin. I was desperate for her, starving. Feeling her naked body slip against mine was heaven and I wound my legs through hers and undulated my hips.

A hiss sounded from Rayla and she pinned my hands above me to kiss down my torso and belly.

I tilted my head back, relishing her touch.

"I will kill whoever did this to you," she growled at my side, kissing up the scar my attacker had left.

I smiled, liking how angry she sounded on my behalf.

She made her way up my body, lacing one of her hands to both of mine. "I missed you, Liz," she whispered before kissing me deeply.

"And I you. I was so afraid when the news came…I–"

"Shhh, close your eyes," she said against my lips. I did and offered my body to her.

Her touch was fire, searing everything away but us. I was helpless not to succumb to her in every way possible, feeling an intense heaviness in my chest.

It did not take long for her to find her way down, making me explode like I had never before.

Shaking and gasping for air, I rolled us around once she worked her way up to my face once more.

"My turn," I said and began exploring her. I learned her body through touch, sight, taste, and smell, committing every tiny detail to memory. Every scar, every freckle, each part of skin. It was elating how her body reacted to me, how much power one touch, one kiss, one nibble had on her. Her muscles clenched underneath me, her moans music to my ears.

I slid down and stroked her lovely, toned legs, settling between them and pushing them apart. Running my fingers down the insides of her thighs, I blew out a shaky breath, forcing myself to drag out this experience, to fully enjoy every last second of it. I parted her with my palms and dragged my tongue up her center, circled, and moaned at the taste. Her legs shook next to my face and hoarse sighs reached me, making me smile.

"You are so beautiful," I told her. Getting nothing but a strangled moan in answer, as I lapped at her.

With fingers and tongue, I made her shatter beneath me, holding onto her legs when she bucked her hips. I did not stop until a long, relaxed sigh left her. Deeply satisfied, I crawled back up, pulling her into my arms and sliding my legs around and through hers, holding her as flush to me as was humanly possible.

"I never want this night to end," she said.

"Me neither." My lids drooped and I let out a happy sigh.

We spent hours holding each other, only interrupted by searching hands and sensual kisses. Finally, as dawn was approaching, we lay arm in arm again. My hands threaded through her hair, her head lying on my chest. She was quiet and when I asked her about it, she stayed silent for a moment.

"I think it was my fault, Liz. Somehow that orb wasn't able to hit me, and the shattered pieces caused disaster. What if I caused it?"

"You can't think like that. We have no idea why it happened the way it did and you had no way of predicting anything. It was not your fault. Please don't let it bother you in this way."

She didn't answer.

"Rayla. Promise me you'll not let it go to your head."

She shrugged. "I'll try."

Chapter Twenty-Two
Kay

Princess Fabienne sat in a large dining hall, all by herself, when a manservant led me to it. Rayla stood next to one of the doors, silent and stoic. I waved at her and got a small nod back.

"I hope you have slept well," the princess said upon seeing me.

"I tried, but the memories from our escape kept getting in the way." I walked over to the only other set place, opposite from her. The whole length of the table was between us now. I shrugged, took my plate and carried it to her, sitting down at her side.

She watched me, clearly surprised.

"I don't intend to shout at you across the table," I said.

Fabienne grinned. "I didn't know we felt the same on this."

We didn't talk, but ate in relative silence, then she stood, grabbed a cane propped up on her armrest and asked me if I wanted to see the castle.

We strolled through countless halls and she told me about the history of Chardour and the House of Vaster. All of it was very educational and I paid close attention to her words. Rayla lingered behind us, always watching. From time to time, I saw Fabienne throwing her looks over the shoulder and wondered what it was about. Generally, seeing them together yesterday had been strange. They seemed to get along very well, and the connection and trust they shared was obvious. No wonder Rayla had told me she would end me if I ever

251

harmed her charge. Her words made a tad more sense to me now. And yet, something felt off. I could not place my finger on it, but eventually decided it had to be something between the two and none of my business.

Fabienne asked me to call her by her given name because she despised the whole titles thing, as she called it. I offered for her to call me Hamon, which she happily did.

We strolled on and found ourselves in the throne room at the end of her tour. It was grand and splendid, with many windows allowing light inside, different from the throne room in Sif. Even the floor was fair, as were the ceiling and the walls, glittering with reliefs, which caught my eye the most. The whole place radiated a serenity and peacefulness rarely found in Sif.

"Stefan," she addressed her steward, who was sitting at a table by the stairs leading to the thrones. "Any news from Khoras?" The question was simple, but I could hear the worry in her voice.

"None, Your Highness."

"Very well." She took a deep breath. "I would like to see my family now. Rayla?"

Her guard appeared at her side a second later. "Your Highness?"

"Where are they?"

"In the catacombs, Your Highness. They are being prepared for the funeral."

Fabienne sank at those words and all color left her face. "Will you take me there?" she asked, her voice frail.

Rayla nodded and offered her arm. I let go and stepped back, unsure of what to do next.

"You are free to explore, Prince Belenet," Fabienne said. "We will find you later."

Just like that, I was dismissed and watched the women walk away from me. I was glad in a way. I did not want to intrude upon her saying goodbye to her family.

I wandered around the throne room, the only sound my steps and the scratching of Stefan's quill on paper.

Walking the length of the walls, I took in the story told before me. The opening of the mines. One side was dedicated to Siveil, one to Gern. It was astounding how great the craftsmanship of the artists was, bringing the people and scenery to life.

"Steward!" someone called from the entrance and when I turned, I saw the captain of the guard enter the hall. The older man – who I remembered was called Jentz – looked stricken as he strutted through the hall, heading for the steward.

Stefan rose from his seat, his features drawn.

"A messenger from Captain Richard just reached us," Jentz said.

"And?" Stefan asked. "What news does he bring?"

"It's…uh…gone."

"What do you mean, gone?"

"Khoras. The entire surrounding land. Only a huge hole is left, one can apparently see straight down to the acidic ocean."

I jogged over to the two men, who looked aghast and terrified. "All of it?" I asked, nervousness and anger building in my chest.

"Well… The Foundan looks unharmed. But it is floating in the distance, cut off from every bit of land," Jentz said.

"What?" Stefan exclaimed. "How is that possible?"

"No idea, steward, but it means that…all those people…the entire garrison… They are lost."

Anger seared through me, and the utter helplessness at doing something about it weighed on me. Cynthia, Henry, my entire entourage, and the people of Khoras. I could not believe it.

"Where is Princess Fabienne?" Jentz asked.

"With her family," I said.

"We have to call on her," Stefan said. "After she is done."

****

Sitting in the same study, we had conversed in yesterday, Jentz told his princess the news. Her already pale face, whitened even more. Her eyes were red, probably from crying, and tears welled at the news once more.

"I can't believe it," she whispered. Then she cleared her throat, wiped her face, and straightened in her seat. "Call on the inventors, see if they have a way of bringing us across to the Foudan. Build a bridge, something…"

"If I may, Your Highness," I said.

"Please." She inclined her head at me.

"We reach Sif via hovering plateaus. I am sure I can give your inventors the combination of crystals used for it, but I don't know the exact composition."

"That would be a great help. Thank you, Prince Belenet."

I nodded and listened while the conversation wore on.

I hadn't known what to expect of Princess Fabienne, but it certainly wasn't who I beheld across the room. There was no trace of a reckless wild child, or an immature princess. She faced everything head on, even after just having seen her whole family dead for the first time. I could not imagine how hard it was to be in her skin right now. I could respect her drive and her will to do what was necessary. However, she radiated something I had only ever experienced once. As though she was sharper, cut more clearly from the fabric of reality than others. And I recognized the despair she felt at loosing loved ones, something no one in my family related to. It was the sort of understanding born from sorrow. She had deep sorrow in her eyes.

I was not ready to be a king, but she certainly was ready to be queen. Who was I to stand in her way?

When the steward and her captain of the guard left, I stayed behind. "I would like to speak with you in private, if that is fine with you, Your Highness."

Rayla looked at me, her eyes narrowing.

"Of course, Prince Hamon," Fabienne said. "Rayla, will you please wait outside."

The Dovani still glared at me, but nodded once. She walked from the study and closed the door behind her.

I cleared my throat and stood. Walking from my seat, I traversed the study and sank into the armchair next to Fabienne. "We both know why I am here, Fabienne. You asked my father to continue relations between Chardour and Leozar through marriage. I agreed to come and offer my hand, in duty to my kingdom and house." I looked at her, her green eyes meeting mine in a steady gaze. She looked tiny in her seat, but not at all weak or faltering. "I do offer my hand to you, but there are certain things you should know about me before you accept or decline."

She held up a palm. "Hamon, I doubt there is anything you can say that will make me decline."

My brows rose in surprise.

"If you offer, I am saying yes."

"Just like that?" I asked. "You know nothing about me, you…"

She leaned forward in my chair. "I know what I must. You are a prince of Leozar and you will be my king. A troubled man, but good and with compassion, if Rayla is to be believed."

"She said that about me?" The ghost of a smile flashed across my features, but it didn't manifest. "I does not matter, Fabienne, I still have to tell you about myself. I am the firstborn of my father King Onis, but a bastard. Your court will give you grief for choosing me, as will your people. I have a reputation throughout the ruling houses of Iyune and to be frank, that reputation is true in most cases."

"And you think I care?"

I frowned at her in confusion.

"Let me tell you a bit about myself, Hamon. I lost my world the day the messenger came from your father, telling me my family was gone. Every step of the way thereafter, I have been questioned. My choices, my right to rule, not to mention, my ability to do so. I have to learn day in and out how to lead. I have to marry a complete stranger," she gestured at me, "to even be able to claim what is mine. Who knows what the court and the senate will have to say about what happened at the Foudan? My kingdom is in danger from more than the looming war, it seems. And I intend to protect it. As queen. It was a decision I had to make. I made it. And you can damned-well bet your ass I will do anything it takes to stick by that decision. To serve my people and the memory of my family. I saw them today. Cold as ice. And got the terrible news of more death among my people. A tragedy. I will not sit idly by while my people are in danger."

I sank back in my chair and blinked several times. "You are unusual, to say the least. Maybe we will fit because of it. Maybe we will both be miserable. But I promised to offer my hand." I rose from my chair, rounded the table between us, and knelt before her. I took her hand and looked at her. "If you will have me, I offer myself to you. As a husband, a king, and whatever else we decide to be to each other. I only want one thing in return."

"Name it," she said, her breath hitching.

The same anger from before rose inside of me. I needed to find out if the people who had chased me and Rayla had anything to do with the one who ordered the death of my mother. In both cases Obsidian was at the center of it, so the conclusion seemed valid. "We find whoever is responsible for what happened at Khoras and bring them to justice."

"Agreed."

I brought her hand to my lips and kissed it, our gazes never leaving one another.

"Thank you, Hamon."

"No need," I said. "We will work together and bring justice to those who deserve it."

Her features changed into a mask of determination. "That we will."

The Stones and their Properties

Clear – *Sinu* = to control water
Clear with yellow tint – *Sinusai* = to capture light
Yellow – *Micra* = to warm
Brown – *Rigna* = to travel
Gold – *Insa* = to float
Orange – *Meren* = to spark/light fire
Light-blue – *Grift* = to strengthen – material
Blue – *Hivan* = to call forth – material
Dark-blue – *Kinesh* = to summon/alarm
Green – *Driton* = to shield
Leaf-green – *Doran* = to control metal
Blood-red – *Sangus* = to mend wounds
Cherry-red – *Illain* = to travel – multiple people and objects
Dark-red – *Krais* = to lift heavy loads
Light-red – *Krias* = to add weight to objects
Violet – *Rani* = to taste sounds
Black with red tint – *Obsidian* = to bring destruction

About Victoria Larque

Victoria Larque writes Paranormal Romance and Urban Fantasy. Her love for the genre is rooted in the fact that she has rules to go by, but they can be bent and even broken if need be. She was born and raised in the wonderful country of Namibia and is now residing and working in Germany where she lives in the woods with her adorable, grumpy husband. She has learned the amazing craft of being a car-mechanic, but her passion is writing, telling stories and dreaming up impossibilities. When she gets home from work, she writes. On the weekends she writes. Her goal is to, one day, be able to do nothing but indulge in her passion.

Other BDP books by Victoria Larque

Terrifying Love - A Halloween Anthology
Beautiful Tragedy - A Halloween Anthology
Demon Rising (Embers Duology Book One)
Lakeborn
Princess of Stone (Fractured Queendom Trilogy Book One)
Golden Tattoo A Halloween Anthology